When Bruce Met Cyn . . .

Also by Lori Foster in Large Print:

The Secret Life of Bryan
A Hot Summer (Un cálido verano)
A Marvelous Lover (Una amante maravillosa)

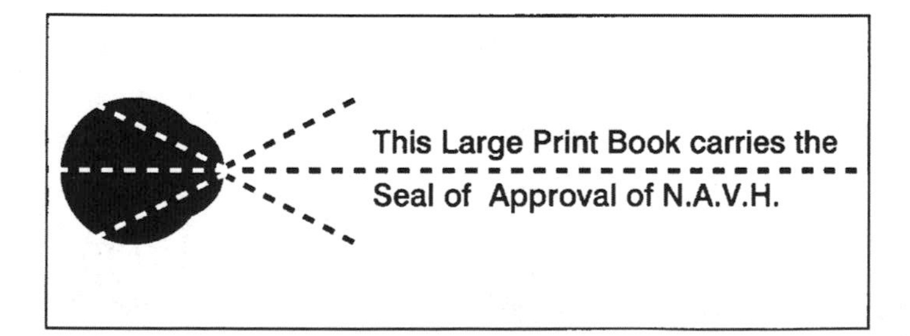

When Bruce Met Cyn . . .

Lori Foster

Thorndike Press • Waterville, Maine

Published in 2004 by arrangement with Zebra Books, an imprint of Kensington Publishing Corp.

Thorndike Press® Large Print Basic.

The tree indicium is a trademark of Thorndike Press.

The text of this Large Print edition is unabridged.
Other aspects of the book may vary from the original edition.

Set in 16 pt. Plantin by Myrna S. Raven.

Printed in the United States on permanent paper.

Library of Congress Cataloging-in-Publication Data

Foster, Lori, 1958–
When Bruce met Cyn — / Lori Foster.
p. cm.
ISBN 0-7862-7005-5 (lg. print : hc : alk. paper)
1. Difference (Psychology) — Fiction. 2. Large type books. I. Title.
PS3556.O767W48 2004

2004054138

When Bruce Met Cyn . . .

National Association for Visually Handicapped
serving the partially seeing

As the Founder/CEO of NAVH, the only national health agency solely devoted to those who, although not totally blind, have an eye disease which could lead to serious visual impairment, I am pleased to recognize Thorndike Press* as one of the leading publishers in the large print field.

Founded in 1954 in San Francisco to prepare large print textbooks for partially seeing children, NAVH became the pioneer and standard setting agency in the preparation of large type.

Today, those publishers who meet our standards carry the prestigious "Seal of Approval" indicating high quality large print. We are delighted that Thorndike Press is one of the publishers whose titles meet these standards. We are also pleased to recognize the significant contribution Thorndike Press is making in this important and growing field.

Lorraine H. Marchi, L.H.D.
Founder/CEO
NAVH

* Thorndike Press encompasses the following imprints: Thorndike, Wheeler, Walker and Large Print Press.

Prologue

Her eyes flared open and she gave a silent, gasping start — silent, because she'd learned to make no sounds, to hold her fear deep inside, protected. The night was as black and cold and empty as ever. What had awakened her?

Rain softly drubbed the window beside her bed, and frigid air seeped in around the warped frame, but it wasn't the nasty weather that left chills on her exposed arms.

Out of necessity, Cynthia Potter had learned to know what would happen before it did. She picked up clues, learned to read body language.

Even the dumbest animal learned how to survive.

Her heart rapped painfully against her ribs as she strained to listen, but she couldn't hear past the awful rushing of blood in her ears. Her eyes encountered only shifting darkness, molded and moved by shadows of the moon.

Then, suddenly, a thump sounded in the hallway.

A footstep.

A creak of the floorboards.

Because she recognized the soft noises all too well, they assaulted her fractured nerves like gunshots and twisted her stomach into a painful knot.

Palmer Oaks was coming to her bedroom.

A sob crawled up her throat, but she ruthlessly gulped it back.

She'd known it would happen, and she'd already decided to do something about it. She had to take control of her life. She was seventeen now, a grown woman. That was both the problem, and a solution. A woman's body took his hateful attention in a new direction, but a woman's mind ensured she could make her own way.

Until now, she'd had no choice. She'd been small and young, no match for Palmer at all. Her neighbors had openly pitied her, but didn't want to get involved. The school's attempt at intervention had backfired. Reverend Thorne . . . no, he was more warped than Palmer.

Regardless of what they claimed, she knew she wasn't evil. She didn't deserve them. She didn't deserve any of it.

As if in slow motion, her doorknob turned, tightening her panic and calming it at the same time. She'd reached her limit.

She would not be a victim anymore.

As she slowly turned her head to watch the door, hot tears tracked her face. Blindly, she reached out for the nightstand and her icy fingers knocked against the small glass lamp. Before it could fall, she clenched it in her fist and scooted up in her bed, curling her legs under her, prepared to lunge.

Resolve weighed heavy in her chest, forming a lump, agonizing but solid. She'd planned this scenario many times. She knew the lamp was solid enough, and her determination would carry her through. The alternative was unthinkable.

Without further warning, the door swung open and banged against the wall. Palmer often did that, hoping to take her by surprise, to terrorize her. He liked it when she screamed, when she tried to run. This time she didn't move, not even to draw breath.

He stood there, a looming, imposing shadow against the cracked wallpaper. She knew he'd be smiling in gleeful menace and she knew his rheumy eyes would be alight with excitement.

Sick bastard.

He started to say something in his coarse, mean way. Accusations, insults, warped justifications. The words meant nothing to Cynthia now. They couldn't hurt her anymore.

She waited until he moved, then rage brought her off the bed with a surge of incredible power. Taken by surprise, Palmer lurched back and banged into the doorframe.

Satisfaction roared through her. For once, Cynthia didn't feel helpless. Adrenaline pumped through her veins, giving her awesome strength. She was in charge, she was almighty.

The lamp struck his face and shattered, sending razor-sharp glass shards into his flesh and around the room. She relished the raw shriek of stunned pain that gurgled from deep in his throat. He held up his hands, turned his face half away from her as if to protect it.

Using the base of the now broken lamp, Cyn landed a solid thunk against his temple. His hands batted at her, but they were ineffectual against her fierce vengeance.

Unable to stop herself, her blows occurring without her mind's input, Cyn struck him again, and again, then once more. His corpulent body slumped to the floor, but she didn't register what it meant. Panting, she stood just out of his reach, gulping air, crying silently, her nightgown twisted around her body, her short, curly hair half hanging in her eyes. The now broken lamp was still held aloft with both fists. Ready.

Cynthia waited for his curses, for his fists, for anything . . . but nothing happened.

She sucked air so hard, she felt lightheaded, her chest heaved, her throat burned. Oh, God. The seconds ticked by, each one reverberating with her frantic heartbeat — one, two, three . . . and finally, with new fear she crept closer, slowly, so very slowly.

She expected to be grabbed at any second, pulled to the floor, punished . . . touched. She tried to stay prepared, but her legs were shaking horribly and her eyes blurred, her lungs hurt. Palmer was a large, terrifying lump on the floor. Unmoving. Silent.

Too silent. She couldn't hear him breathing, when usually his weight made him wheeze.

How long Cynthia stood there, she couldn't say, and then she heard her mother fumbling with the front door. As a barmaid, Arlene Potter worked late, and played even later. She'd be drunk and even if she weren't, she'd be no help. "It's for your own good," Arlene always said, and Cyn knew she believed it. That's what made it all the more frightening.

Galvanized into action, Cynthia turned on her dim overhead light and surveyed the damage done to the man her mother had brought into their ramshackle home two years ago. Stripped clean of emotion, she took in his mangled, unrecognizable face. There was so much blood, so much swelling and bruising, she couldn't make out his hated features.

She felt no remorse — *she didn't.* She felt only a sense of being very, very alone.

Knuckling aside the useless tears, she forced herself to think. She knew nothing of first aid, but it didn't take a genius to see he wasn't breathing. And there was so much blood — on him, on the floor, and on her. Using the bare toes of her left foot, Cyn nudged him.

Nothing.

Not a sound, not a movement. Her arms curled around herself and she bent double in pain. Not for him, but for herself.

She'd killed him.

Pity became an acrid taste in her mouth — pity for herself and for what she'd been forced to become. It worked its way up her throat until she sobbed, but she immediately stuck her fist against her quivering mouth to silence herself.

She could hear her mother in the kitchen, pouring another drink, singing to herself in her drunken slur, as oblivious, as uncaring of her daughter's welfare as ever.

God, how Cyn hated her.

At least, that's what she tried to tell herself as her heart shattered into small pieces, causing so much hurt it was a wonder it didn't kill her, too. In her mind, she *was* dead, dead and buried so that a new Cynthia could be born. After tonight, the pain would go away.

She'd *make* it go away.

She drew a deep breath to calm herself. The future opened up before her with warm, colorful possibilities.

Pushing aside the revulsion, Cynthia dropped to her knees and dug in Palmer's pants pockets until she located his wallet. It held a hundred dollars. To Cyn, it seemed like a fortune.

Thanks to the recent driver's education classes at her school, she had her birth certificate and social security card in the top drawer of her dresser. No one had been more surprised than Cynthia when her mother agreed to let her take the classes —

until Arlene explained that it'd make her life easier when Cynthia could do all the shopping.

Within two minutes, she'd dressed in her warmest clothes and gathered a few necessities. At the last moment, she dug beneath her mattress and pulled out the notebook she'd kept hidden there. With trembling hands, she laid it atop the rumpled blankets, knowing it told everything, all the things she didn't dare tell while she was still living with him.

Maybe someone would understand. Maybe, when they found his body, she wouldn't be blamed.

As she climbed out her bedroom window into the damp, cold spring night, she glanced back at the cramped room, at what she was leaving behind, and at the body on her floor.

He was dead and good riddance. She wouldn't, couldn't care. As far as she was concerned, Cynthia Potter died with him. The scared young woman was gone, and a new, free woman had emerged. A better life awaited her. It might not be great, but no way could it be worse.

Chapter One

As the vivid dream faded, Cyn stretched awake on the narrow, lumpy mattress. A spring rain pattered against the window, and for a brief moment, a sense of *déjà vu* settled over her. She turned her head to stare out the window. This soft, late-April rain smelled fresh and held numerous possibilities. She waited, yet there was no sense of danger, no threat, and her heart swelled with relief, with honest happiness.

She sat up and shoved the window all the way open, letting the cold air blow in, dissipating the scent of stale sex.

Thanks to the compelling dream that had filled her sleep for the past month, she'd made some decisions. As of last night, she'd turned her last trick, and knowing that sent a bounty of energy surging through her. Perched on the side of the bed, she flipped her head forward and gathered her impossibly long hair in her hands. After retrieving a cloth-covered band from her nightstand, she secured the unruly mass into a high ponytail, then left the bed to take a shower.

She lingered, washing away every trace of the men who'd paid for her body, and at the same time, she washed away the past.

She didn't rue the things she'd done, because she'd survived, and if she could claim nothing else, she knew she was one hell of a survivor. Regardless of what others might think or how society would label her, she was damn proud of herself.

Wrapped in a terry cloth robe, she left the bathroom and made coffee. Her home for the past year was an efficiency apartment with a minuscule bathroom, a double bed, and a hot plate for cooking. It was so small, she barely had room to turn around, but compared to some of the other places she'd slept, like the park and alleys and one-night motels, it was nice. It was also cheap, which meant most of the money she made, she could save.

She'd decorated it with pictures from magazines and flowers that grew wild, and she'd loved the independence it had provided. For the first time in her life, she'd been able to call a place home. But she was now twenty-two, and she had enough cash saved to start over.

She'd managed it once before when she'd been no more than a kid of seventeen, afraid and alone. She was still alone, but fear was a luxury she couldn't afford these days. By necessity, she'd taken risks that no woman should ever take, and they'd paid off.

Little by little, she'd learned to fend for herself, to protect her body and her mind, and to separate the two. She wasn't wealthy, and a lot of people might scoff at a mere twenty-five hundred dollars.

To Cyn, it was a fortune, a future, and independence.

She sipped her coffee while daydreaming of what was to come, the things she'd do. When she closed her eyes, she saw a shadowed man, standing among tall trees, and a blinding sun with birds singing. Now familiar things.

The urge to make changes had been eating away at her for a month, when normally she didn't allow herself the pleasure of daydreaming. It was the oddest thing, but she'd felt compelled to ponder it. Whenever she slept, visions of the man and a place far away, with water and fresh air and friendly people who didn't know her, played in her mind with the same clarity as a movie show.

She didn't recognize the man or the place, but both had become real to her. She knew them as well as she knew herself.

Somehow, she'd find them.

She skinned on jeans, shoved her feet into flat sandals, and tugged on a long-sleeved T-shirt. Many of her clothes would be left behind. She couldn't see herself wearing hot-pants and fishnet in her new life.

Grinning at the thought, she folded away her jeans, tees, and sweaters, then packed up her makeup and toiletries.

She eyed her collection of books, considered leaving them behind because they'd certainly be heavy, but she couldn't do it. They'd saved her, and they were like her trusted friends. When she needed comfort, she revisited them. She had to remove a sweatshirt to fit the books into the suitcase, but it seemed a small price to pay. Her stash of money was hidden in the lining of her purse.

The box of condoms got tossed in the trashcan. She wouldn't need *those* for a long time, if ever.

With everything else ready, Cyn opened the map that she'd swiped from the gas station and carefully spread it out on her bed. Feeling giddy with the pleasure of it, she closed her eyes, drew her fingers over the crinkling paper until it felt *right,* and then, finger pointed, she opened her eyes.

Visitation, North Carolina.

Oh, she liked the sound of it, the way it felt on her tongue when she said it aloud. She even laughed. So be it. Her days of running were over. It was time for a rebirth.

For the first time since she'd left her old life five long years ago, Cynthia slung her purse over her arm, rolled her suitcase to the door, and allowed the fates to guide her.

After spotting a cockroach beneath his chair, Bruce Kelly ruled out the soup. Cautiously, he stirred his coffee, and found nothing swimming inside it. He tasted it, and decided it wasn't too awful. After doctoring it with sugar and creamer, he sat back to revive himself with some much-needed caffeine.

The cracked plastic seat of the booth snagged against his behind every so often, forcing him to shift around until he faced the window.

Evening had settled over North Carolina hours ago, bringing with it a black velvet blanket studded with stars and a chill that could cut to the bones. He should have been in bed by now, and usually he was, but he'd been too tired to continue driving without a break. He had another fifty miles to go, and he wasn't fool enough to make the trip half-asleep.

His visit back to Ohio had been a pleasure, and he'd lingered too long chatting with friends. There was a time when he'd felt deeply rooted to his projects there, but in less than a year, Visitation had become home.

He was lost in thought, his cup nearly empty, when a semi pulled up outside the diner. The headlights briefly blinded Bruce before the truck swung around and stopped. As he watched, the passenger door jerked open and a young woman tumbled out in haste, almost falling to the broken concrete lot. His attention caught, eyes narrowed, Bruce absorbed the sight of her. She seemed to be all luxuriant, tangled hair, long legs, and defiance.

Leaving the big rig idling, the trucker threw open his door and thundered toward the woman. He was a large man, in both stature and girth, dressed in a flannel shirt with jeans that belted below his protruding belly. He seethed with aggression.

Hastily, Bruce laid enough change on the table to cover his coffee and slid from his seat. His gaze never wavered from the unfolding scene.

As the trucker drew near, the woman didn't back up. No, she grabbed a suitcase and shoved it behind her, then, strangely enough, she took a stance. The disparity in their size was ludicrous, and yet she squared off with the big bruiser as if she intended to duke it out with him.

Bruce couldn't hear the argument, but he could tell by their postures that emotions were high and driven by anger. The young lady practically bounced on her toes in provocation, amusing Bruce even as he feared for her safety.

From one second to the next, things escalated from a verbal confrontation to physical combat. The trucker grabbed her by the arms, jerking her forward and into his chest. The woman's mouth opened on a silent cry.

And Bruce bolted for the door.

He'd seen plenty of violence against women, but it hadn't made him immune. Just the opposite — more than ever, it infuriated him.

With all the recent changes in his vocation, protecting women was no longer his job. Yet, the instinct remained as strong as ever.

Ignoring the other customers who watched him curiously, Bruce shoved the glass door open and was halfway across the lot before his mind registered the scene before him.

The trucker had dropped to his knees with his hands cupped around his testicles, his face a twisted mask of excruciating pain. Surprise didn't slow Bruce's stride, and he reached the woman just as she drew back her foot to kick the trucker in the chin.

Catching her from behind, Bruce swung her up and away from the other man, then set her back down out of striking range.

The second her feet touched the ground, she rounded on him, drew back a bent arm to plant her elbow in his face — and paused with a look of mute surprise. Their gazes clashed and locked for long seconds that to Bruce, felt like an eternity.

He was captivated.

She appeared more than a little wary.

Blinking away his astonishment, Bruce came to his senses first. He felt like a fool, and no wonder since he was acting like one. "Are you all right?"

Breathing hard, she shook back her long black hair and demanded, "Who are you?"

Many of the bulbs in the diner's outdoor lighting had burned out, but they still provided enough illumination for Bruce to fall headlong into her exotic features. Pale, icy blue eyes were tilted on the outside corners, heavily lashed and direct. Never in his life had he seen eyes like that.

Her petite body had generous curves enhanced by snug jeans and a soft cotton top. Long limbed, delicate but lush, she was a male fantasy come to life. Because the night air was cool, her nipples had stiffened. Bruce felt his stomach muscles clench as he watched her chest, now rising and falling in agitation — and suddenly her elbow connected.

Not on his nose, thank God, but against his solar plexus, stealing his wind and making him gasp while staggering back a step. *"That hurt."*

She tossed her hair again. "The first ten seconds of ogling were free. But you went way past that."

Pressing a fist to the ache she'd caused, Bruce swallowed, cautiously drew two more painful breaths, then rasped, "My sincerest apologies."

Her incredible eyes narrowed. "Are you for real?"

He almost smiled at the irony of the situation. "I saw your predicament from the diner and had some vague notion that you might need assistance."

"Yeah?" She glanced behind her at the trucker, who was making noises of renewed life. "I still might."

The trucker staggered to his feet with a lot of grunting and grimacing. With his right hand, he pointed a short, meaty finger at her. "Fucking whore," he spat. His left hand continued massaging his crotch.

Offended, Bruce said, "That language is unnecessary."

The trucker snarled. "She promised to —"

"I didn't make any promises." The young lady didn't raise her chin, but instead tucked it in and looked down her narrow nose at the trucker with icy disdain. "I was nice, and you made assumptions."

"I gave you a ride and even bought you lunch!"

Her rosy lips curled in a taunting way. "And you thought a hamburger and fries got you special favors? Get real."

"They sure as hell weren't free."

"Perv."

Fuming, the trucker reached for her again; she physically prepared herself, and Bruce, feeling like the biggest idiot alive, got between them.

Quickly, before the trucker tried to take

him apart, Bruce asked, "How much does she owe you?" Then he held up a hand. "And don't mention sex, because that's obviously out of the question. And besides, prostitution is illegal here and there's a cop sitting right inside the diner."

The trucker, with one worried glance at the restaurant, subsided. He pushed his ball cap back on his head and scratched at his ear. He seemed undecided, but finally said, "Forty bucks oughta cover it."

Bristling indignation brought the woman to her toes. "Forty bucks! Are you out of your friggin' —"

"Fine." Bruce located two twenties. "Here. Now go. We're drawing a lot of attention."

Hearing that, the woman looked over her shoulder, and grinned. The front window of the diner had at least ten noses pressed to it. "So we are. Probably the most excitement any of them have had in a decade. Oh and look. There *is* a cop." She waggled her fingers at the mostly disinterested officer before turning back to the trucker. "Get lost, Tarzan."

The trucker folded the bills Bruce had given him into his wallet, then tucked it into his back pocket. "Cock tease," he muttered with pure venom and headed for his idling semi.

In saccharine-sweet tones, she shot back, "Buffoon." But the trucker wasted no more time in throwing the big rig into gear and grinding his way out of the lot.

Bruce exhaled his relief, gave himself a few seconds to prepare for her impact, then returned his attention to the young lady. Her features were as devastating now as they had been moments before, but at least this time he wasn't taken unawares. "You're okay?"

"Fine and dandy." One arched brow lifted. "You?"

"I'll live." But his chest still hurt from the blow she'd delivered. She might be small, but she wasn't helpless.

She looked around her with interest. "I don't suppose you'd want to buy me something to eat? That hamburger was hours ago and I'm starving."

Her brazenness might have put another man off, but Bruce had spent most of his adult life in the company of brazen women. His mouth twitched and he said gently, "Not here, no."

She took that on the chin. "Sure, Gallahad, whatever." Readjusting the satchel-type purse she carried, and grabbing up the handle to her suitcase, she started for the diner. "Maybe some other Good Samaritan will feel differently."

Bruce stopped her. "They have cockroaches."

She twisted to look at him over her shoulder. Her grin made his stomach knot with unheard-of sensations. "No problem. Most of the people I know are probably related."

Sympathy saved him, brought out his more professional persona. If she didn't mind eating with bugs, she must truly be hungry. And he knew from experience that her joking attitude was no more than bravado, anyway. "I'm heading to Visitation."

She paused.

"It's an hour south, but at the next gas station, I can buy you something prepackaged."

Slowly, she turned to face him. Her lush lips pursed, and then formed the word, "Yummy."

Bruce's stomach took a free fall. He rubbed the back of his neck and tried to ignore her blatant sex appeal. "Once we hit town, if you can wait that long, I can get you some real food."

She cocked out her hip and crossed her arms under her plump breasts. "You offering me a ride?"

"As far as Visitation, yes."

"Well, what about that?" Her wide smile left twin dimples in her soft cheeks and had her eyes warming with surprise. She shifted the handle of her suitcase into her left hand, and held out her right. "I'm Cyn, Cyn Potter."

His automatic "nice to meet you" froze on his tongue. *Sin?* What was her middle name? *Temptation?*

As if she'd read his thoughts, she smirked. "Short for Cynthia, though I haven't used that name in a long, long time."

"I see." He needed to get his thoughts in order, fast. He folded her slender fingers into his. "Bruce Kelly."

Her hand was small and warm and her handshake held no reservation, no uncertainty. Bruce gestured to the side lot. "My car is over here."

She'd been rolling her suitcase along, but the uneven lot, littered with rocks and other debris, made it difficult. Bruce took it from her, lifted it with ease, and led the way. He knew she'd follow.

Where else did she have to go?

He started to put the luggage in the back of the aged station wagon, but Cyn stopped him. “Put it in the backseat. Not that I don’t trust you, but if I have to make a fast exit, I don’t want to leave my stuff behind.”

Bruce didn’t question that, he just did as she asked. “This thing weighs a ton.”

“Books.” She shrugged. “I like to read.”

“Me, too.”

Her mouth quirked. “Somehow I doubt we share the same interest in topics.”

Bruce was well used to untrusting women and he always did his best to reassure them. He opened her door for her, and without a word, she checked to make sure the lock hadn’t been tampered with.

He was wondering how many cars she’d been trapped in when she explained. “I read in a book that some sickos fix the door locks so once you’re in, you can’t get out.” Her eyes slanted his way. “Hope you don’t mind me checking.”

“Not at all. I think it’s smart.”

“Yeah — me, too.”

He wanted, needed, to know more about her. But he’d learned patience and wouldn’t push her. Simple questions seemed the best, and he’d ask them whenever the opportunity arose. “You ever find yourself in that situation?”

“Nope. And I don’t plan to, either.” She

fastened her seat belt, kicked off her sandals, and slouched down comfortably. Bruce watched her a moment more before closing her door and circling the hood. He dug his keys out of his pocket.

Before seating himself, he pulled off his windbreaker and offered it to her. "I noticed you were chilled."

She laughed and accepted the jacket. "I noticed you noticing." She pulled it up over her like a blanket. "Man, you must be like a furnace. It's still hot from your body." She gave a soft, contented groan. "Feels good."

The things that tripped out of her delectable mouth would set a man on fire. He merely nodded and gave his attention to the car.

Once he'd left the lot and entered the main road, he asked, "So what do you like to read?"

"Depends."

"On what?"

"Where I'm at, what I'm doing. I've read books on self-defense, on psychology, safety, and on self-help." She turned her face toward him. "What about you?"

Her choices surprised him, but he hoped he'd hidden his reaction. He didn't know what he'd expected, but heavy reading about serious issues never entered his mind.

In comparison, his genre reading seemed almost silly, and he smiled when he said, "I'm partial to mysteries." He meant her as much as the stories he read. "Where are you headed?"

"Visitation, with you." The night was dark and quiet. The lights of the console barely limned her face.

He shook his head. "I meant ultimately — where are you going?"

"Now that's the funny part." She idly coiled and recoiled a long, ebony tress around her finger. In nervousness or out of habit?

Or because she knew it was a feminine, sexy gesture and it turned him on?

He cleared his throat and divided his attention between her and the road. "Funny — in what way?"

"Fated, maybe. Like destiny or karma. Whatever you want to call it." She turned her head to face him. "Believe it or not, I was going to Visitation."

"Really?" Bruce didn't look at her again, but with every fiber of his masculine being, he was aware of her. Her scent, soft and warm, stirred the air in the closed confines of the car. "Why?"

"If I tell you, you'll laugh and I'll be pissed and our peaceful time together will be ruined."

Cyn in a teasing mood was almost more than his libido could take. "I won't laugh, I promise."

Still, she hesitated, playing with her hair, watching him . . . making him twitchy. "I have a vision of it in my mind."

"And what does your vision tell you?"

"That it's beautiful. A good place to be." Her thick lashes lowered and she smiled. "I see wide open spaces and wildlife and I can almost smell the fresh air . . ." Suddenly she twisted her mouth, making a face. "That sounds pretty lame, doesn't it?"

"Actually, it sounds like Visitation."

"Really?" She half twisted in her seat to face him. "So tell me more about it."

"What do you want to know?"

"I don't care. Anything."

How could she be going to a place she didn't know? "Do you have relatives there? Or a new job?"

The animated curiosity left her. She turned away to watch the blackness beyond the passenger window, and though she answered, Bruce still felt shut out, as if she'd slammed a steel door in his face.

"Nope, no relatives, and no job. But I'll find work after I get there."

"Work?"

Her laugh was nasty, hurt. "I don't mean working the streets, so don't get your hopes up."

"You're assuming you know my thoughts when you don't."

"Bull. You're a guy. I know what you're thinking."

God, he hoped not. It was bad enough that *he* knew the way his imagination had gone. "I only meant to inquire about your skills."

She laughed again. Worse and worse. He was never this rattled with women in need. He just had to remember that Cyn was a needy woman — despite the protestations she'd no doubt make.

Ready to groan, or bite off his own tongue, Bruce said, "Forget all that. Let me start over."

"Good idea."

He drew a breath, getting a grip on himself. "You're awfully young to take off on your own. So I was naturally concerned." Bruce was a good judge of age, but Cyn could have been sixteen or twenty-six. Her confident air was that of a mature woman, but something else about her, some indefinable nuance, told him that she had the same insecurities as a child might.

"I've been on my own for five years now." Her fingertips touched the window, exploring her own reflection there. "And what's it to you anyway?"

So defensive, Bruce thought sadly, but he'd already suspected as much. She must have been alone when she was still a child. "What do you think that trucker might have done to you tonight if I hadn't been there?"

"Nothing that hasn't been done to me before."

It pained him to know that much. "Cyn . . ."

Her fragile shoulder lifted. "You *were* there, so it's a dumb question. Forget it."

"You could still run into more problems, you know." And once they parted ways, she'd be on her own. He didn't like that idea much at all.

She pulled her bare feet up onto the seat and put her chin on her knees. "You believe in destiny, Bruce Kelly?"

"Why?"

"Because I'm thinking maybe we were destined to meet, that's why."

He liked that idea. "I'm a preacher. I believe God has a plan for all of us."

Her eyes widened like saucers. "No way."

He grinned at her shock. "I also believe we hold responsibility for our own lives, and for those who come into our lives."

His statement angered her. He felt her temper crackling in the air. "I'm responsible for myself, so don't start getting any ideas."

Bruce ventured forth carefully. "You could use my help."

"Right. I've had all the help I can stomach from your kind, so forget it."

"My kind?"

"You said you're a preacher."

Her words were issued as an accusation. "That's right." Absurd as it seemed, Bruce thought she might be afraid. He'd told her his vocation in the hopes it would reassure her, but the opposite had happened. She'd become more disgruntled and defensive than ever. "Why does it bother you?"

"I've changed my mind."

Bruce lifted a brow. "About what?" Her moods were jumping all over the place, and he had to go slowly until he figured her out, until he could understand the way her mind worked.

"I don't want to go to Visitation." Her piercing gaze never left his face. "Not with you. You can let me out here."

"Here?" They were in the middle of nowhere. Literally. The moon was bright, the sky filled with stars, but they weren't enough to combat the thick, heavy shadows of the night. The car headlights shone into endless darkness. There was nothing but mountains and trees and more trees.

Bruce had slowed the car in deference to the black night. The road was so twisted, winding this way and that, anyone with a weak stomach would probably get carsick. "That doesn't make any sense."

Slowly, she pushed her feet back into her sandals and hefted the strap of her purse back up on her shoulder. "Just let me out, okay?"

No way could he do that. "Calm down. Talk to me. Tell me what's wrong."

Her anger sizzled between them. "You won't let me out?"

Her escalating temper forced him to plain speaking. "No, I won't. I can't. I'm sorry, but it's too dangerous. You'd have hours and hours of walking before you even came close to reaching a town. There are critters of all sorts, and the occasional coyote or bear sometimes shows up —"

Bruce heard a click, and knew it was her seat belt opening.

"Cyn, stop it." Impatience made his voice sharp. What in the world was wrong with her? She'd been cocky only moments ago, confident in her ability to control the trucker, the situation, and him. Now she acted as if she'd found a bloody ax in his backseat.

He slowed for a sharp bend in the road. Gently, hoping to reassure her, Bruce said, "It's all right, you're safe with me —"

And her door swung open.

Bruce slammed on the brakes. The smell of burning rubber and the squeal of tires filled the quiet night. The old car jerked hard and came to a grinding halt.

Cyn had already rolled out.

"Oh, my God." Bruce twisted to look over the back of the seat. His brake lights left a red glow on the narrow road, and plainly showed the small body curled there.

His heart shot into his throat, his muscles clamped in alarm, and then he saw her push to her feet and take off in a hobbling, hurt run — into the thick woods at the side of the road.

Dear God, he'd worked with a lot of emotionally wounded women, but none who had ever feared him like this. She tried to hide the fear — she was brassy and bossy and full of obnoxious command. But he saw through that.

He couldn't let her get lost. He couldn't let her go.

Bruce opened his door, and silent as a ghost, went after her.

Chapter Two

Cyn could hear the awful soughing of her own breath in her ears as she slapped past branches and bramble and twigs. Damn, but she'd been such an idiot.

A preacher! Few things took her by surprise anymore, but she sure hadn't seen that one coming. She'd have believed almost anything else, but not that. The man was too rugged and sexy and handsome to be a preacher. No, she wasn't buying it. He had to be lying.

And why would he lie, unless it was to lull her, pull her in? That's what scared her.

Even as she thought it, she recalled how he'd come dashing to her rescue when no one else would have. He'd taken her blow to the chest without retaliation, and he'd even apologized for eyeing her boobs.

Other than that one slight, he hadn't leered as other men usually did. Mostly, he'd been watching her with gentle, concerned brown eyes. . . .

But she'd sure never seen a preacher who looked like him. Streaked blond hair that touched his collar, deep brown eyes framed by black lashes and low brows. Wide shoulders, trim hips. He was deeply tanned, physically fit. Muscular, sexy . . . In no way did he look like a man of great moral rectitude. A sinner, sure, but not a man of God.

Her foot caught on a gnarled root and she pitched forward, hitting the ground hard and getting several scratches and a mouthful of dirt. Pain shot up her leg. Reflexively, she curled into a small ball and held still, straining to hear. Nothing.

Odds were, he'd given up and gone on. Who wanted a looney tunes broad to deal with? Her reaction was nothing short of insane, she knew that, but even though Palmer Oaks was long dead, old memories were deeply inbred and impossible to shed.

She struggled to calm the wild drumming of her heartbeat so she could concentrate. She was safe from her past — had been safe since that night she'd left long ago.

However, her current predicament was not safe. She hurt from her toes to her ears, she'd left her suitcase behind, and she was all alone in the woods, as Bruce had said, hours from reaching a town.

She'd screwed up big time, so now what should she do?

Very slowly, every movement as silent as she could make it, she pulled into a crouch.

"Cyn."

The scream was startled right out of her. She flailed around and landed on her ass. Eyes wide, she stared in the darkness at the hulking shadow of his body standing a few feet away.

He made no move toward her, which was a good thing considering she'd probably scream again and she felt idiotic enough as it was. She didn't need to add to the drama.

Bruce let out a long sigh. "Don't run, okay? I swear I'm not going to hurt you." He took two steps back. She heard — and felt — his retreat more than saw it. "Are you all right?"

Her thoughts ran this way and that, making it impossible to speak. How the hell had he crept up on her like that? How did a man his size, easily six feet tall and she'd be willing to bet he weighed at least two hundred pounds, move without making a sound?

"You fell hard," he continued in that calm, gentle voice — a voice she realized was a lot like the Reverend Thorne's, the man Arlene and Palmer had taken her to see.

Cyn pulled back more, and hated herself for showing that much weakness.

Still, Bruce held himself immobile. "Did you hurt anything?"

She shook her head, then felt even more moronic because he couldn't possibly see her. Well, she'd quit acting dumb and cowardly right now. "No."

"Good. I'm glad."

Jesus, what type of man was he?

He knelt down too, and Cyn felt her spine collide with the rough bark of a massive tree.

Determined to brazen it out, she straightened her back and shoulders. It was unfortunate, but while he remained so close, she totally forgot the different ways that she knew to defend herself. She could have maced him. She could have drawn her knife.

Instead, she glared at him in the darkness, buried in confusion and exasperation and yeah, still some healthy fear. "What the hell do you want, anyway?"

"I just want to help you."

Yeah, right. And then he'd sell her a bridge. He didn't know her, had no vested interest in her — unless he hoped to get laid. Ha! Fat chance. He looked like he was poor, driving that old rattrap car and dressed in faded jeans.

She clenched her hands into fists. "I'm not screwing you."

"I didn't ask you to." And then, with some sort of warped amusement, he added, "I'm not that easy."

"Oh, give me a break," she said, more to herself than to him.

"That's what I'm trying to do. I offered to drive you into Visitation. But if that won't do, then at least let me get you to a gas station." She started to shake her head, and he continued. "But if you don't want to do that, either, then I'll leave your suitcase on the road for you."

She wasn't buying it. "You'd really do that?"

"Yes. But I'll also call the deputy of Visitation. His name is Scott Royal and he can come by and give you a ride."

Worse and worse. No way in hell did she want the law involved. "Thanks, but no thanks."

"Why?"

Was he an idiot? "I don't want any trouble with the law."

Bruce was silent for a moment, then asked quietly, "Why would there be trouble?"

Because she'd killed a man.

Only, Bruce didn't know that, and she

wasn't about to tell him. In five years, no one had come after her. She'd hidden her trail as best she could, but she knew, if the law had been after her, they'd have found her.

With her fear all but gone, Cyn looked around the murky interior of the woods. Bugs scurried by, owls hooted, leaves rustled. She'd been in some strange situations in her lifetime, but sitting here now, with a hunk claiming to be a preacher, no less, and carrying on a whispered conversation, had to take the cake.

Again, her lack of a reply prompted him to more discussion. "Scott's a friend, and more than that, he's a good man, a man who cares about people. He'll make sure you get someplace safe."

"You expect me to believe that all these saints are just running loose, waiting to help little ol' me?"

Bruce's dark shadow stretched out and then he was standing over her, tall, strong, and she sensed, oddly protective. "I understand you have reason for cynicism."

"Do you?" She was deliberately sarcastic, but damn it . . . he did sound understanding. Something about his voice, the emotion behind it, was beginning to reel her in.

She could feel his consideration, his acute attention on her, before he asked, "Do you need some money?"

Anger saved her. Using the tree for support, Cyn pulled herself upright. Her right ankle protested the movement, but she ignored it. "Why in hell would you want to give me money?"

"Because I'm concerned about you."

"Why?"

He hesitated, then finally said, "You're young."

"Twenty-two, buddy boy. Plenty old enough to have earned a living for five years now."

That surprised him, she could tell. "You look younger."

"Not to most men." Shut up, Cyn. She bit her bottom lip and held herself still.

"Twenty-two is definitely young to a thirty-five-year-old." His white teeth shone in a smile that didn't reassure her one bit, and he gave up. "You're also small, and female. I'm sorry, I don't mean to sound sexist, but you're vulnerable here alone. You're vulnerable just about anywhere alone right now."

Never in her entire life had she known anyone like him. She felt so damned confused her head hurt as much as her ankle.

His exasperation was expressed in a long, exaggerated sigh. "Look, Cyn, it's obvious that you're running away from something or someone. You're afraid."

She tried to square her shoulders again, but she was just too tired. "Maybe I'm running *to* something. Did you think of that?"

Rather than scoff, he asked, "Visitation?"

"And why not?" Did he think his little Podunk town was too good for her?

His sympathy washed over her like a gentle, warm wave. It was the weirdest sensation, as if she were being drawn to him, as if she knew him, even though they'd just met. He wasn't the man in the recurring dream, but still, she was starting to believe him.

How stupid could she be?

Okay, so he wasn't your average run-of-the-mill guy. He sure as certain wasn't a run-of-the-mill preacher, either. But he did seem genuinely kind. And caring, and sincere.

"You left your luggage in my car."

"I know." She rubbed her face tiredly. "It was stupid of me." Because she'd always prided herself on *not* being dumb, it hurt to make that admission. But everything she really needed was in her purse anyway. She wore the strap across her body and over her neck. No one would be able to yank it off her shoulder, not without taking her head off, too.

"You're afraid of me now," Bruce pointed out, "but you weren't. Not until I mentioned I was a preacher."

There was an unasked question there, and she supposed, given her behavior, he deserved an explanation or two. "Yeah, well, it doesn't add up. You and church pews . . . nope. It feels suspicious."

Incredulity rang in his tone when he said, "Suspicious enough to make you leap out of a running car?"

Though he couldn't possibly see, Cyn made a face. "You weren't going that fast and you refused to let me out."

"If you asked to jump off a bridge, I'd refuse to let you do that, too." He waited, huffed at her continued silence. "All right. You think I'm lying? Why?"

"Preachers don't look like you."

She saw his teeth again, and felt his amusement. "Is that so? Are you giving me a compliment or an insult?"

Cyn snorted. In some respects, men were all the same. Little by little, the sense of threat had entirely evaporated. She'd overreacted — she knew that now. But she wouldn't keep feeling foolish because of it. Better to make too much of something than to be caught with deceit.

She pushed away from the tree and dusted off her bottom. "Don't let it go to your head, but you have to know you're gorgeous."

He continued to grin. "Thank you." Casual as you please, he produced a hanky and used it to wipe her face. "You're a mess."

The gesture so took her by surprise, she froze. His touch was light, gentle, as if he worried he might hurt her.

Some strange, exceptional sensation expanded inside her. It was a dangerous feeling, stealing her breath, making her heart race. It made her weak — and so she rejected it.

She shoved his hand away. "How the hell can you see?" She narrowed her eyes and strained, but could only see the dark shadows of his body.

"You're very white," he said in a near whisper. Then louder, with a smile, "Except for all that long black hair."

"Witchy hair, I know." She turned her head and spit. "Ugh, I ate so much dirt, I shouldn't be hungry anymore."

Again, with unfamiliar tenderness, he smoothed her hair back, handed her the hanky, and then took her arm to start her back toward the car.

Like a zombie, Cyn found herself following. But really, what other option did she have? She didn't want to walk miles and miles in the dark, in the cold, in her skimpy sandals. She was already beat. And sleeping in the woods with the threat of wild animals didn't sound all that great, either.

Bruce propelled her forward with gentle, concerned insistence. His hand was big and hot, like the man himself. He didn't hold her tight, but rather just as a gentlemanly gesture.

He continued to chat as if he weren't retrieving her from the woods. "My twin brother is, or rather used to be, a bounty hunter. Is that more the type of occupation you had in mind for my mug?"

Amazed at such a disclosure, Cyn stared toward him. "Yeah. That'd work." God knew he was big and solid enough to chase down criminals. His nearness was somehow comforting and secure, not threatening. Then, just because she wanted to keep him talking so he wouldn't ask more questions, she said, "So you have a twin?"

"Married not too long ago. He and his wife, Shay, just settled in their new house in Visitation. We all used to live in Ohio. I ran a safe house there for prostitutes."

Cyn tripped over her own feet, and gasped as pain shot up her leg. "The hell you say?" Now *that* was just too damn much coincidence.

Bruce hauled her upright, then slipped his arm around her waist when she almost collapsed again. "Okay?"

"Quit asking me that." She shoved him back a safer distance. When he got too close, her heart did funny little flips and her stomach curled in an odd, unfamiliar way. "I'm fine." At least physically, she wasn't hurt. But mentally, she was reeling. "You want me to believe that you housed hookers?"

"When they needed a safe place to go, yes. I was able to help many of them start new lives."

As far as hints went, he wasn't all that subtle. Cyn tucked in her chin. "What if they didn't want to start a new life?"

Her challenging tone didn't faze him one bit. "Then I helped them deal with the life they had."

Unbelievable. It almost sounded like he truly cared, like he didn't judge them as the sludge of humanity. She peeked at his heavily shadowed form, and couldn't quite dredge up an image of him beating the evilness out of a woman.

"Shay also did some community work," he said, pulling her from her thoughts. "She opened a bigger, nicer safe house in the same area where I had mine. A dear friend of hers runs it now, and things are going great, so I thought I'd try my hand at something else."

Like saving recently retired hookers from annoyed truckers? She shook her head at herself. "Like what?"

"Easy there, watch your feet. There are sticker bushes."

His gallant consideration got on her nerves. It wasn't what she was used to. It sure as heck wasn't what she expected. "You can see pretty good in the dark, can't you?" The cold tried to sink into her bones, making her entire body shiver, but Bruce pulled her closer and his warmth settled over her, as comforting as a heated blanket.

"Well enough." And with tons of innuendo: "Being a preacher doesn't make me blind."

He led her over the bushes, and then she could see his car on the road, the headlights still on, sending scant illumination around the area. He stopped and turned her to face him. For a long moment, she got lost in the dark mystery of his eyes, until he said, "So, what'll it be?"

He wanted to know if she'd ride with him. But he'd already told her he wouldn't just leave her alone, and she'd been dumb enough for one night.

She shrugged. "Sure. Why not?"

An increasing breeze, damp with the threat of rain, lifted a long tress of her hair, sending it past her face and against Bruce's throat. She watched him draw in a deep breath, then mentally shake himself. He smoothed her hair back, tucked it behind her ear. The moon shone down on him, giving his masculine form an almost divine aura.

Damn, but he took her breath away.

His warm fingertips grazed her cheek, and then he dropped his hand. "I don't want you to do anything you don't want to do."

Odd, but what she wanted most at that moment was to curl into him and beg to be held. No one had ever really held her, not without expectations. No one had ever really cared about her, about what she wanted and needed, and suddenly, she craved his comfort.

But she hadn't begged for anything in years, not since she'd gone off on her own, and she sure as certain wouldn't start now.

Besides, she'd known since she was sixteen that her looks presented her as a sexual being, not merely a female. If her mother and Palmer Oaks hadn't made that clear, the Reverend certainly had. He blamed her for the way Palmer reacted to her. He told her that her soul was carnal.

Reverend Thorne was wrong, she knew that now, but men did look at her and get ideas. She wouldn't encourage those ideas with too much touching. Not anymore. Not even a man who seemed genuinely kind. She just didn't know enough about honesty to judge him.

"Naw, I'd rather ride than walk." And to dismiss the moments past, she laughed. "Sorry I freaked on you."

Bruce accepted her decision with a nod and they continued on toward the car. When she limped again, he asked, "Are you sure your leg's okay?"

"It's nothing."

"You're limping."

Her laugh sounded loud in the otherwise quiet area. "I've limped worse after being on my back all day."

His gaze zeroed in on her like a homing beacon. "Meaning?"

He knew damn good and well what she meant, but she said only, "You're a preacher, right? So I better not melt your ears with my sordid tales of debauchery."

"You have a colorful way of putting things."

"I'm a colorful kind of gal."

"I'll take a look at it if you want."

"No."

"Okay, then."

The idle chitchat distracted her. She needed to plan out the rest of the evening.

"I'm building a church," he said, as if the last fifteen minutes hadn't happened.

He treated her like any other woman he might have encountered, not as a crazy ex-hooker who leaped out of cars, not as a woman who looked like the original temptation.

It was . . . nice. "You mean in Visitation?"

"Yes. The closest one is almost two hours away, and a lot of the locals use that as an excuse not to attend service. Because I always liked working in the streets, I haven't limited myself to a single church in a very long time. But now, I don't know. It feels right to build a church right in the town proper. I feel the . . . *pull* to be there again, addressing a congregation, delivering a sermon. Do you know what I mean?"

He opened Cyn's door for her and she sat down, but kept her legs out. The interior lights spilled out in a soft arc, exaggerating Bruce's features, sharpening his bone structure, making his hair lighter, his eyes darker.

So many contrasts the preacher had.

"Sure. I felt the pull to come to Visitation."

"That's why you're here?"

It was probably past midnight. By the minute, the air grew heavier with the scent of an approaching storm. But Bruce seemed in no real hurry to be on their way.

Cyn wasn't sure what to think of that. "Yeah. Like you with your church, I'm ready to change my life, too."

"And you chose to do that in Visitation?"

"Visitation was the place that chose me."

He smiled again. "Maybe you're right. Maybe fate is lending a hand. For both of us."

Cyn licked her dry lips. All things aside, a girl couldn't be too careful. "I've gotta ask you something, Bruce."

She'd kept her tone light, but his look was full of serious regard as he stared down at her. "Of course. Anything."

She nodded, thought about how to put her question, then just blurted it out. "You into hitting women or kids? For any reason?" She watched him closely, waiting for any telltale sign that might give him away as a liar or a fraud.

There was no hesitation. "Never." His fingers touched her chin, tilting her face up to his. His thumb brushed at a little dirt on her jaw. "And I'd do anything in my power to stop anyone who did."

Cyn wasn't sure about that. No one had ever really intervened on her behalf before — but then again, she remembered the trucker and how Bruce had rushed out to defend her.

Just as he had before, he dropped his hand the moment he realized that he touched her. "Good men don't abuse others, and I wouldn't want to think of myself as less than a good man. Not perfect, mind you, because God knows I have my flaws."

Cyn nodded. "Picking up strangers is one of them."

He grinned at her quip. "I have nothing but disdain for anyone who deliberately hurts another person." He paused, his eyes narrowing. "Is that what you're afraid of? That someone will hurt you?"

She shrugged, wary of dredging up the past and the ugliness of it. It was incredible that she'd told him so much already. She'd never shared her awful secrets with anyone. "If a man thinks he's justified, then who's to stop him?"

Bruce shoved his hands into his pockets. The fact that they were alone on a deserted road in the middle of the night didn't disturb him. "There is no excuse, none, for ever hurting a woman or child. Unfortunately, bad people are everywhere, hiding behind occupations, wealth, social standing, and fanatical convictions. A mean spirit isn't something exclusive to the ugly or the poor — it's not something you can easily see in a person's eyes."

He'd be good at delivering the sermons, she decided. He had a real passionate way of sharing his opinions and beliefs. "I can sometimes tell."

He stared down at her so intently, she felt it like a tactile touch. He looked big and imposing, but she wasn't afraid. Not now.

"You couldn't tell with me."

"You just took me by surprise, that's all." She tried a halfhearted smile. "If you say you're a saintly sort, then who am I to argue?"

He wasn't appeased. Just the opposite — her words seemed to set him off. "Tell me something, Cyn. You're obviously an intelligent woman. Why are you taking so many chances? When you know the risks, why are you hitchhiking and —"

"I don't have a car." She felt like saying, "Duh," but didn't.

He gave her a look of incomprehension.

By necessity, her view of such things was philosophical. "I needed to travel."

"But it scares you."

"Most times, fear is a luxury, so it doesn't matter if you're afraid." She shared with him what she'd always known. "And I don't really have a choice."

Bruce rubbed his face, stared up at the heavens, and muttered something under his breath that she didn't quite catch. Then, in an almost angry stride, he headed to his side of the car.

Cyn had learned to read people, especially men, and Bruce Kelly was as sincere as a man could be. She would have seen that before, if his odd vocation hadn't taken her by surprise.

He slammed his door and started the engine. "Ready?"

"*Ready* is my middle name." She swung her legs into the car, shut the door, and let out a long breath. She'd been up for too many hours to count, which maybe had contributed to her earlier panic. As she fastened her seat belt, she asked, "I think I'll sleep while you drive. I'm pooped."

Bruce knew that Cyn wasn't really asleep. With his jacket pulled up over her chest and shoulders like a blanket, she dozed. But anytime he moved — to adjust the radio, to turn down the heater — she opened those pale eyes just enough to watch him.

It broke his heart to see such a young woman so vigilant and fearful. She was stretched out as much as a person could be in a car while still sitting upright. She kept her purse looped across her neck, with the purse tucked securely under her arm, but otherwise her limbs were loose and relaxed.

Her face was half turned toward him, her long, silky hair teasing her breasts, hanging almost to her elbows. Her nails were short and blunt, unpainted. Her feet were small and narrow. She wore no makeup at all.

And she was so incredibly sexy she made his heart race. Half asleep, she should have looked like a child.

Instead, she looked . . . wanton.

Her features were exotic, so delectably carnal and earthy that she needed to do nothing at all to make a man think of rumpled sheets and sweat-damp bodies straining together. Bruce had no doubt that she'd had more than a few men anxious to bed her.

In all likelihood, she'd sold them the privilege on a regular basis. He also knew, given her reserve and probable background, that some of those men had hurt her.

Yet, they hadn't broken her spirit. That bespoke an uncommon inner strength, and gave him hope.

Despite her fortitude, the exhaustion was plain in her boneless posture and the weariness etched in her face, so Bruce drove straight home. After parking on the gravel road in front of the half-finished church, he turned off the headlights and cut the engine. "Cynthia."

Her eyes opened and she straightened with a luxuriant stretch and a lusty yawn. "Where are we?" Curious, she glanced around, saw that everything was dark and empty, and gave him a suspicious frown.

"My place." He got out and circled the hood to open her door.

Eyes wide, she scampered from the car so fast, she forgot her shoes. She faltered a moment on her hurt ankle, then breathed deeply of the cold night air. Bruce watched her toes curl against the chilly, dew-wet grass.

"This is Visitation?" She looked around with a sort of silent awe.

Bruce felt his lips twitch. She said "Visitation" with the same reverence one might give heaven. "It is. Part of it, at least."

He reached in the car for his jacket and wrapped it around her, then fetched her sandals. She braced a hand on his shoulder as she slipped them on her feet, saying a distracted, "Thanks." She was too busy soaking in the sights to pay much attention to her feet.

He pointed down the street. "There's a nice diner where you can catch breakfast in the morning, but they're closed for the night now. Around the block, about two minutes from here, is a small motel. The town's small, with one strip mall, a few small businesses, and a factory farther out. Fact is, you can drive completely through town in under ten minutes, but if you go back about an hour from where we came and take the exit into —"

"No." She closed her arms around herself to ward off the April chill and favored him with a bright smile that made everything masculine in him stand at attention. "I'm here and I'm staying. In Visitation. Nowhere else."

Bruce cocked a brow at her quick insistence.

Her smile turned whimsical. "I've dreamed about this place so many times. I want to see if I recognize it in daylight, if it feels as good as it did in my imagination."

"All right." Bruce had learned long ago when to push and when to let things ride. "I can take you to the motel after you eat."

She gave him a calculated look. "If the restaurant's closed, how do you plan to feed me?"

Because he couldn't help himself, he flicked the end of her nose. "I can cook."

"No kidding? I mean, I didn't expect you to do that, but a starving woman doesn't quibble." She nodded toward the building. "So these are your digs?"

Bruce relaxed. Finding herself alone with him in a less-than-public place didn't seem to alarm her at all. Other than her brief, overwhelming fear on the road, she'd been as at ease as a long acquaintance.

"This will eventually be my church." Pride filled him as he gestured to the two-story, red brick house now sporting a very large, not-quite-complete addition. Because he'd been gone overnight, he'd left the porch light on and it showed the destroyed lawn typical of new construction. The building wasn't fancy, but he loved it.

God didn't need fancy, and neither did Bruce.

"It doesn't look like a church."

He watched her smooth her unruly curls, tossed by the wind. It distracted him, and made him think of things he shouldn't. He shook his head. "In the same way that I don't look like a preacher?"

"Just the opposite. It's too plain to be a church." She lightly elbowed him. "And you're too hunky to be a preacher."

Plenty of women had teased and flirted with him, but he'd never paid much attention, never lost sight of the fact that they needed him and depended on him. With Cyn, it was different and he had to deliberately keep his mind off taboo speculation. With her, he didn't just see the bravado of a woman covering past hurts. He saw long, silky hair and warm, smooth skin. He smelled her — the scent of woman, more provocative than any manufactured perfume. He enjoyed her bold gaze, the tilt of her sexy mouth . . . "Did I mention that my father was a preacher, too?"

Thank God, she'd been unaware of his intimate perusal. She smiled without a care. "Does he look like you?"

Mentioning his family would hopefully help him keep his head. "Not really. He's darker. My brother and I got our fair hair from our mother, but our brown eyes from Dad."

"Dad's gotta love the bounty hunter, huh?"

Bruce enjoyed her teasing. "We're very proud of Bryan. He helps people, same as we try to do. It's just that his methods are . . . a little different."

"Yeah, I can imagine." She winked at him. "So, where are we going to eat?"

"The construction crew's managed to leave most of my living quarters around back untouched. It's small, but then I'm only one person. I don't need much space."

"Lead the way." But when Cyn went to take a step, she stumbled, and Bruce saw a grimace on her face.

She was hurt more than she wanted to admit, stubborn woman. "Lean on me, and I'll help you inside." He put his arm around her waist and pulled her against him.

Even though she held herself stiffly — due more to pride than discomfort at his closeness, he was sure — he was very aware of her softness, of how slight she felt against his side, the heat of her small body. The top of her head aligned with his mouth, and he fought the instinct to plant a small kiss on her forehead.

She was dead tired, had probably been on the road for hours, but she still smelled fresh and spicy and so much like a woman that Bruce almost stumbled, too.

As they passed the side of the church, she noticed the crumbled wall where plastic had been tacked up to protect against the weather. "You sleep in there with your house open?"

"Visitation isn't exactly a hotbed of crime, and it's not for long. They're saying within a month, but it'll probably take longer. I'm learning that in construction, a month often means three months. A very nice glass block niche will go there. Shay, my sister-in-law, donated the money for it. We'll use it as a sunny play area for the little ones who come to church with their parents."

"She donated that, huh?"

"Did I mention that Shay was filthy rich?" He grinned. "She could probably buy the whole town, but instead, she's been running amuck making improvements everywhere. Thanks to her, we've been able to hold services in the basement of the only local bank. She's paying the rental fee until the church is complete."

Bruce unlocked the door that led into his kitchen. Warmth greeted them, along with the scents of sawdust and drywall. He flipped on the inside light. "Here we are. Why don't you sit down and rest your ankle."

He glanced at her, winced at the dirt still on her face and clothes, and pulled out a kitchen chair for her. "You're a mess, young lady. Sit still and let me get you a few damp cloths."

"Thanks." Once Cyn was seated, she kicked off her sandals again and bent to look at her ankle, while saying, "You're a man who housed hookers, with a preacher for a father, a bounty hunter for a brother, and a wealthy sister-in-law. Your life must never be boring."

What an understatement. Much of the past year had been chaotic, sometimes frightening, and full of change. "You should meet some of my friends here in Visitation." He returned to her with two damp dishcloths. "Hold still."

She held up her hands. "See these? They make it easy for me to do my own bathing."

Bruce winced. "There's no mirror down here, and I doubt you're up to climbing the stairs. As to these hands . . ." He laid the cloths down and caught both her wrists, examining her palms. In places, they were scraped raw, probably from her fall in the woods. She had dirt under her nails, scratches and scrapes.

Bruce pulled her upright and practically carried her to the kitchen sink a few feet away. Her bulky purse was between them. "You can leave your purse on the table."

"It goes where I go."

"What about when you sleep?"

She patted it. "Makes a nice pillow."

Bruce rolled his eyes. She must have something mighty important inside that she thought to protect with her person. "Suit yourself, but it pains me to be thought a thief."

"Yeah, well, it'd pain me more to lose it."

Did she have her entire life in that bag? It was possible, so Bruce let it drop. Trust would come in time.

Feeling bedeviled by his own wayward musings, he stood beside her, supervising while she washed away the dirt and small streaks of dried blood on her tender palms.

When she saw his frown, she said, "Relax, Lancelot. It's no biggie."

How many hurts in her life had she dismissed as *no biggie?* Her stomach rumbled, breaking his troubled thoughts enough that Bruce laughed. "I can take a hint."

While she finished washing, he opened the refrigerator and took out a covered container. "Left-over chicken, broiled potatoes, and string beans sound good?"

"Like heaven." She returned to the table, pulled a chair around, and propped up her legs, making herself at home. "So tell me about your friends."

Bruce began preparing a plate to go in the microwave. "There's Joe Winston. Now, you want to talk about a man with a colorful past, Joe fits the bill. He's been a police officer, a PI, a bounty hunter, and a bodyguard. Now he's married to Luna, and together they run a recreational lake here in Visitation. It's further out, very private and very beautiful." He turned and watched her running her fingers through her hair, attempting to untangle it.

Wishing he could do that for her, he

cleared his throat. "You remember the deputy I told you about? Scott Royal."

"Cops tend to stick in my mind."

"Scott's a deputy, but you seldom see the sheriff, so if you need the law, odds are it'll be Scott. He's a nice guy, but he goes bonkers whenever Joe's sister, Alyx, is in town."

"How come?"

"They rub each other the wrong way. Or maybe the right way — with those two it's hard to tell." He laughed, remembering their last encounter. "The Winstons are pretty outrageous, and they have a lot of presence. When one is around, you know it. But watching Alyx and Scott spark off each other is entertaining."

"Alyx doesn't live here?"

"Not yet, but I expect her to move to Visitation any day now. So far she's restricted herself to monthly visits, which is probably all that's saved Scott's sanity." Bruce put the plate in the microwave and turned it on. "I can't tell you about Visitation without mentioning Jamie Creed."

Cyn cocked her head to the side. Curiosity shone from her light eyes. "Jamie Creed?"

He opened the refrigerator and surveyed drinks. "Jamie has never come right out and said it, but he's a psychic of some sort. Or maybe more specifically an empath."

"He picks up on others' emotions?"

Bruce frowned at himself. "Yes, but actually, it goes beyond even that. Jamie somehow knows things, even before they happen. And he knows how they'll happen, how to manipulate events so they work out the way he wants them to."

"Sounds spooky."

"Not really. The women in town see him as a dark, romantic mystery. The men, from my observations, are both jealous and leery of him."

"Why would they be leery?"

Bruce poured her iced tea, which was about all he had to offer other than water, then joined her at the small oak table. "Jamie has this habit of only showing himself long enough to shake things up. He lives up on the mountain — where, exactly, I'm not sure. One minute he'll be here, then he'll be gone, and he only comes back when it suits him to do so."

Cyn's expression became pinched. "He lives in the middle of tall trees with no one else around?"

Because he watched her so closely, with so much fascination, Bruce noticed how the mention of Jamie affected her. "As I said, I don't really know. I suppose so, though. The mountains here are so thick with trees, they're almost impenetrable."

Cyn slowly licked her lips. "He's tall. Dark hair, a beard. Trim but muscular."

Bruce leaned toward her. "You've met Jamie?"

"No." She shook her head. "But he has the darkest brown eyes, not sexy like yours, but almost black and empty and sort of eerie . . ."

The microwave dinged, and Cyn nearly jumped out of her chair.

Bruce reached for her hand. "You haven't met him, but you've seen him?"

She avoided his gaze. "This'll clinch it. You'll definitely think I'm nuts."

"I know Jamie, who fades in and out, and I don't think he's nuts. Trust me, nothing you can say will shock me after meeting him."

"All right, you asked for it." She gave him a crooked smile. "It's this strange dream that I keep having. Remember I said Visitation pulled at me? Well, I didn't know it was Visitation, I just knew what it looked like and how it felt. I'd see this big, clean lake and so many trees that sometimes you couldn't see the sky and I saw . . . Jamie Creed. I didn't know his name, I just saw him. But unlike the other things, like the lake and the trees, he was always vague. There, but not real defined."

Beyond fascinated, Bruce rose from his seat to get her plate, giving himself a moment to think. Was it possible that she knew Jamie from somewhere? Maybe Jamie's mysterious past was somehow tied in with hers. "What did he say to you in this dream?"

"Nothing. He was just there. Quiet and not really frowning, but not smiling, either."

"No, Jamie doesn't smile much." Too many times to count, Bruce had pondered Jamie and his too serious, too sober outlook on life. Jamie seemed to feel responsible for everyone, even though it was plain he wanted to keep himself separate from others.

But now Cyn had some sort of connection to him.

"Will I get to meet Jamie, do you think?"

He set her plate in front of her and watched her inhale the scent of roast chicken with great anticipation. "That's up to Jamie. If he wants to meet you, he'll show up."

She accepted that with a nod. Before Bruce realized what she was doing, she'd dug a small pill bottle out of her purse and had two round tablets ready to toss in her mouth.

He caught her wrist. "What are you taking?"

She stared at his restraining hand, and slowly, her gaze moved up to his face. They had a visual standoff, but Bruce didn't relent, so finally she said, "It's aspirin. For my ankle."

"Let me see."

She stiffened and her chin tucked in. "You're calling me a liar?"

Her wrist felt slender, almost fragile, with his fingers wrapped around it. "I don't like drugs."

She jerked away from him. "And I don't like pain."

"What pain?"

Her foot got thrust in his face. "You saw me limping. You even kept harping about it. Remember?"

Bruce wrapped his fingers around the arch of her small foot. He lowered it to his lap so he could inspect her ankle. It was swollen and bruised and she sucked in her breath when he touched it. "I don't think you broke anything or you wouldn't have been able to walk at all, but it's probably sprained."

"So do I have Your Majesty's permission to pop some aspirin?"

Leaving her foot balanced on his thigh, Bruce again caught her wrist and pried her fingers open. Two small, chalky-white pills were on her palm. He recognized them as brand-name aspirin.

She started to jerk her foot away, but Bruce held her still. "I'm sorry."

She didn't soften one bit. "I'm not a drug head."

He'd already apologized, and by her comment, he knew she understood his concern. "I'm glad."

His simple but sincere sentiment took the heat from her eyes. She licked her lips. "I know a lot of the other girls took drugs, but I never did."

"Other girls?" She made sarcastic comments, but hadn't outright admitted to being a prostitute yet.

She met his gaze without flinching. "From the time I was seventeen, until now, I was a hooker. But you already knew that."

"I thought it was possible." It took all his resolve to keep his expression impassive, when inside his emotions churned. Seventeen. It hurt him to even consider it. "Why?"

"The usual reason — I needed money."

"Why prostitution? Why not some other job?"

"Whoring is easier?"

He chastised her with a frown. "No, it's not."

She laughed. "You're right, it isn't." She turned her head, giving him a long look, then shrugged. "I tried to get other jobs, but I was young, dumb as dirt when it came to skills, and even the most basic job wanted some sort of ID."

It was a typical story for runaways, one he'd heard many times. "You couldn't give any ID?"

"Nope."

"Because you didn't want to be taken back?"

"That's about it."

He closed his eyes, pained for her. "And so you sold yourself."

"I didn't have much else to sell. And it wasn't like I wanted to do it." She half laughed, showing no signs of real humor. "But I got hungry, ya know?"

"Yes. I know."

"I'd watched some girls turning tricks. I saw what they were doing and how they dressed and the stuff they said. Guys are notoriously easy. You stand there, smile, show a little leg or cleavage . . ."

"I understand." But he couldn't bear to visualize it.

"Anyway, I watched them, what the drugs and the flesh peddling did to them, and I knew I never wanted to be like that. So I was more careful and I stayed away from the pushers."

Her idea of caution would make most people faint in fright. Still, he understood her — and he admired her. "Good for you."

"It doesn't take a rocket scientist to see that drugs mess up your head. And like you said, being a small woman puts you at a disadvantage from jump. I didn't need to be loopy on top of it. Besides, I wanted to save all my money, not waste it on getting high." After saying that, she popped the aspirin in her mouth and washed them down with tea, the topic dead by her decree.

Bruce accepted that. He patted her hand. "I'll get you some ice for your ankle. Use my chair to keep it elevated while you eat."

"Yes, oh-mighty-one."

The variety of names she called him weren't exactly complimentary, but they weren't outright insults, either, and Bruce was too relieved to have her good humor restored to say anything about it.

The rain started not two minutes later. The sky opened up and the storm hit as an angry torrent, accompanied by wailing winds and a spattering of hail. The lights in the kitchen flickered, but didn't go out.

He was glad. Never before had he felt so entertained watching a woman eat. Cyn was small, but she had a hearty appetite. He'd realized while watching her that her manners were surprisingly refined. In his past experience, hookers were deliberately crass and uncouth. If Cyn tempered what she said, no one would ever suspect her of being anything other than an exceptionally appealing young lady with a middle-class background.

She ate every bite on her plate, but refused seconds when Bruce offered them. "Any more and my jeans will pop a snap. But thanks."

"You're welcome."

She pushed her plate back and slouched in her seat with her hands laced over her flat belly. "There's nothing in this world like home-cooked food."

Bruce was good at picking up on clues to a person's background, but as clues went, that one was pretty in-your-face. "You normally eat at restaurants?"

"I've never had a kitchen, so yeah."

"Never?"

She met his surprise with an expression of negligence. "Not since I was a kid, and my mother sure as hell wasn't Suzy-homemaker, you know?" She stood up and stretched, flexed her ankle experimentally, and frowned. "I'd better be on my way. I don't want to abuse your hospitality."

It was three in the morning, it was storming, and she looked exhausted as well as hurt.

After giving her a long, thoughtful look, Bruce came to a sudden decision. Only moments ago, he'd had his intentions all planned out. He'd told himself it'd be for the best for her to go the motel. He'd told himself it wouldn't look right, for *her,* if she stayed with him. He'd check in on her, offer her assistance, and keep in touch. A good plan. A solid, typical plan.

But suddenly, things felt different.

He didn't want her to go.

He stood in front of her, hating the way she abruptly turned defensive and watchful. "I'll drive you to the motel," he told her, holding her gaze with his own. "But if you'd prefer, you can sleep here for the night."

Chapter Three

Barefoot, still half-asleep, Jamie Creed stepped out onto his wooden porch. The trees surrounding his hidden home blocked his view of the stars.

But he could see *her.*

She was here, at last, in Visitation. Safer, but not out of danger, not yet. He closed his eyes and concentrated, but it didn't help. He could see her, smell her, practically feel her warm flesh and the trembling of her most secret fears, but he couldn't see the threat. Not clearly enough to help.

Frustration bit into him, making him tense. He brought his fists lightly against the railing. The wood was slick and wet once again with another spring rain. Soon the wildflowers would be blooming and the birds would all return. The woods would be alive with newborn wildlife: deer, beaver, fox . . . It was a time of year he loved, but now, he felt weighted down with the unknown.

He had to help her, *but how?*

Already she'd touched him in ways he

didn't like, calling out to him, connecting with him when few people ever tried. Not anymore.

The whistling wind cut through his T-shirt and unsnapped jeans, ruffling his beard and sending his too-long hair into his eyes. He'd awakened with her need, a need he couldn't yet understand. He'd hoped a breath of cold, crisp air would clear his head. It hadn't, but he realized that she was with Bruce, and for now, that was enough. Bruce was a good man. He'd keep her safe.

Tonight.

But was Bruce strong enough to protect her forever?

Cyn woke with a small stretch — and her foot bumped into a hard, masculine thigh. Memories ran through her like a flash fire, memories of Palmer Oaks, numerous faceless men after him . . . She bolted upright in alarm and dread. Her heart was racing, her head spinning — and she saw Bruce.

Slumped more upright than otherwise at the other end of the sofa, he stirred, got one eye open, and stared at her. Their gazes held.

"Good morning," he rumbled in a sexy,

sleep-deep voice that sent shivers all through her.

Oh, no. *No, no, no.* Cyn blinked, praying he would disappear. But he didn't. "You slept there?" she accused. "All night?"

His attention moved from the top of her wildly tangled hair, to her shoulders, breasts, and abruptly to the ceiling. "It would appear so. Sorry." He sat up and scrubbed his hands over his face. "I meant to go upstairs, but I guess I fell asleep."

"What kind of lame-ass excuse is that?"

He shrugged, stretched, and yawned. "We were talking, then you dozed off and I was listening to you —"

"*Listening* to me?"

One side of his whiskered mouth lifted in a slight, self-conscious smile. "You sounded very peaceful in your sleep."

Get a grip, Cyn.

His gaze burned into her, and his brown eyes looked doubly sexy when heavy with fatigue and coupled with an unshaven jaw and rumpled hair. He shrugged again, half-apologetic, more than a little pensive. "I guess I dozed off at some point." He looked away and ran both hands through his hair, smoothing the overlong, sun-streaked locks.

Cyn couldn't quite take it in. She'd sort

of slept with a man who hadn't paid her. And he hadn't touched her. He'd just . . . listened to her?

What if she'd snored?

She remembered using his bathroom upstairs to wash up and change into one of his sweatshirts. It had been storming so hard, she'd refused to let him run out for her suitcase, and he'd been equally adamant that she not go after it. So, she'd borrowed his shirt.

It was clean, fresh from a drawer, but still it smelled of Bruce, and her stomach had done that funny twisting thing again after she'd pulled it on over her head. She'd hugged it to her, somehow comforted until she realized what she was doing and forced herself to stop.

She didn't need his comfort.

She didn't need anybody.

After she'd washed up and cleaned her teeth, he'd brought her blankets and a pillow so she could nest on the oversized couch in the room used for watching television and reading.

The kitchen and TV rooms took up only a small portion of the first floor. The rest, with the addition, were designated for church services. By necessity, the rooms were small, which meant that even if Bruce weren't on the couch with her, they'd have been in close proximity.

Cyn tried to quit staring at him. "Last I remember, we were gabbing . . ."

Bruce nodded. "You looked more asleep than awake, but you asked me a lot of stuff about Visitation, and so I answered."

Cyn nodded as snippets of memory crept back on her. She'd been curled up under the blankets, warm and drowsy, while rain continued to batter the house and the wind whistled through the trees and rattled the plastic covering the unfinished wall. The next thing she knew, she woke up and Bruce was still there.

He turned slightly to face her, and his denim-covered thigh brushed her bare feet again. She'd left her jeans on, and he still wore all his clothes, but it felt more intimate than anything she'd ever experienced.

And she'd pretty much experienced it all.

Or so she'd thought.

She felt crippled by confusion and conflicting emotions, and pulled her feet beneath the blanket, well away from him and his heat and his masculine perfection.

Though nothing escaped Bruce's notice, he pretended not to see her reaction. "How's your ankle?"

She hadn't thought about it until he mentioned it, and then she realized a dull, throbbing ache traveled up her leg. "It's great."

"Fibber. Keep that up and your nose will grow." He stood, scratched his stomach and yawned.

Her gaze zeroed in on impressive morning wood straining the front of his jeans. Her mouth went dry.

Oh boy. She'd seen plenty of erections on plenty of guys in the past few years. Some of the men were handsome, some were pigs.

They all paid.

They all left her feeling cold and empty.

She didn't feel cold or empty now. She didn't mean to stare, but she couldn't get herself to look away, either. He was *so* fine, so incredibly good-looking, and now, despite knowing he was a preacher who sermonized on sins and sinners, he had a boner — which made him all man, as far as she was concerned.

She'd kept her purse beside her through the night, and now she hugged it to her chest.

"Want to take a shower while I fix breakfast?"

Finally, Cyn elevated her attention to

Bruce's face, and wanted to melt on the spot. He wasn't leering, he wasn't even going to acknowledge the perfectly normal morning function of his body or her less-than-casual reaction to it. Well, he could keep his face as expressionless as he pleased, but he couldn't dim the heat in those dark bedroom eyes.

She saw it, and for some unknown reason, a reciprocal heat burned deep inside her. "A hot shower would be heaven." If she hadn't turned over a new leaf, she'd have invited him to join her. But all things considered, he probably would have refused her anyway.

"When you finish bathing, get the antiseptic ointment from the medicine cabinet and put some on your scratches."

Cyn touched her neck and discovered a sore spot and a few nicks. She shoved her thick hair back from her face, knowing she looked a fright . . . Oh, for crying out loud. Who cared?

She didn't.

She didn't want him to be attracted to her, anyway. "Sure, thanks."

After untangling herself from the blankets and readjusting the strap of her purse, she stood. Her ankle felt better today, and she gingerly put her weight on it. Her hair hung in long, twisted ropes down her back, and more muscles ached than didn't. Getting dressed and ready to go job-hunting was going to bite.

Bruce didn't touch her. He just crossed his arms over his chest and watched her. "You have more aspirin?"

"Yeah."

"Do you need help up the stairs?"

"Hardly." Damn him, she'd make it if she had to crawl. Did he have to be so caring and helpful and . . .

"Then I'll go get your suitcase."

Guilt nearly choked her. It wasn't his fault that she didn't know how to deal with nice people. "It's not raining any-more?"

He looked toward the window, but the curtains were drawn. "Not hard, if it is. I don't hear anything."

It still looked dark to Cyn, but in her former profession, where the night meant work and the day was dead, she'd kept the hours of an owl, not an eagle. "What time is it?"

Glancing at his watch, he said, "Almost seven. It's supposed to clear up today. The sun will be out before you know it." He turned and headed for the door. "I'll be right back."

* * *

Bruce found her upstairs, sitting on the edge of his bed, her purse in her lap, and it floored him. He'd stood outside in the cold long enough to get his body under control, but his thoughts were another matter.

The second he saw her, urges and images converged on him in a tidal wave of heat and need. Cyn could stand in a pile of mud and give men thoughts. Seeing her on a bed — *his* bed — was like throwing gas on an already blazing fire.

The urge was there, prodding him to step in, to ease her onto her back and cover her with his body, to taste her, take her . . .

He was going to have to get a handle on his reactions or else keep his distance. No other option was permissible.

And he didn't want to stay away from her.

He started to speak to her, and belatedly he saw that her head was bowed, her shoulders slumped. Lust fled in the face of concern. He took two silent steps into the room. "Cyn?"

Immediately she straightened and gave a small, brave smile. "Sorry. No place to sit up here but on the john and I thought you might want to make use of that before I get in the shower."

"Right." Her blunt speech didn't put him off. After years of running the safe house, he was well used to women saying just about anything. Still, he'd never shared a bathroom with any of those women. And, at least in his mind, none of them had looked like Cyn.

He set her bag beside her. She looked more worn than any woman ever should, especially a woman so young. She'd attempted to comb her hair but she still suffered bedhead, and dark circles were under her vivid eyes, the contrast lighting them like the pale blue of a flame.

She hadn't had enough sleep, but Bruce didn't know what to do about that. He had an appointment, and if the weather cleared, men, both paid contractors and volunteers, would show up to work on the church.

He couldn't, wouldn't, leave her alone to deal with them. Cyn was both skittish and provoking. He refused to borrow trouble.

Added to her obvious fatigue, she now had the small scratches on her throat and her mouth was pinched with pain, no doubt caused by her ankle. Should he insist she go to the doctor to get it checked?

One look at her stiffened spine and he

knew she'd do just as she pleased. He managed a smile. "It's stopped raining and the sun's peeking out, but it's still chilly. You have warm stuff to wear?"

"You're worse than an old lady, you know that?"

Feigning offense, Bruce said, "Concern is part of my stock and trade. Be nice and tolerate it, okay?"

She laughed, dropped her suitcase on his bed and opened it to produce a sweater set. "I promise I'll be warm enough."

Bruce would prefer she wear a coat, but maybe she didn't have one. He frowned, realized she was watching him with a sort of rebellious regard, and got hold of himself. If he got too smothering in his worry, she might bolt on him. Best to retrench now before he pushed her too far. "Give me just a minute and then the bathroom's all yours."

He was in and out in less than two minutes. He didn't bother to shave yet, but he did splash his face and brush his teeth. Cyn was waiting for him in the narrow hall when he stepped out. He felt her closeness like the brush of warm breath, and his guts tightened.

Not since his high school days, before he'd decided to become a preacher, had he felt such volcanic sexual need. Back then, he'd have talked the girl into going to the gravel pit, or the drive-in — anyplace that ensured privacy where they could indulge their healthy desires. He'd been young and undisciplined then, like most testosterone-ridden youths.

These days, his healthy desires were well under control. Or at least they were the day before.

He started to edge past her. "I'll head to the kitchen and get breakfast going."

She didn't move out of his way. "Shouldn't it be my turn to cook?"

"Do you know how?"

Amazingly enough, her face colored. It was the first time he'd seen her blush. "Not really. But I'm not stupid. I can read directions."

He was close enough to kiss her — scratch that. He managed a brotherly smile. "Next time, okay?"

Her brows lifted the tiniest bit. "Next time?"

He had to put some distance between them before he did something even dumber than coddling her. "Sure, you can pay me back. You're not leaving Visitation anytime soon, right?"

"I don't plan to leave ever."

God help him. "There you go." He stepped past her, and his chest brushed against the lush fullness of her breasts. Bruce couldn't bring himself to look at her again. "Don't linger too long, okay? I don't want your pancakes to get cold."

As he trotted down the stairs, he felt as if the hounds of hell were on his heels. Lust had no place in his life right now, but he had a feeling that as long as Cyn hung around, he'd be dealing with it.

He had the table set and a platter of buttered pancakes ready when he felt her presence. He looked up, and his breath caught.

Silly girl.

Did she really think dowdier clothes could mask her appeal? She wore the sweater set, dark green and high-necked and a size too big, over loose-fitting khakis and slip-on shoes. Her long hair was still damp and had been woven into a thick braid. She wore no makeup and her eyes showed her uncertainty.

Bruce straightened and crossed his arms, pretending to survey her when in fact his gaze had devoured her the second she appeared. "Very nice. Very professional. I expect you'll get hired on the spot."

"Right. Don't overdo it, okay?" Her

words were teasing, but couldn't hide her discomfort.

It broke his heart and made him desperate to reassure her. "Definitely."

She held out the hem of the cardigan and looked up at him with hopeful eyes. "It's . . . *blah* enough?"

A surprised laugh escaped him. Miss Cynthia Potter couldn't be blah, even when so obviously trying. "No, not blah at all. I'd say . . . classy. Sedate."

"I don't look like a tramp?"

His breath caught. *"No."* Anger at her, and at himself, rippled through him. "Why would you say something like that?"

"Because I usually do, no matter what I wear. At least that's what I've been told." She pulled out a chair and dropped into it. "Dressing down isn't what I'm used to. I had a hell of a time picking out these clothes."

They needed to explore her awful declaration, but Bruce couldn't help but be grateful for the change of topic. "When did you shop?"

"Before hitching here. I had to toss out a bunch of my old clothes." Her nose wrinkled. "I figured anything spandex, animal print, or fake leather had to go."

He sat opposite her, forked pancakes

onto both their plates, and did what he knew he should do. He encouraged her to talk. “What kind of job are you hoping to get?”

She picked at the edge of one pancake, her gaze averted. “I don’t care, as long as it’s a real job.” Her eyes lifted to lock with his. “A legitimate job.”

Before Bruce even knew what he was going to say, the words were out. “I’d like to help.”

Her soft mouth formed a crooked smile. “Now, why doesn’t that surprise me?”

Derision masked a lot of hurt, he knew. He warmed to the idea. “I could give you a job helping here at the church.”

She stared at him, a little stunned, then gave a burst of surprised laughter. “Me, in a church? Now, wouldn’t *that* set the good people on their ears.”

“You’re a good person, Cyn.”

“You don’t even know me.”

“I’m a good judge of character.”

As if he were simple, she said succinctly, “I was a *hooker.*”

“You did what you had to do — you said so yourself.” Bruce leaned forward in his chair. “But no one knows what you did before coming here. No one has to know. Your business is your own.”

"Right." She drowned her pancakes in syrup. "Reverend Thorne would disagree with you."

Bruce could feel himself tightening, but he kept his tone calm. "Who?"

"Reverend Thorne, this creepy, cleric guy I was taken to see, sort of like intervention."

"When was this?"

"Long time ago, when I was a kid. You don't think I'd have gone on my own, do you?" She snorted over the absurdity of that. "He said I look like a whore. Always have and always would. Something about my harlot's soul manifesting itself in my appearance."

Bruce wasn't a violent man under normal circumstances, but this wasn't normal. If the reverend were here right now, Bruce would have happily beat him to a pulp.

How dare a man, especially a man pretending to do God's work, tell her such a cruel thing? How dare he emotionally abuse a young girl?

Bruce's hands curled into fists, but there was no anger in his voice when he spoke. "Thorne sounds like an idiot."

"Yeah, I know. Stupid and mean. I'm not really sure what faith he was supposed to be, but he and Palmer got along great."

"Palmer?"

Her lip curled. "Palmer Oaks. The guy my mother shacked with. Talk about colorful characters. Those two'd take the cake."

Emotion tightened his throat, and Bruce reached across the table to take her hand. "I haven't known you long, but I already know without a single doubt that you're a very intelligent young lady."

"Damn right — and thanks for noticing."

She was in a talkative mood this morning. Bruce hoped that meant she was beginning to feel at ease with him. "Modest, too."

That had her laughing. "Modest, smart, *and* strong. I don't need any handouts. I can make it on my own. That's the whole point."

"I understand that, and I commend you." It was a typical response to proffered help, one he'd expected, especially from Cyn. "But that wasn't what I meant."

"No?"

He hesitated, weighing his words. "As I said, you're smart. You have to know that Thorne and Palmer were sick men. They're not the norm. The world is filled with good people."

As if placating him, she said, "Like you?"

"And you." He laced his fingers with hers. He'd often made a point of offering physical contact, hand-holding, shoulder-rubbing, to help give comfort to the distraught.

With Cyn, his motives were murky at best. He had a feeling that the physical contact was more for his benefit than for hers.

"You're smart enough to know that the biggest step toward changing your life is talking to someone. Sharing the things that hurt you, that helped mold you. In order to move forward, you need to let the past go, and the best way to do that is to purge yourself of the memories."

"Right." Her expression soured into cynicism. "You wanna hear all the gruesome details, is that it?"

Want to hear them? No. But he believed she needed to talk, and he wanted to be the one she talked to. "If you're comfortable with me, I'm a very good listener."

"They teach you listening skills in preacher school?"

She had a biting wit that would have been more amusing under less tragic circumstances. "Yes, and I aced my classes."

"Why would you want to listen to people whine and complain? I got my fill of that with the johns who paid me. Pathetic bozos, all of them."

"But I'm not a pathetic bozo, right?" He didn't give her a chance to answer, just in case her answer wasn't what he wanted to hear. "I just want to help, that's all."

"You'd have been a helluva lot more help when I was a kid." She slipped her hand away.

"I wish I'd been there." He wished that more than anything.

Her disbelief was plain, and fired by anger. "It wouldn't have mattered. Problems like that are a hell of a lot easier to ignore. Neighbors don't want to get involved. Relatives look the other way. What makes you think you'd have been any different?"

A heavy weight settled around his heart. "It's unforgivable not to intervene if you know someone is hurt."

"Yep. *Un*forgivable." She pinned him with her shrewd gaze. "You got that much right."

"They don't deserve your forgiveness, Cyn, that's true. But *you* deserve to forgive and move on. To let it go from your life so it can't bother you anymore."

She eyed him, then shook her head with a rusty laugh. "You're not going to let this drop, are you?"

He didn't want to. He stared into her mocking eyes, searching for the right words, when suddenly she pushed to her feet.

"I'm going to show you something."

The abrupt change took him by surprise. "All right."

She turned and headed back upstairs. Bruce watched her exit, saw she was still limping a bit, but also saw the anticipation in her body language. She wanted to share — she was ready to take that next step.

He was grateful to be the man she confided in.

Cyn returned moments later with a stack of books. Out of all the things Bruce had expected, books hadn't figured in.

She plunked the pile on the table. "You wanna know about me? Well, here I am." She indicated the books with a wave of her hand. "This is why I don't need you or your sympathy or your help."

Dumbfounded, at a complete loss, Bruce watched her pick up one slim volume.

"After I ran off," she said, her eyes still narrowed and her attitude aggressive, "I didn't trust anyone. I couldn't.

It would have been dumb."

Bruce took the book from her. His heart twisted at the title: *The Roots of Child Abuse and Neglect*. He looked at Cyn. "The books helped?"

As if she clenched her teeth, her jaw worked. "Friendships were out. Can't be friends with people you can't trust, and most everyone on the street would steal you blind with a smile. Public places like the movies or malls were too iffy. So I read."

He remembered her telling him that her reading interests varied. Apparently, she educated herself on whatever she thought she needed to know.

"There were two independent bookstores near my corner. One was run by foreigners. They didn't care who bought a book, as long as you had cash. They'd even order titles for me."

Bruce felt such admiration, he couldn't bring himself to look away from her. "This is some heavy reading."

"I guess." She opened the cover on the book, flipped idly through the pages. "Remember I said I watched the other hookers, and knew I didn't want to end up that way? Well, I watched my mother and Palmer, too, and God knows, I sure didn't want to be like them. They disgusted me. So I figured I had to learn as much about them as I could. That way I'd know what to expect, what to avoid."

Bruce was so humbled, so astonished at her resourcefulness, that the urge to hold her nearly overwhelmed him. He needed the contact as much, if not more, than she did.

But he didn't want to scare her off, to interrupt what he hoped would be a cathartic retelling of her past.

He picked up the next book. *The Road to Recovery: After Child Abuse.* Red-hot rage mixed with drowning compassion. His voice rough with emotion, he said, "You're pretty amazing, you know that?"

Sarcasm had her rolling her eyes. "There's nothing amazing about a homeless ex-hooker with a shady past." And before he could protest that, she shook her head. "Every ten seconds, a kid gets abused. *Every ten seconds,* Bruce. You said you would have helped, but even if you did, it wouldn't be enough." A shudder of revulsion shook her slender frame, and her voice went hollow and pained. "I always thought I was the only one."

Bruce watched her shoulders firm, watched her straighten her spine in iron resolve. How many times had she been forced to do that throughout her young life?

"After I found out how many kids are hurt, I wished I *was* the only one. I get ill thinking of it."

She fell silent, then said in a rush, "Did you know most abusers were abused? They grow up and follow some sick pattern." Her words came in a rush, as if a dam had burst. Her hand curled into a tight fist. "I'd sooner be dead than ever hurt someone, especially a child."

Talk of death always alarmed Bruce, but not this time. Cyn was a survivor. He had a feeling she'd been making plans to change her life from the day she left home, whether she realized it or not.

She'd looked ahead to what she eventually wanted by avoiding some of the pitfalls so many desperate people fell into, like drugs and alcohol. She'd educated herself and taken steps to be a better person than those around her.

Despite the prostitution issue, which broke his heart, she hadn't given up, hadn't accepted her fate or grown comfortable with it. Her anger was over the past, not the present. Her views weren't despondent, but determined.

She wanted change, for herself and others, and Bruce had a feeling she'd get it.

It was odd, how comfortable he felt speaking with her. Unlike the other women he'd counseled, his conversations with Cyn were shared, not sermonized. He wasn't trying to alter her views — he was learning more about her. And what he learned intrigued him.

"People either follow a familiar path, or they forge a new one. You're aware of the problem and you'll be able to help others with your understanding." He visually caressed her face, noting the stubborn chin, the soft lips, the intelligent and compelling gaze. "That's why you read literature on the subject."

She toyed with her hair, a sign he now saw as nervousness. "I know it's far-fetched, but you're right. Someday, if I can save enough money, I want to go back to school, maybe even college. I want to work with kids, to help them . . ." She suddenly shut down, as if embarrassed by what she'd admitted. "I can't imagine too many people wanting an ex-hooker around their kids, though."

"I think you'd be a wonderful inspiration to many."

She ducked her head. "Yeah, well, it's mostly just a pipe dream. Besides, I'd probably screw it up somehow."

Bruce shook his head. She could grapple with a bulky truck driver without pause, but compliments made her uneasy. Never in his life had he known anyone like her. "Tell me about Palmer. Was he your step-father?"

"Hardly. Marriage is for normal people, Bruce, not my family. No, Palmer was just Mom's latest shack-up, but he stuck around longer than the others. She was totally impressed with him. He strutted around our dirty little house like a ragtag king." More to herself than Bruce, she muttered, "Stupid fool."

"He abused your mother, too?"

She shrugged as if she really didn't care, about any of it, when Bruce knew she cared too much. "He slapped her around a little. Whenever that happened, she'd blame me."

A mother should protect her child, but instead Cyn's had abandoned her. Very softly, he asked, "How old were you?"

Cyn stared at the far wall. "I'd just turned fifteen when he moved in." The corners of her mouth lifted in a sheepish grin, putting dimples in her cheeks. "Back then, I was still suffering adolescence. You know, baby fat and bad complexion and all that."

Bruce smiled, imagining her as a young, round-faced girl. "I'll bet you were cute."

"No, I was homely. But it was okay because at least Palmer ignored me back then. Occasionally he'd snatch up a weapon and whale on me, but it wasn't all that often."

Ice ran up Bruce's spine. "A weapon?"

"That's just what I called it." She rubbed at her left eye, as if the memories pained her. "You know, a shoe, his belt, whatever was handy. One thing about Palmer, he almost never used his bare hands then. That didn't come till I got older."

Bruce couldn't bear it. He moved his chair closer to hers and put a hand on her shoulder. He had no words to say, no platitudes that could comfort.

She lounged back in her chair, her sardonic mask back in place. "Unfortunately, I couldn't stay a chubby, ugly kid forever. By the time I was sixteen, I'd slimmed down except that I had big boobs and a round butt." She stared down at her own chest in wry disgust. "Man, I hated these things then, but they've kept me fed since I left."

Bruce drew a shuddering breath and kept his attention on her face. "A beautiful body is a blessing, not a curse."

"Spoken as a true guy." She laughed. "You wouldn't have thought so if you were me."

"No, I don't suppose I would have."

"Getting a bod had Palmer looking at me different."

That statement fell between them like a dead weight, and Cyn waited for his reaction. Bruce knew what she was telling him, and he wished he had Palmer at hand. He'd have given retribution for a young girl's hurt without an ounce of remorse.

Words failed him. "I'm sorry," he said, and hugged her up against his chest.

He expected some resistance, but instead, she patted his back, as if giving him comfort. "It's okay. It was long ago."

Hearing about abuse always ripped Bruce up, but this time was worse. His fingers curved around her head, urging it to his shoulder. "He molested you?"

Her fingers moved over his shoulder, smoothing, touching, driving him to distraction. "No. No way. I wouldn't have let him."

Bruce knew she couldn't have stopped

him, but all he said was, "I understand." And he did.

Somehow, Cyn crawled completely into his lap without Bruce even being aware of it. Once he did realize it, it just felt right to have her there and no way would he budge her from his arms.

"He would have raped me," she admitted. "It was only a matter of time." She leaned back to see him. "I only did what I had to do."

Bruce thought it was a miracle that she hadn't suffered that final insult. He smoothed her cheek to let her know it was okay. "What did you do?"

Her eyes darkened with the realization of all she'd shared. He felt her emotional retreat, but tried not to let it bother him. Trust was a hard thing to give, especially for someone with Cyn's background.

Somehow, Bruce decided he'd earn her trust, and in the bargain, she'd learn that there were other people worthy of trusting.

She stared down at her hand, her fingers spread wide on his chest right over his heart. He felt her breath on his throat, stirring emotions that were at odds with their discussion.

He wanted her. It was shameful to admit, and he wouldn't do anything about it, but it didn't change his feelings. She made him feel more like a man than he had in a decade.

Still touching him with a sort of abstract concentration, she remarked, "As bad as prostitution is, as scary as it got at times, at least it was my choice." Her hand smoothed up and over his shoulder. Her fingers slid into his hair, her breathing deepened.

As if collecting herself, she shook her head, smiled, and stared into his eyes. "Damn. I should be embarrassed, shouldn't I?"

"Why?" He was hoarse with need, tense with the struggle to control the reactions of his body. Holding her was about the nicest thing he'd done for himself in too many years to count.

"Duh. I'm curled in your lap like a baby, spilling my guts all over the place."

Bruce kept his hands still on her back, kept his breathing even and low. "I want you to always feel free to talk to me, Cyn."

With a chuckle, her forehead touched his. "Bruce Almighty," she teased, and her breathy laugh slipped over his lips. "You're the nicest, but strangest man I've ever known."

Her teasing eased some of his tension. "Strange, huh?"

She leaned back again, her face bright with humor. "If I sat on any other guy, he'd have a boner prodding my butt and hands going everywhere."

Under other circumstances, Bruce would have been hard, too. He *was* aroused, just not to the degree of an erection. The suffering of a young girl and his own empathy kept sexual thoughts and feelings under control.

"But you . . ." She shook her head with endearing bafflement. "You just let me prattle on and on."

"It's called sharing, and everyone needs to do it sometimes."

She leaned down and planted a chaste kiss on his cheek, and Bruce went as still as a concrete block. He didn't even breathe, taken off guard, fighting urges he hadn't suffered in an eon, and grateful for the meaning behind the gesture.

"Thanks," she whispered. And she pulled away, going back to her own seat.

Bruce ran a hand through his hair. "I take it our talk is over?"

"Oh yeah, dead, buried, with a tombstone on top." She took a big bite of her pancakes, and spoke with her mouth full. "I just wanted you to know why I won't take charity. Well, other than this terrific breakfast, that is."

Don't push, Bruce reminded himself. And still he said, "One more question, and I promise that's it."

"Shoot." She took another bite of her breakfast, then hummed in satisfaction. "Good."

"Where did you come from? What city?"

"Ah ah ah," she warned. She licked sticky syrup from her lips while gifting him with a look of chastisement. "Good preachers shouldn't snoop."

"It's not snooping, just idle curiosity." He didn't count that as an outright lie, because he *was* curious about her. But in truth, he wanted to check into her background, more for her own safety than for any other reason.

"Let's just say Hicksville, Indiana, and leave it at that. I haven't been there in years. I won't ever go there again. When I left, that place and everyone there was dead to me."

"So where did you go?" If he could at least find out that much, maybe the rest would come.

"Cincinnati. It was far enough."

Far enough for what? To avoid being taken back? To escape her painful past? Or to escape Palmer Oaks?

"You got any coffee? I need a jolt to get the motor running this morning. It'll probably be easier to find a job if I'm wide-eyed and bushy-tailed." With a return of cockiness, she winked. "Ladies of the night have a real problem with early mornings."

"*Ex*-ladies of the night."

"Yeah, sure. Whatever."

Bruce checked his watch. "You have time for two cups before I need to head out. I'll drive you into town."

Chapter Four

Cyn stared around the town as Bruce pulled up to the curb in front of a beauty parlor. She didn't see any "Help Wanted" signs on any of the small, quaint establishments, but she wouldn't rule them out. And there was always the strip mall. She had high hopes. She didn't care what the job might be, as long as it didn't involve her stripping naked.

Before now, she'd been afraid to have her social security number registered, afraid to give her full name, afraid to make polite society aware of her in any way. Fear had been a part of her day, her night, her very existence.

But she wouldn't be afraid anymore. Whatever happened, happened. No more running. She trusted Visitation.

Strangely enough, she was starting to trust Bruce Kelly.

He opened her car door for her. Such a gentleman, she thought, amused and touched. He hadn't come on to her, but he had been kind. Did he find her unappealing? Did he consider her good enough to counsel, but beneath his physical notice?

He'd been subdued since their talk, or more appropriately, since she'd kissed him. She hadn't meant to do it. She hadn't even wanted to do it. But at that particular moment in time, she would have given him anything he wanted. Talking with him was so damn liberating, it was like the sun had finally shone down on her.

For years, she'd kept all the pain and unhappiness bottled up inside. The books had helped her to understand it, but dealing with it was different from just understanding. Bruce, God bless him, helped her to deal.

He'd given her what no one else ever had: the freedom to share her darkest secrets. He hadn't been appalled, hadn't passed judgement, hadn't done anything other than listen. And understand.

Of course, he didn't know she'd killed Palmer; that would stretch the bounds of even a saint's understanding.

As Cyn stepped out, agog at the scenery, he asked, "You're sure you're okay on your own?"

She couldn't help but laugh. "You're too funny, Bruce. I've been on my own forever."

Arms crossed over his wide chest, big, booted feet planted apart, he stood in front of her — a habit she'd already noticed — as if he thought to shield her from the world by his physical bulk. He looked too damn good to be a preacher, too fit and strong, and by the hour, he grew sexier.

"Just because you've been alone doesn't make it right or easy."

The sun had crawled out from behind the clouds, displaying Visitation in the best possible light. Enormous budding trees were everywhere. Birds, their feathers fluffed to ward off the chill, sat on every branch and telephone wire. Unlike the alleys where she'd worked, the people she'd associated with, everything here looked and smelled clean.

This was a place where miracles could happen; she knew that's what it would take for her to be able to put everything behind her. The sun bright in her eyes, she squinted up at Bruce. "Nothing's ever easy, but I'll make do."

"Your ankle's not giving you too much trouble?"

"Quit fretting, big boy." She patted his chest in distraction while noticing the drugstore. "I'll be fine." Sunglasses were the first order of business. "You mind if I leave my bag in your car? I want to see if I can find a job before I check into the motel." She wouldn't start spending her savings without knowing more money would be coming in. If necessary, she'd sleep in the park — as she had on other occasions.

Bruce rubbed the back of his neck, glanced around at a few passersby. His fingers were long, his body tanned. His fair hair fell over his wrist, looking silky and warm, before he dropped his arm.

Oh, for crying out loud, Cyn thought. No way was she going to start admiring a guy's damn fingers. "I didn't ask for a cure to world hunger."

She had the feeling he might ask her to stay with him, and despite what she'd just told herself, she secretly crossed her fingers.

He was powerful, but not aggressive. Proud but not arrogant. And unless he was one hell of an actor, he genuinely liked her without making any attempt to get her in the sack.

In the end, he merely nodded. "That's fine. I'll be in town for a few hours at least."

If she asked, he'd let her stay with him — she believed that. But Cyn vowed she wouldn't take advantage of him. A week ago, even a few days ago, she wouldn't have hesitated to try to exploit him. Not in a mean way, but in any way that didn't seriously hurt anyone, yet was advantageous to her. That's how she'd survived, how she'd gotten through the days and the nights . . .

But this was a new life. A new, hopefully better, Cynthia Potter. She was tired of using people, and she was tired of being used.

"Appreciate it." Still she hesitated, until he glanced at his watch and she realized she was keeping him from an appointment. Dolt. "Okay, then. Catch you here around noon?"

"Great. And good luck." He turned and trotted across the street to the diner.

They'd just finished breakfast, so why go to the diner? To meet someone? A woman?

Oh God, she was a horrible person. It wasn't any of her damn business who Bruce might be seeing. The last thing she needed right now was the complication of a guy.

Determined to put Bruce from her mind, she walked to the drugstore, favoring her injured ankle only a little. A small bell chimed above the door when she entered, and an older, heavy man with the thickest gray hair she'd ever seen looked at her over his wire-rimmed glasses. "Morning."

A bit surprised by the brusque but cordial greeting, Cyn nodded. "Good morning."

"Can I help you find anything?"

There was no leer on his face, just a pleasant smile and maybe a touch of curiosity. Huh. Maybe her clothes were like Superman's glasses — one hell of a disguise.

She grinned. "Two things. Cheap sunglasses first."

He walked out from behind his counter and strode to a rotating rack. "Just got a bunch in. Whaddaya think?"

Cyn eyed the glasses, chose a mirrored pair, and checked to make sure they weren't too costly. She slipped them on.

"Handsome," the older man said in approval, and Cyn actually laughed. No one had ever used quite that term to describe her. The day, which had started out pretty gloomy, was going great so far.

"All right. I'll take these." She handed them back to him.

He said, "And a wrap for your ankle?"

"Excuse me?"

"Saw you were limping." He moved to a shelf of medical supplies and took down an

ACE Bandage. "Wrap it up good with this for support. It'll help."

"Oh. Okay, sure. I'll take that, too, then."

"Anything else?"

Cyn realized she was nervous, which was dumb, except that she'd never asked for an honest-to-goodness, legitimate job. Forcing herself not to stammer, she met his gaze and said, "I'm looking for work. I didn't see a sign, but I was hoping —"

He turned and headed for the register. "You new to town?"

"Just got in last night. I was hoping to find a job first thing today. I'm not picky. I can clean, run the register —"

"Sorry, but I don't really need any help right now. Come the summer, I'll be hiring part-time help if you're interested then." He rang up the glasses and bandage and gave her the price.

Deflated, Cyn dug in her purse and handed him money. She kept a spot of spending cash in her wallet, with the rest still safely hidden away in the lining of her purse. "Do you know anyone who might be hiring now?"

He tugged at his ear. "The restaurant was, a while back, but I think they found someone already. You could check the mall, but it's slow for them right now. And there's always the lake. Joe and Luna will do a lot of business this summer, so they might be gearing up already. Worth a try."

The bell chimed again and more customers walked in. Cyn glanced over her shoulder, and discovered two men giving her the once-over. One of them gave a silent whistle and nudged the other.

Now *that* she expected. Idiots. She turned back to the pharmacist.

He was kind enough to give her directions to the lake. The biggest problem Cyn could see was the distance. Walking was impossible. It'd take her half a day just to get there. She wouldn't mind a bus; it was how she'd gotten around before. But far as she could tell, Visitation didn't have much in the way of public transportation.

In the next two hours, she tried the beauty salon, the hardware store, the grocery and a pastry shop. Male managers at the grocery and the hardware store let her leave applications, but mostly just so they could question her with heated gazes and loose lips and a lot of speculation. She did her best to behave properly, despite the urge to tell them off.

In the mall, she filled out applications everywhere, but as the pharmacist had told her, no one was hiring at the moment. She suffered through several pick-up lines, a few come-ons, and more leering. The nicer people suggested she come back in early June, when they'd be picking up summer help.

Cyn headed for the diner. She'd used up so much time already — Bruce would soon be leaving and she needed to get her bag out of his car. He wasn't outside when she reached the diner, so she went in.

She spotted Bruce right off.

He was so big and so handsome, he naturally stood out in a crowd. He lingered near a table with a tall, very beautiful blonde on his arm. From what Cyn could tell, the woman was about to leave. Then Bruce leaned forward, cupped the back of her neck, and kissed her right on the mouth. And what a kiss. It might have been brief, but anyone looking, and several smiling people were, could see he was a natural-born sensualist.

He'd all but turned to ice when *she'd* kissed him, but for this other woman, this amazon, he was all smoky machismo.

Cyn felt . . . betrayed.

It was stupid. Beyond stupid. Not once had Bruce told her he was available, and even if he had been, she wasn't the type a preacher got involved with.

But he could have explained that he had a relationship. She'd opened her heart to him and he'd listened . . . but of course, he'd done the same for a lot of hookers. And that's probably all she was to him — some pathetic scrap of humanity he wanted to help because that's what he did. He helped people like her.

She felt sick, demoralized — then annoyed.

After all, he was a *preacher,* for crying out loud, or so he'd claimed. What did he think he was doing, indulging in blatant public displays of affection?

Before the woman could leave, Cyn marched in — that is, she marched as much as someone could with a painful ankle. She heard a whistle behind her, felt eyes on her back, but she easily dismissed them all. Her gaze was locked on Bruce as she made her way forward around tables and patrons and a few harried waitresses. When she stopped in front of him, he merely looked at her, one brow raised.

Cyn could feel the other woman, as tall as Bruce, staring down at her.

"I need my things from your car."

Bruce said, "Excuse me?"

All his natural warmth and open caring

were gone. His dark eyes no longer seemed gently accepting, but rather sharp, as if an inherent danger simmered just below the surface of his handsome façade.

If he wanted to warn her off, he could forget it. She wasn't afraid of him.

Cyn cocked out a hip and readjusted her purse strap. "No job yet, but I don't want to hold you up. Don't worry, I'll find somewhere else to sleep tonight. I won't bother you." Her gaze slanted toward the blond bombshell. "Either of you."

Strangely enough, the blonde became purely titillated. "Where, exactly, did you sleep last night?"

Cyn frowned, a little thrown by the woman's wide smile and delighted attitude. She tipped her head toward Bruce. "At his place." *With him.* She sniffed. "He was a complete gentleman."

Laughing, the woman said, "Oh, I never doubted that. But you say you slept in his house? That's incredible."

Instead of leaving, as she'd been about to do, she gestured to a chair. "Please, why don't you join us and then you can tell us all about last night."

Bryan Kelly took in the petite confection fuming her discontent beside his wife. She was short, but then standing next to Shay, most women looked short. She was also stunning.

A thick, glossy black braid hung over her shoulder. Her tilted cat eyes, challenging him with a bold stare, were incredibly sexy and the lightest blue he'd ever seen.

He thought, no, it couldn't be. And still he asked, "Are you by any chance confusing me with my brother?"

Those sensual eyes widened. Lush lips parted. And a slim, pale throat worked as she swallowed.

Yeah, she had killer looks, but . . . Bruce didn't care about that. His brother had been around plenty of attractive women and had barely given them a second look.

The little sweetheart groaned. "Oh, no. He couldn't . . . you couldn't . . ." She gave a wan smile. "Your brother, you say?"

Oh, this was rich. "Bruce. Looks just like me." Bryan grinned, then reached for Shay and pulled her into his side. "Hard as it is to believe, it had to be Bruce, because honey, I slept with my wife last night."

Her sooty lashes sank down until her eyes had closed in an expression of pained embarrassment. "Oh, shit — I mean, shoot."

Snickering, still grinning like a loon,

Shay patted her shoulder. "I made the same mistake many times. Even kissed the wrong brother once."

Bryan didn't like that reminder. He glared at Shay, but she wasn't paying him any attention.

"Come on," Shay said again, "join us." After all but forcing the poor girl into a chair, Shay dropped into her own and said, "Bryan, sit. You're making her nervous looming over her like that."

Bryan snorted. "Never worked on you."

"You don't loom over me."

"I'm sorry," the girl interjected in a disconcerted rush. "I thought . . ." She stared at Bryan and shook her head. "You two look *exactly* alike. Well . . ." She looked at him a little closer. "Maybe there's a slight difference in the eyes. Yours are . . ."

She trailed off and Shay said, "Meaner?"

The girl winced. "I wouldn't say that. But yeah, Bruce's are more compassionate."

"Compassionate. That's our Bruce."

Bryan gestured for a waitress. "You want some coffee?"

She rubbed her forehead, pushed her long braid over her shoulder, and nodded. "Sure, why not? That'd be great."

Conversation was suspended until the

waitress had poured another cup of coffee and walked away.

"So." Shay held out a hand. "I'm Shay Kelly, Bryan's wife and Bruce's sister-in-law, and this, of course, is my not-so-mean husband, Bryan."

The girl gave a sheepish grin and accepted handshakes. "Cynthia Potter. 'Cyn' to my friends."

Bryan still struggled with disbelief. "You say you spent the night with Bruce?"

"On his couch," she clarified. She doctored the coffee with cream and sugar. "He gave me a ride into town and it was late and so he let me crash. I'm hunting up a job today." She glanced up and grimaced. "And a place to stay."

Bryan saw his wife go on the alert. Shay couldn't resist helping people, and he loved that about her, but her efforts to save the world sometimes exhausted him. Since they'd finished their house, a huge undertaking all on its own, she'd been on a regular rampage of town improvements. From the fire department to the sheriff's office to the schools, Shay wanted a hand in making everything better.

"Any luck finding a job yet?"

Cyn shook her head. "Not even a nibble. I guess I need to get settled first so I can give a place of residence and phone number and all that. I'd wanted to get the job first, but . . ." She shrugged like someone well used to adversity.

A wolf whistle was heard above the din of conversation and Cyn stiffened. Chagrined, she glanced toward the men ogling her, then away again.

Bryan, too, looked at the men, and his smile wasn't nice. It was the same look he used to discourage men from ogling his wife. And as always, it worked like a charm.

Shay laughed. "Yep, mean."

Bryan disregarded her teasing; he knew Shay enjoyed his more possessive tendencies. "Sorry about that," he told Cyn. "Some guys have no manners."

"It's because you're beautiful," Shay said. "I imagine you get that a lot."

Cyn looked more pained by the moment.

Sympathizing with her, Bryan folded his arms across his chest and settled back in his seat. "Shay, didn't you need to be on your way?"

She waved that off. "In a moment." And then to Cyn: "If you don't mind me prying —"

"As if anyone could stop you," Bryan

said, and got an evil look from Shay in return.

"What type of job are you looking for?"

Cyn relaxed at the change of subject. "I'm not in a position to be picky. Anything would do, as long as it pays enough that I won't starve."

"My do-gooder wife and saintly brother would never let that happen."

Shay kicked him under the table and Bryan jumped. "Damn it, woman, that hurt."

"Then behave and it won't happen again."

Cyn laughed. "You and your brother may look alike, but you're plenty different."

Bryan rubbed at his shin. "In some ways, yeah, but don't let him fool you too much." He scooted out of reach before Shay could land another kick.

"He told me you're a bounty hunter."

"Used to be, yeah. I like being with my wife too much — when she's not violent — to be on the road for weeks at a time, and that's what it takes to be a bounty hunter. You go where the criminals go. Now I'm a domesticated lamb."

Shay gave a rude hoot of laughter over that exaggeration. Bryan just grinned.

"Actually, I own a warehouse that distributes security equipment. It's about an hour north of here."

Glowing with pride, Shay added, "The business is new, but Bryan's drawing customers from everywhere. He's used most of the equipment that he sells, so he knows what works and what doesn't. People trust him. He's got a mail order catalogue and Web-based sales, too."

Suddenly Bruce appeared beside the table. He was with Julie Rose, the schoolteacher. The two saw each other whenever Julie Rose was available, and though she was engaged, she was available more often than not.

Sometimes, Bryan wondered if they were romantically involved. Not that Bruce would poach on an existing relationship, but . . .

His curiosity was put to rest the second Bruce looked at Cyn. His brother had the strangest expression on his face, an expression Bryan hadn't seen on him since the more rambunctious days of their youth. It was a look of hunger.

Well, what do you know? Bryan grinned, prepared to enjoy himself.

"Cynthia," Bruce said, and he sounded more like a clergyman than ever.

Bryan noticed that the girl, who really was a knockout, twisted to face Bruce with naked happiness. She grinned, saw Julie, and her slim brows came down in a frown.

Supposedly, they'd just met last night, but they were both showing possessive signs already. Interesting.

Bryan stood. "Bruce, Julie. Should we all move to a bigger table? Or since Shay's about to leave, maybe we could just grab another chair?"

"I'm not going anywhere," Shay protested.

"But you have an appointment," Bryan reminded her, doing his best to swallow his grin.

"It'll wait," she all but hissed, and Bryan couldn't help but chuckle as he reseated himself.

Bruce cleared his throat. "I was just walking Julie out." And then, because Bruce was always a gentleman, he did introductions. "Cynthia, this is Julie Rose. Julie, Cynthia Potter."

"A pleasure." Julie held out her hand.

Bryan could understand Cyn's jealousy when she spotted Shay. After all, his wife was about the most delectable woman he'd ever met. But Julie? She was a stereotypical teacher-type. Plain. Medium brown hair, puppydog brown eyes. Skinny, nondescript bod.

He'd give Cyn credit for trying to hide it, but she looked murderous. Wearing an insincere smile, she accepted Julie's slender hand in a very brief shake. "The same."

Bruce nodded to Cyn's bag. "So you did a little shopping?"

"Just an ACE Bandage for my ankle. The pharmacist suggested it."

"How's it feeling?"

"I'm ignoring it."

After that conversational gambit fell flat, things came to a screeching halt, so Bryan decided to stir things up a bit. "Bruce, Cyn was just telling us that she spent the night with you."

Bruce went rigid as hot color crept up his neck. "I offered her a place to sleep, yes."

Julie, never one to get involved with rumor or gossip, never so much as blinked. "You're new to town?"

"Brand spanking new."

Bruce turned his gaze down to Cyn. Bryan watched his brother, so he didn't miss the way Bruce's attention grew hot and sharp with pure masculine awareness.

Bryan exchanged a glance with Shay. She, too, had noticed the change in Bruce and she looked as amazed as Bryan felt. It was about time his brother rediscovered his masculinity. Not that Bruce was a wimp. Far from it. But he spent all his time helping others, with no consideration for his own needs.

In a voice as soft as butter, Bruce asked, "How did the job hunt go?"

For the first time since she'd walked into the diner, Cyn looked vulnerable. "Not so great — yet. But the day's not over. After I check into the motel, I'll start looking again."

Julie, always nice if too puckered up, said, "The motel is okay, but costly, especially if you're planning to stay any time at all."

Cyn's smile looked like a feminine warning. "I'm moving here for good, but I don't have much choice on the motel." She looked at Bruce. "I've got to sleep somewhere."

"I know a place," Julie said, before Bruce could even get his mouth open. "It's not far from here."

She pulled a pen and paper from her very organized purse and jotted down an address. "Mary Donniger, a lovely lady who works day care, needs someone to care for her horses now that her husband has passed on. She's offering a small salary plus a room that was put into the loft of the barn. It's not fancy accommodations, but it is less costly until you find something better."

Bruce looked from one woman to the other. "But . . . a barn?"

"It's finished off," Julie promised, and handed the piece of paper to Cyn. "She showed it to me the other day, and asked me to spread the word around. You'd have your own bed and bath, but no cooking. I'm afraid you'd have to rely on the local eateries for meals."

"No sweat." Cyn read the address and frowned. "I don't know much about horses."

"Mary can teach you. The work is physical, but you look young and healthy."

"Her ankle is hurt," Bruce protested.

"It's nothing." Cyn gave him a quelling look that Bruce visibly ignored.

Julie dismissed their sniping with little notice. "From what Mary told me, the chores won't take up much of your time." She shrugged. "You feed the horses twice a day, muck out the barn, throw down new straw, stuff like that."

"So I should have plenty of free time to work at another job, too?"

"If you can work out the hours. I know Mary wouldn't mind that at all. Unfortunately, there's not much work opportunity in Visitation. Have you tried the factory?"

"I didn't know there was one." Cyn, the paper clutched in her hand, returned her attention to Bruce. "Where is it?"

"We passed it coming into Visitation, but you were almost asleep then. It's assembly line work."

"No skills needed — right up my alley." Cyn's eyes lit with optimism. "It would be too perfect if I could get both jobs."

Bryan had never seen anyone so thrilled at the prospect of hard work. Knowing his wife was about to burst, he asked, "Any other ideas, Shay?"

Shay pounced on the chance to contribute. "As a matter of fact, yes. There are still all kinds of things to be done for the new church, jobs that aren't part of the contractor's agreement, but are more than the volunteers can handle. There's regular cleaning, bookkeeping, lawn maintenance, stuff like that. And I could use help with some of my other projects. There's —"

"That's generous of you," Cyn interrupted, polite but firm. She pushed back her chair and stood. "But I don't want to impose."

"You'd be doing me a favor," Shay insisted as she, too, came to her feet.

Bryan could tell by Cyn's expression — she didn't believe that.

"I appreciate it, I really do. Still, if it's all the same to you, I'd like to check out the horse care and the factory first."

Shay subsided, but she didn't look happy about it. "Of course." She dug a card out of her purse. "Here's my number, in case either of those don't work out. You can call me anytime, okay?"

With some reservations, Cyn accepted the card. "Okay. Thanks again."

Bruce let out a big breath. "If you want to check out those places, I'll take you."

"No, that's —"

"I'll take you."

Bryan raised his eyebrows at his brother's unusually commanding tone. Wow. He'd never heard Bruce be quite so forceful, especially not with a woman. Cajoling, yes. Sympathetic and gentle, all the time. But not insistent.

Mutinous, Cyn said, "Fine."

"Good."

Julie looked between the two of them and laughed. "I'll call Mary and tell her you're stopping by today. She'll be thrilled. Now, I'd better be off." She waved a hand at Bruce when he started to follow her. "No need to walk me out. I'll see you tomorrow."

With everyone else standing, Bryan scooted back his own chair. "Looks like things are all taken care of, then." He offered Cyn his hand. "It was nice meeting you. Don't be a stranger. And really, don't hesitate to call on my wife if you need anything. She lives to interfere in others' lives."

Shay pretended affront, but her eyes were filled with laughter. "I call it making friends."

Chapter Five

The factory job fell through. Bruce waited in the hall while Cyn sat on a plastic couch and filled out an application form. He could see and hear her through the open office door, and he noticed right off the way the woman behind the desk watched Cyn with disdain. Jealousy was an ugly thing, but he supposed with Cyn being so beautiful, it was something she'd have to learn to deal with.

At the moment, she had her bottom lip caught in her teeth, her braid hanging over her shoulder, her brows beetled in thought. The form couldn't be that complicated, but for someone with no past history of work and no references, it probably felt intimidating.

After Cyn finished, she approached the woman's desk and handed in the form with an optimistic smile.

The woman glanced over it, said something low, and Cyn's face fell.

Bruce went to the door, feeling helpless to assist her.

The woman said, "You must have some past work experience."

Her expression wiped clean of emotion, her chin tucked in, Cyn said, "Nope. You're saying the job requires special skills?"

Rather than answer, the woman's mouth pursed. "Were you in school? Do you have a college degree?"

"No."

"Then what have you been doing with yourself since high school? Oh wait, it says here that you don't have a high school education, either? Oh my."

Very slowly, Cyn straightened. "I never completed my senior year."

Smug, the woman pushed back in her chair. "Perhaps you should at least get your GED before applying for work again?"

She was nasty, even vicious in her satisfaction, and Bruce wanted to slap her. Instead, he stepped into the office and took Cyn's arm. "Let's go."

Cyn straightened her purse strap, thanked the woman with haughty disdain, and walked out with her head up and her shoulders back. Thanks to the Ace bandage, there was no noticeable limp to mar her grand exit.

Bruce admired her spunk in the face of rejection.

"You're better than her," he told Cyn, and meant it.

Cyn's *yeah, right* look was there and gone before he could comment on it. She didn't say a word.

Her silence chewed on his peace of mind. Everyone deserved the chance to start over, to correct mistakes and make a better life. His sister-in-law Shay had given many of the women at his safe house just that type of opportunity. But Cyn was determined to make her own opportunities, not have them given to her. Her obstinacy would make things that much more difficult, when Bruce knew they'd be hard enough already.

He had a feeling Cyn knew it, too, but she wasn't going to let it stand in her way. One way or another, she'd accomplish anything she set her mind to.

The urge to protect her, to offer to care for her, beat inside him. *Stupid.* He couldn't ask to take her in like a stray pup. She was a grown woman — smart, proud, determined.

He knew as well or better than most that what Cyn needed was some form of independence, a way to regain confidence in herself.

Once they were on the road, Bruce

cracked. He just couldn't bear letting her stew in silence. "There'll be other jobs, Cyn."

"Sure. I mean, isn't everyone looking to hire a gal with my experience? Maybe I should test out mattresses or fishnet or —"

"Stop it, Cyn."

She exhaled a long breath, as if preparing herself, then blurted, "That woman took one look at me and she knew who I was and what I'd done."

"Baloney." Bruce could have laughed at such an absurd, paranoid observation, but somehow he knew the truth wouldn't make Cyn feel much better. "She took one look at you and was shriveled with envy."

Incredulous, Cyn stared at him. "Envious of *what?*"

"Maybe it's escaped your notice," Bruce said, "but you're an incredibly beautiful young lady. And that woman . . . well," he laughed, "she's most definitely not."

She stared at him in mute surprise for a moment before laughing. "That's not a very Christian observation."

"It's the truth. And a mean spirit sure doesn't help make a body prettier."

She chewed her bottom lip. "So. You think I'm beautiful?"

"Don't be coy." She was so beautiful that

men and women alike would make notice of her, everywhere she went, whatever she did. Bruce cleared his throat. "I imagine a lot of women will treat you differently. Men, too. But not because they know your past or suspect a black soul as Thorne accused. Forget that nonsense."

His tone must have been harsher than he realized, because she saluted. "Yes, sir."

He didn't relent. "I mean it. People are human, Cyn, and jealousy is a normal reaction. You should just get used to it."

She was silent a moment, then asked, "Do you think I'm sexy?"

Bruce's hands flexed on the steering wheel. What a loaded question to put to a man struggling for good intentions. "Yes," he said, but tempered that with the admission, "I think Shay and Luna are both sexy, too."

"Luna?"

"Joe Winston's wife. Sexiness is something that comes as much from a woman's attitude as her looks. It's appealing, not sinful, not something to be ashamed of."

She surveyed him from head to toe. "Julie seems nice."

Now where were her thoughts headed? Second-guessing Cyn would keep him busy, that's for sure.

"She's very nice," he ventured, but with a lot of caution. "She takes people at face value. You can count on her to always be kind and generous."

"Do you think she's sexy?"

How in the world had they gotten onto this conversation? Bruce glanced at her, and saw the speculative gleam in her eyes. He felt the trap closing around him but was helpless to avoid it. "I've never really thought about it." As if it explained anything, he stupidly added, "Julie is a good friend."

"But you don't think she's beautiful?"

He wanted to ask her why she cared, but knew that'd take him down a path better left to his imagination. "Outwardly, Julie might seem plain to some, but when you get to know her better, you'll see her backbone and conviction and her generous heart."

"And those things make her attractive?"

"To me, yes. To people who look beyond the surface."

"Men don't."

"You're too smart to spout ridiculous platitudes. *Good* men do, and Cyn, you need to trust me that the world is filled with good people."

Her mouth flattened in disbelief, but she

refrained from disagreeing with him. "Your brother must have been looking at the surface when he married Shay."

"You only think that because you don't know Bryan."

"How do you mean?"

"Bryan's been with plenty of beautiful women. Don't doubt it. If that's all Shay had to offer, he'd have been able to resist her." Memories brought a smile to his face, and he decided to tell her about them. He glanced at her to watch her reaction to his tale. "When they first met, Bryan thought Shay was a prostitute, and it made him nuts trying to keep his hands to himself."

Her eyes widened. "Why would he think that?"

"Because Shay wanted him to." He laughed. "She had some trouble and didn't want anyone to know her real identity."

"But if he thought she was a hooker, why didn't he just —"

"Cyn." Bruce interrupted her before she could finish that damning thought. "You haven't known many good men, or you wouldn't have to ask."

Eyes narrowed, she sneered, "So a good man wouldn't dirty himself with a whore. Gotcha."

"Maybe I should reassess your intelligence." He didn't give her a chance to get offended. "When Bryan met Shay, he was impersonating me."

"Just for the fun of it?" she asked in that same nasty tone. "Or was there a reason?"

To avoid a long discussion, Bruce condensed the story enormously. "Someone had targeted my safe house with threats, and it made it easier to figure things out with both Bryan and me involved."

That got her mind on a different track. "Did you find the person?"

"Yes, and everything's all right now. But while Bryan was being me, he met Shay. He mistook her for a prostitute, she believed he was a preacher, and neither corrected the other. Bryan fought it because he knew it wouldn't be ethical to get involved with a woman he thought had come to him for help."

"But he wanted to?"

Nodding, Bruce reiterated, "Not so much because of how she looked, but because of her outlook on life, how she treated others." Bruce turned down the gravel drive to the twenty-acre home where Cyn would apply for work. "Bryan likes to say that Shay has a beautiful heart. And he'd be right. She's pretty incredible."

Skeptical, Cyn asked, "He thought Shay

was a prostitute and he still married her?"

"No, he knew the truth before they married. But not before he fell in love with her." Bruce parked the car, grateful to avoid more difficult questions. "We're here. Ready?"

Instantly diverted, Cyn looked around at the fenced acreage, the immaculate two-story house, and the enormous barn out back.

"Wow. We've arrived at Tara."

"Remember, Julie said Mary was a nice person. And Julie would know."

Nervousness had Cyn smoothing her sweater and tidying her braid. With a wince, she added, "Whatever. Nice or not, the worst she can do is not hire me, right?"

"True, and if she doesn't, there's always Shay. Now let's go."

Cyn fell instantly in love with the horses, and given how they kept nibbling on her hair and butting her shoulder with their muzzles, they liked her, too.

Bruce stood back and watched her with an indulgent smile as she petted and spoke with the animals. It was clear she knew very little about horses, but she wasn't afraid of them. If anything, she seemed to strike an instant rapport.

After her disappointment at the factory, her animated happiness now was a welcome relief.

There were two mares: Satin, a black with a white star, and a gray named Silver Bells. They were fifteen years old and kept strictly for pleasure, not for showing or breeding. Their stalls were clean and roomy, the horses obviously well cared for.

Mary Donniger, a very nice lady in her mid-sixties, wanted to keep it that way. "They adore you," Mary said with wonder.

"I'm amazed. I mean, they're *huge*. And so beautiful. I hadn't realized." Cyn smoothed her hand along the gray's back, then patted its shoulder. The black protested being ignored, and with a laugh, Cyn moved to the other stall and treated that horse to the same attention. "I've never been around animals much."

"You're a natural." Mary watched her crooning to the animals, then smiled. "I love them both very much."

"I can see why." Silver Bells let out a whinny, and Cyn laughed in delight. "You're both spoiled, aren't you?" She took turns stroking the horses, talking to them as if they understood her, praising them.

Mary gave them a little more time to interact, then suggested they tour the space above the barn that served as living quarters. Bruce took that as a positive sign, and given Cyn's look of cautious expectation, she did, too.

The main entrance to the apartment was by stairs outside the barn, but a steep ladder from the barn floor also led to an interior door into the loft. The space was indeed small, but tidy and warm.

Bruce hated to admit it, and he didn't like himself for it, but he had half hoped it would be unsuitable to give him a reason to take Cyn home with him again.

Hands in his pockets, his heart strangely full, Bruce said, "It smells a little of the horses."

Cyn closed her eyes and breathed deeply. "And leather and hay. Clean, natural smells. I like it."

Everything she did seemed to incite him to lust. He cleared his throat and tried not to watch her so closely. "It's not an unpleasant smell at all."

Mary leaned in the doorway. "I've always enjoyed it and if I was younger, I'd relish spending time out here working. It makes me feel closer to my husband."

The room included a very small refrigerator, an electric coffeepot, a microwave, and a tiny television. The telephone was an extension of the main line, so if Cyn used it, she'd be sharing with Mary.

But as she said, she didn't have anyone to call, anyway.

"What do you think?" Mary asked.

Cyn looked as if she were standing in the middle of a palace. "It's great."

"It has everything you'd need, but probably not everything you'd want." Mary smoothed her hand over the quilt on the twin-sized bed tucked into one corner, opposite the appliances. "My grandmother made this quilt. My husband and father worked together to turn the loft into an apartment. My mother and I could hear them laughing all the way up to the house."

Bruce felt her pain. "I'm sorry for your loss."

She gave a slight smile. "Before Dave's health deteriorated, we'd planned to travel. We were going to hire someone to tend the horses to give us more free time." She walked over to the window that overlooked the backyard. "We thought we'd have years, until a heart attack took him."

To Bruce, her loss only emphasized the value of life, and why you should never waste a single moment. He glanced at Cyn and saw the sympathy in her pale gaze. She looked injured by Mary's pain, as if she shared it. And indeed, Cyn certainly knew more about loss than most people would ever have to learn.

Mary sighed. "Since then, I've been caring for the animals myself, but it's not easy on me. I want to ride them, to love them, but I'm afraid I need someone else to do the physical work."

Cyn licked her lips, determined, anxious. "I'd love to take the job. I'll be honest — I've never been around horses. But I'm more than willing to learn and I swear I'll be good to them. I'll do the best job I can."

Mary continued to look out the window a few seconds more, then she turned to Cyn. She was smiling. "For tonight, the horses just need to be fed and watered. In the morning, I can show you how to clean the stalls and lay out new hay."

Cyn caught her breath. "I have the job?"

"The horses like you, and that's what's most important. They're a good judge of character." With a laugh, Mary added, "Everything else can be learned."

Cyn squealed in excitement, but tamped down on her enthusiasm when Mary's cell phone rang. She looked ready to burst as she hugged herself tight and jiggled in place.

Her happiness proved contagious, and Bruce wanted to laugh with her.

Mary fished the phone from her jacket pocket to check the caller ID. "I'm sorry, I need to take this. Look around all you want, move in your things, then come up to the house and we can go over your schedule."

She turned away while answering the phone and a moment later, the door closed behind her, leaving Bruce alone with Cyn.

Slowly, Cyn turned to face him, so alight with joy that he couldn't help but grin. He winked at her. "Congratulations."

Her smile spread into a wide grin, then she impulsively threw herself into his arms. Bruce staggered back before gaining his wits and wrapping his arms around her slight, soft frame. Cyn was laughing, squeezing him, her hands on his shoulders, his nape, along his spine.

Her breasts pressed into his chest, her thighs rubbed his, and she was happy. Wonderfully, deliriously happy — for the simplest thing that most people took for granted: a chance to work and make her own way.

From one moment to the next, his body

reacted predictably to holding an attractive woman he wanted.

Her laughter was a powerful aphrodisiac, and combined with the feel of her body in his arms, it was enough. More than enough.

Right and wrong didn't play into it. He wanted to lower her to the narrow cot behind them and claim her as his own.

His mind was still fighting that image when Cyn turned her face up to his. Tears of happiness made her pale eyes glassy. The second their gazes met, he was a goner. He cupped her face, relishing the warm softness of her skin, breathing hard with growing need. "Cyn."

He tried to say her name as a warning, wanting her to shove him away, slap him, elbow him in the chest again. Anything that would shake off the overwhelming need.

She stared at him with confusion, then dawning awareness. Her breath caught, and slowly, very slowly, her thick lashes dropped over her eyes in a sign of permission and acceptance.

That did it.

His control cracked and Bruce took her mouth, soft and damp, her lips opened just enough for his tongue to glide inside.

Oh God, she tasted good and it felt right, so right to touch her this way . . .

Cyn went perfectly still, her breathing fast but her body immobile. She was pliable in his arms, not fighting him, but not really taking part, either.

His muddled mind couldn't register anything beyond the need for more. He readjusted his hold, aligning her slender body with his muscular one, pulling her closer. Her nipples stiffened, teasing him, wringing a groan from deep in his chest. Oblivion set in, blocking out their surroundings, the impropriety of the moment.

Cyn's hands clenched into his shirtsleeves over his biceps and she gave the softest, most compelling moan he'd ever heard. He realized his hand was fisted around her braid, holding her right where he wanted her, that his tongue was in her mouth and his hips were pressing against hers, and he was instantly appalled.

He pushed back — and Cyn, taken unawares, put too much weight on her injured ankle. She stumbled and would have fallen if Bruce hadn't caught her again.

He held her shoulders and got iron control of himself. His jaw clenched, his lungs labored. He knew, damn it, he *knew* what she'd been through, and still he'd all but attacked her.

Guilt burned like acid in his gut and left his voice raspy. "I'm sorry."

She lowered her face, hiding her expression from him. With a shaking hand, she touched her mouth.

Her lips were swollen, reddened . . .

Gripping her shoulders tighter, he gently shook her. "Cyn, talk to me." He bent to see her face, horrified that he might have frightened or insulted her.

She stared at him, bewildered, maybe a little awed. "I had no idea."

That whisper-soft voice nearly took him to his knees. He was still so hard he was shaking, and his reply was sharper than he intended. "No idea about *what?*"

"Why people enjoyed kissing."

Her sentiment hit him like a blow.

Her hand lifted and now it was his lips she touched, featherlight and curious. "It was just something that was sometimes required, something a few guys paid for. A way to help get them off."

Jesus, he couldn't hear this, not right now. Bruce squeezed his eyes shut. "Cyn, don't."

She stepped away from him and turned her back. She, too, was trembling. "I'm sorry. I didn't mean . . ."

He jerked her back around to face him. "Don't apologize!"

Shocked, she stared at him, and he wanted to kick his own behind.

"That's not what I meant," he tried explaining, but she looked completely befuddled, and now ashamed. Bruce released her and ran both hands through his hair. It took an effort, but he moderated both his tone and his emotions. "I'm attracted to you, Cyn." He laughed at such a grave understatement. "I'm sorry, but it's true. It's not what I'm used to . . . but that's no excuse. I shouldn't have done that."

"Kissed me?"

He gave a stiff nod. "Yes."

"But . . . I liked it." And then, "Didn't you?"

God help him. His groan was harsh with self-loathing; her words made him want to kiss her again, longer and deeper this time. Everywhere.

"Yeah, I liked it. Too much." To be safe, he moved a considerable distance from her. "But I don't want to take advantage of you."

Incredulous, she laughed at him. "Take advantage of *me?*" She laughed again, more than making her point. "That's hardly possible, all things considered."

Just that quickly, Bruce was back to standing inches from her, her face held in his hands, his nose almost touching hers. "That's exactly what I'm talking about, Cyn. At the moment, you don't realize how special, how beautiful you are, inside and out. And until you do, until you accept what a lovely, intelligent woman you are, until you see what I see, I don't want to crowd you or confuse the issue."

One brow lifted in mocking interest. "The issue being . . . ?"

"That you're as good as anyone, as good as you want to be."

Time seemed to stand still while she weighed his words, and then the cynicism left her and she pressed close again, hugging him in an entirely platonic embrace. "Thanks."

"For what?"

"For being a guy I actually like. And let me tell ya, *that's* unusual." She smiled up at him, kissed his chin, and stepped back. "Let me get my stuff out of your car and you can be on your way."

He didn't want to be on his way, blast her. He should have been pleased to put the unnerving encounter to rest, but instead, he wished for different circumstances. He wished for a time and a place where he wouldn't have to hold himself back.

He had considered sex over the years; God knew, he was human and he was male. But he'd only thought of it in the abstract, not in such a definite, desperate way. He didn't just want relief, he wanted Cyn. In every way known to man. He didn't only think of coupling with her, he thought of taking her for long, heated hours. He thought of hearing her cry out in a climax, he thought of exploding inside her . . .

Vivid, burning visuals that now tormented him. He ran a hand through his hair, unsure what to do.

After dismissing sex for years, he now wanted the one woman who was off limits. He could probably make her understand, convince her . . .

But she'd made her preferences clear and they took precedence over his at the moment. Bruce cleared his throat. "Stay put. Rest, put your feet up. I'll bring your things in."

"I'm not —"

"Helpless, I know." God, he couldn't quibble with her right now. He needed a breath of fresh air and a moment away from her. "You're one of the most ingenious people I've ever met, but you still have a sore ankle."

"Ingenious?"

Turbulent lust turned to irritation. "Do not insult yourself again, Cyn. I mean it." He waited, but she held herself in wide-eyed silence and finally he nodded. "Your ankle is hurt and you've been on your feet all day. Ignoring it is only going to get you so far, and if you want to be up to working tomorrow, you'll have to take it easy today."

"Well, don't get in a lather. You want me to sit, I'll sit." She stomped to the small dinette, dropped down onto a chair, and sent him a smarmy smile. "Happy?"

Far from it. "Your books will go nicely on that shelf below the microwave."

She knew exactly what he was doing, but she didn't argue the point. "Instead of cookbooks, I'll have *Famine of the Child's Soul* on display." She lounged back in a sensual sprawl and grinned. "Guaranteed to ruin most appetites."

Time, Bruce reminded himself. She needed time, and somehow he'd make sure she got it. Today had been a wonderful start filled with amazing strides. She had a job, a place to stay.

Soon she'd have a new, more rewarding life.

And then, maybe, just maybe, he could quit denying himself.

Less than an hour later, Bruce was ready to leave. It hadn't taken near that long for Cyn to unload her meager belongings from her one suitcase, but Bruce hung around while Mary showed her how to feed and water the horses. In the morning, she'd show her how to clean the stalls and spread new hay. Then Cyn would be on her own.

She was excited, exhilarated — but nothing compared to the kiss she'd shared with Bruce. Wow, that had been an eye-opener of epic proportions.

Why the hell hadn't any of her books told her how awesome a kiss could be? After Bruce had pulled away, she'd half expected to melt into a puddle on the loft floor. She'd been kissed, more than she wanted to remember, but never with that effect.

Apparently, she needed to broaden her reading horizons.

Despite Bruce's arguments, she walked him to his car. Every additional second she got to spend with him felt like a gift.

Instead of getting in, he leaned on the

door. "Will you call Shay?"

Cyn hated to do that. She wasn't a dummy and she knew Shay would be creating a job for her. It wouldn't be legitimate work, and that's what she craved.

"Just until something else comes along," Bruce urged, and Cyn knew he'd read her thoughts. That was a little disconcerting, that he could see inside her mind. But at the same time, it showed how attuned he was to her as a person, not just to her body. When she talked, he actually listened. And that was as different as his kiss had been.

Maybe the job with Shay wouldn't be such a bad thing. It'd give her a chance to spend more time with Bruce and she was just selfish enough, just hungry enough, to grab the opportunity with both hands. "You're sure you're okay with that?"

He didn't smile. He hadn't smiled since kissing her. "Why wouldn't I be?"

He was the strangest man — placid one moment, hot the next, always concerned yet often teasing. "Shay said we'd be hanging around the church."

He nodded. "Working, helping out."

"Whatever. I wasn't sure how you'd really feel about that. You don't have to be nice, you know. If I'd make anyone uncomfortable — given my background and all — then I wouldn't want to be there." She didn't want to do anything to cause him trouble or sully his good reputation.

Bruce's dark eyes narrowed. He tried to hide his annoyance while tugging playfully on the end of her braid. "On the contrary. I'd enjoy seeing you."

Her heart seemed to leap right from her chest. But was he just being nice? He said he'd worked with hookers. Was he only trying to help her get her life together?

Her skeptical look was met with a frown. Fair hair fell over his brow as he shook his head. "So doubting. I don't lie, Cyn — remember that, okay?"

"Sure." She'd tell him whatever he wanted to hear, just to keep him around a bit longer.

He looked toward the heavens, as if unconvinced. "You'll enjoying working with Shay. And it'll give you a chance to get to know some of the other town folks better." He pulled out his cell phone and punched in Shay's number. "Talk to her now. I know Shay — she'll be thrilled to hear from you."

With a roll of her eyes, Cyn accepted the phone just as Shay answered the call. And as Bruce had predicted, she seemed genuinely happy to hear from her. Without Cyn having to mention her lack of a car, Shay volunteered to pick her up in the morning after she'd taken care of the horses.

In all of five seconds, Shay had a full day planned, and Cyn, caught up in the whirlwind of Shay's excitement, agreed to everything.

Satisfied, Bruce accepted his phone back and tucked it away after Cyn ended the call. "Shay's a charmer."

"She's a bulldozer," Cyn corrected, but her grin told Bruce that she didn't mind. Truth was, she liked Shay. She liked Bryan, too. And even Julie had seemed nice enough.

She wouldn't have admitted it to anyone, but she felt intimidated by people who weren't from her world — good, normal people. But Bruce's friends made it easier than she'd expected.

Bruce glanced back at the barn where her apartment had been built. From the driveway, you could barely see it. It was a good stretch of the legs from one structure to the next. "Promise me you'll take it easy and let your ankle rest."

She crossed her heart. Once he left, she'd have nothing to do but rest. "Sure thing."

"And keep your doors locked at night. That loft doesn't look all that secure to me."

"Mary loves her horses. Weren't you listening when she said there's an alarm on the barn? If anyone breaks in, she'd know it."

"Good." He shifted, tossed the keys in his hand, then gave a nod. "I'd better go."

"See you tomorrow?" The second the words left her mouth, Cyn felt lame, like Polly Puritan setting a damn date.

She was a whore, no longer practicing but in the scheme of things, she wasn't sure that mattered for much.

Bruce was a preacher, very much the wholesome, goody-two-shoes type. They might as well have been from different planets.

She had no business indulging an infatuation. Damn it, she knew better.

But when Bruce leaned forward and touched his mouth to her cheek in a butterfly, somewhat brotherly caress, her knees wanted to buckle.

She would never get used to his kisses — but she wouldn't mind trying.

"See you tomorrow," he murmured low, then got in his car and seconds later drove away.

A soft swell of contentment settled around Cyn as she watched his car disappear from sight. Already she missed him. But thanks to Shay, she'd see him tomorrow and maybe even the day after that.

In school, shame had forced her to shy away from everyone. Friendships left you vulnerable, and she couldn't risk anyone knowing about her secrets. She'd had no friends, so she'd had no boyfriends. On the street, she'd given men her body, but never her thoughts, most definitely never her heart.

Bruce had touched her. Physically, sure, but it was so much more than that. So much more than she'd ever had, or ever expected to want.

But now, the wanting threatened to eat her up.

The sun was bright in her eyes, the breeze brisk but so damn fresh it took her breath away. She turned and headed back to the loft, distracted, distraught . . . and falling in love for the very first time in her life.

She'd achieved so much in such a short time. She was in Visitation, she had a job, and she had a place to stay. She should have been happy.

If she could rule out her past, somehow

erase it from her memory, everything would be almost . . . perfect.

The idea was too scary to let her be happy.

Arlene Potter stared into her coffee cup and concentrated on not moving. A late night and too much whisky had left her brain throbbing and her stomach cramping. She was half-asleep, about to give up on going in to work, when a heavy hand fell on her shoulder.

Twisting so fast and hard that she sprawled on the floor, she screeched out her surprise. She'd slept in her clothes after coming in during the wee hours of the morning, but they were soured with alcohol and sweat so she'd pulled them off when she'd awakened. Now she wore only a ratty housecoat that parted up to her knees.

Heart in her throat, her head splitting, she slowly brought her fearful gaze up to the man's face standing before her.

Terror tightened like a fist around her throat. What was *he* doing in her house? Dear God, she'd thought he was —

"Stupid woman, you wrote me off, didn't you?" His grin wasn't friendly, nor was the narrowing of his small, mean eyes.

"You can't be rid of me that easily."

Arlene put her hand to her throat. It felt like her heart had lodged there. She tried to speak, but nothing came out.

Abruptly he crouched down in front of her and she screeched again, scrambling back in a panic until he caught her ankle and jerked her forward so forcefully that her head fell back and clunked on the floor. He wore black leather gloves, and they looked obscene against her pale skin.

"Arlene," he growled in the way of a reprimand, "where is your lovely daughter?"

Cyn? He wanted Cyn? Oh, thank God. Frantic, gasping, she shook her head and gave the only reply she could. "I don't know."

His fingers tightened on the bones in her ankle. "Don't lie to me, Arlene."

Pain traveled up her shin, and she gasped. "I'm not. She's gone."

His eyes were bright and hot as the fires of hell. "Gone where?"

Arlene clutched at her leg, her expression pleading. "I don't know," she swore in a shrill voice. "Both of you disappeared at the same time. I'd tell you if I knew where to find her, but I haven't seen her in years."

"She's never come back here?"

"No." She shook her head hard. "I haven't heard from her, not once."

His expression thoughtful, he sat back and Arlene scurried into the corner against the grimy cabinets. Knowing what he was capable of, knowing he could do almost anything, brought whimpers of fear from deep inside her.

After a moment, he stood, towering over her, deliberately dominating. She'd always found him cruelly handsome, intimidating and powerful. He crossed his arms and again, he fashioned that evil smile that made Arlene's skin crawl and her heart shudder, even while heightening her awareness of him as a man.

"Pity, because I only know one way to find her."

Her eyes widened in confusion. "But . . . why do you want Cyn so bad?"

He laughed, the sound raw and ugly. "If you were a man, instead of a pathetic bitch, you'd already know the answer to that."

A calculating gleam entered her eyes and she pushed herself upright. "I'm a woman."

His gaze moved over her, from the gaping top of her robe that showed a lot of her naked breasts, down to her knees and bare, dirty feet. He wanted her, she was sure of it. He'd always wanted her, regardless of his fascination with Cyn.

Arlene inched closer. "If it's satisfaction you want . . ." She let the offer dangle out there, hoping for enticement. She'd been too long without a man. Much too long. Why should her daughter have all the attention?

His eyes narrowed and he sucked something from one of his teeth as if in indecision. Then he shrugged. "Come here."

Triumphant, Arlene swayed toward him — and he grabbed her, jerking her around so her back was to his chest. Excitement had her melting, lava-hot and ready . . .

In one smooth movement, he gripped the worn cloth belt to her robe and slid it free. Material parted, exposing her, exciting her more.

She moaned in encouragement.

"If you're dead," he whispered against her temple with cheerful menace, "Cyn will have to be notified, right? Someone will find her. She'll come here, and then I'll have her."

Fuzzy with a hangover and arousal, it took a moment for the awful words to register. Arlene's eyes flared open, but the belt was already wrapped around her throat.

Laughing at her struggles, he squeezed, and cut off her air supply.

Arlene clawed at the back of his hands, gagging, gasping, trying to beg — and she heard his laughter roughen with excitement. Her vision, sound, emotion, all faded away, more and more distant, until she slumped, dead in his arms.

He let her drop to the floor in an inelegant sprawl. Adrenaline flowed through his veins and for a time, he relished the rush, the sense of majestic power. It was almost orgasmic — just the way little Cyn had made him feel.

After several deep breaths, he drew Cyn's journal from inside his jacket. She'd made a mistake in leaving it behind, because the police hadn't found it. She'd have no allies.

He dumped two kitchen drawers before locating a pen and paper. Copying the delicate script from Cyn's journal, he wrote a note. It was heart-wrenching, a cry for help from a young girl, and he snickered as he penned it.

Oh yeah, the cops would find her for him. Soon, he'd have her again.

And then, finally, they could pick up where they'd left off.

Chapter Six

Jamie swung the ax hard, felt it sink deep into the wood, like a hot knife in butter. The wood split into sizeable chunks. He always enjoyed physical labor, and despite being labeled a hermit, he was determined to stay in prime shape. How long his anonymity would last, he didn't know, but never again would he ever be caught unawares.

He jerked the ax free of the chopping block, raised it over his head — and stopped cold. Emotions, warnings, images, rippled through him, making his vision compress and his senses grind to acute sharpness.

The warnings settled around him with all the comfort of a horsehair blanket. They nettled him, but he accepted them. They were part of him. The uglier part.

Shit. It was time. Maybe past time.

He had to make a trip into town. He couldn't put it off any longer. He lowered the ax and rested both hands against the handle. Closing his eyes, he concentrated on Bruce, trying to decipher the best time to make his appearance.

Midweek, he decided, would work out. Nothing would happen for a few more days at least, and that'd be the best time to catch Bruce away from town.

The citizens of Visitation weren't his friends — they couldn't be, but they were friendly acquaintances. For that reason, he preferred to speak with Bruce on the road rather than go into town where he always felt exposed and out of place — where they wanted to engage him in idle chitchat.

Bruce would take a drive, and Jamie would warn him then. Unlike the others, Jamie had a feeling that Bruce would be more receptive to what he knew. If for no other reason than out of concern for Cyn.

Jamie paused and stared up at the towering trees. There was no one around, and Bruce's situation was definitely amusing, but even so, Jamie couldn't quite bring himself to smile. He rarely did smile — except around Joe or Bryan. Those two could supply endless forms of entertainment.

He shook his head.

Cyn had been in town only two weeks, but already Bruce was falling for her. Hard. And in the ways of all men, Bruce looked for opportunities to be alone with her. He was smitten, and fighting it the best he could. Jamie could have told him it was useless, that their union was unavoidable, but for now at least, he'd keep that information to himself.

Using a forearm, Jamie pushed sweat out of his eyes and smoothed away a hank of hair that had escaped his rubber band. His hair had gotten so long that a ponytail was customary with his jeans and tees. If the folks from the institute saw him now, they wouldn't recognize him — and that was the point.

He raised the ax, ready to get back to work. He had enough wood to last him through three winters, but he liked chopping the dead fall, being outside, feeling his muscles strain and letting his mind rest.

The only problem was that, until Cyn was safe, there wouldn't be much rest. And she wouldn't be safe . . . until Bruce made her so. He wanted to give her time, but time was something she didn't have. Bruce would have to step up to the plate. Now.

That was how it had to be, whether Bruce accepted it yet or not.

Bryan nudged his brother hard. "You're staring again."

Bruce pulled his gaze from where Cyn wielded the broom with more energy than was needed. Each sweep jostled her breasts and caused her rear to swing. The sun glinted down on her dark hair and put color in her cheeks. "What's that?"

Laughing, Bryan said, "You're so obvious."

"About what?" But he asked it in distraction because once again, Cyn had caught his notice. She bent to sweep the pile into a dustpan, and Bruce absorbed the sight of her heart-shaped rear. *Such an invitation* . . .

He heard Bryan chuckling and turned to him with disgust. "This is harder than I ever imagined."

"So do something about it." Bryan clapped him on the back. "I know women, and I'm pretty damn sure she's willing. Hell, she looks at you like you're God."

Bruce closed his eyes on a groan of pain. "I can't."

"Why the hell not? You're single, she's single . . ."

"She used to be a prostitute."

That blunt disclosure wrought a shocked silence. "The hell you say." Bryan leaned past Bruce to look at her. "She's so damn young —"

"Twenty-two. And you know that doesn't have a thing to do with it." Bruce stalked into the kitchen for a glass of iced tea. Watching Cyn heated him more than the afternoon sun and he just couldn't torture himself any longer. "She's here to start a new life."

Bryan leaned against the counter. He accepted the icy glass Bruce handed to him, but didn't take his gaze from his brother. "It bothers you?"

"Of course it bothers me." He rounded on his brother in frustrated fury. "Her life has been hellish up until now. She needs friends and acceptance and . . ."

"And?"

Bruce gritted his teeth. "And I want her. I don't want to give her time. Being with her is . . . more difficult than I ever imagined." He swallowed hard. "She's still so insecure, though she does her best to hide it."

"Shay noticed. She thought it was because she was young and new to the area."

Bruce downed half his drink, hoping it would cool his body and his temper. "She thinks men look at her and miraculously know. She knew some crazed minister who told her that her soul was black and others could see it."

"Bastard."

Bruce laughed. "You have no idea. If I

could get my hands on him . . ." He let the ugly threat trail off. In the normal course of things, he wasn't a violent man. But like most male animals, he'd fight to the death to defend his mate, and with each day that passed, he became more and more certain that Cyn was the one woman he wanted.

But Cyn had told him no more about her past or her demons or the men who'd hurt her. It made him crazy with frustration. He wanted her to trust him completely, to let him help heal her heart. Logically, he knew and accepted that she needed more time.

In his heart, he couldn't bear waiting.

Bryan's voice was low when he asked with idle interest, "Want me to check her out?"

"No." Then he added, "Not yet anyway. That would be an intrusion into her privacy and I don't want to do that."

"Yet?"

He nodded. "If I ever think she's threatened in any way, I might feel differently."

Bryan considered that, took a long drink and nodded. "Just let me know."

"Thanks."

"Wanna know what I think?"

Bruce again closed his eyes. "I don't know, do I?"

Bryan shrugged, because they both knew he'd give his advice whether Bruce wanted to hear it or not. Bruce would have done the same in a reverse situation. In fact, he *had* done the same when Bryan had been fighting his attraction to Shay.

"I think love conquers all." Bryan held his arms out to his sides and grinned. "Look at me. I was a miserable bum until Shay loved me."

Bruce eyed him askance. "And you're now what?"

"Deliriously happy and sexually fulfilled. Don't ever discount the sexual fulfillment part. It counts for a lot."

"I do not want to hear this."

"Tough. Because at the moment, you look like a miserable bum, too, and frankly, it turns my stomach. I like you better when you're all pious and righteous, instead of moping around. It's not what I'm used to. Go after her. Let her know how you feel. Trust her to know what's best for her."

"I can't do that."

"Why not? Much as you might want to think otherwise, and despite how Cyn treats you, you aren't God. You aren't all-wise and all-knowing. You can't take care of the entire world."

Bruce sighed. "You don't think she deserves to enjoy her own life before I push my way into it?"

"You planning to make her miserable?"

He was planning to make love to her, long and hard and forever. Oh God. "No, but I don't know if she's ready."

"Why wouldn't she be? She seems happy enough to me."

"She was . . ." Bruce swallowed, struggling to get the words out. "Abused. As a child." It still ate him up to think of what she'd gone through. He put the empty glass in the sink before he broke it. "She says she wasn't raped, but if that's true, it's the only indignity she didn't suffer. You know what she reads?"

Bryan just waited.

"Books on child abuse, how to heal, how to avoid becoming an abuser. Even as a kid, she knew she wanted to stop the chain."

"Sounds like she survived it all with her spirit intact. I don't think you're giving her enough credit."

"She has secrets that she won't share. I feel it." He dug the heels of his hands into his eye sockets. "I kissed her."

Bryan's eyebrows shot up. "And?"

His laugh was harsh and filled with self-loathing. "She was stunned. She said she didn't know kissing could be nice." He dropped his hands and stared at Bryan. "She's been used most of her life. Her experiences with men aren't pleasant."

Filled with sympathy, Bryan put his arm around his brother's shoulders. "So you'll show her that there are a lot of nice things between men and women. You'll help her forget the past. You'll be there with her as she moves on." He squeezed Bruce hard enough to break a few ribs. "Trust me on this. I've watched her watching you in church. She's got it worse than you do." He released Bruce and grinned. "Shay loves it. She's hoping to see you all settled and happy."

It had surprised Bruce to see either of them there. Bryan wasn't a big churchgoer, but Shay had dragged him in. Not long after, Cyn had crept in, trying to be inconspicuous as she seated herself in the middle of a crowd.

But she couldn't be near without Bruce knowing it. His eyes were constantly drawn to her, and all through his sermon, his attention had veered back to her again and again.

Bruce wanted to take Bryan's advice, he really did. "I don't know."

With a frown, Bryan said, "You're going

to force me to get all mushy and stuff, aren't you?"

"Mushy?"

Bryan sighed. "All joking aside, you're a terrific, intuitive person, Bruce. You'll know if you're pushing too hard. I'm not saying to toss her into bed tonight. But I don't think letting her know how you feel will hurt anything. Cyn's not exactly shy, despite her past, or maybe because of it. She'll let you know if she's not interested."

A memory intruded, bringing with it a grin. "When I first met her," Bruce confided, "she elbowed me. Right here."

"Ah." Bryan grinned with new admiration. "In the solar plexus. Good place to land a blow. Even a small woman can immobilize a big guy that way."

"Yeah. She's read some books on self-defense, too."

"Smart girl." Respect filled his voice.

"But still just a girl," Bruce felt pressed to point out.

Bryan glanced out the window at Cyn. "Looks like a woman to me. A really hot babe, in fact, and if you don't make a move, someone with fewer scruples is likely to. Then where will you be?"

Bruce whipped around. Sure enough, two of the workers were chatting with Cyn and she was smiling back. It made his blood boil. "I was going to have dinner with Julie tonight."

Bryan rolled his eyes. "So ask Cyn to go along. Afterward, you can drop Julie off and spend a few private minutes with her. Let nature take its course."

"I have spent time with her. I've ridden with her when she's exercising the horses."

"Well, unless you're an acrobat, I doubt you can accomplish much on the back of a horse."

Which was the point, as far as Bruce was concerned. He'd done his level best not to be with her where opportunities might arise. He'd never had his moral strength tested the way it was around Cyn. Truth was, he didn't trust himself to do what was right.

Bruce continued to watch out the window until the two men walked away and Cyn returned to work. He came to a sudden decision. "All right. I'll do it."

He wasn't sure if he could only kiss her. If ever a woman was designed to push all his buttons, it was Cynthia Potter. But he could at least invite her along for dinner. With Julie there, he'd be forced to be on his best behavior.

And after he dropped Julie off? Well, he'd just have to see.

* * *

In the two weeks she'd spent in Visitation, Cyn had changed in many ways.

Working with the horses had made her physically stronger, thanks to using a wheelbarrow, big shovel, and manure pick. On a daily basis, she removed horse "apples" and cleaned up the stalls, the barn, and the area around it. Mary told her she was almost too meticulous, but Cyn adored the animals already, and she enjoyed being with them.

Once a week, she completely emptied the stalls, replacing the bedding and making everything fresh. It was dirty work, but she didn't mind at all. As Mary had said, it felt good to use her body, to feel the stretch and ache of new muscles. And being near the horses brought its own kind of peace.

Feeding them was a pleasure because they were always so happy to see her. She checked on them several times a day, and Mary was teaching her how to ride. She wasn't very accomplished yet, and Bruce laughed at her efforts, though he wasn't much better.

The first time he showed up, she was stunned. He'd brought her a book on horses to add to her collection, but then hung around for over an hour. When Mary suggested they exercise the horses, Bruce had been quick to agree. Since then, he'd been over several times, but only when it was time to exercise the horses. And he never accepted her invitations into the loft.

If Cyn didn't know better, she'd think he was afraid of her.

Thanks to Shay, when Bruce didn't come to her, she went to him. After Reverend Thorne, she'd had great reservations about attending Sunday service. But Shay had convinced her to show up, and she was so glad she had. Twice now, she'd heard Bruce speak, and his sermons were not what she had imagined.

He spent his time praising people who had done good deeds for the community. He never failed to say a few prayers for Scott Royal, the deputy, or men from the fire department, asking that they be kept safe in their duties.

He praised Joe Winston for hosting benefits at the lake, Shay for her donations, the children who had written letters to the president. He'd asked the congregation to remember a neighbor who was in the hospital, and after some discussion on that, they agreed to send a variety of flowers and cards to cheer the elderly man.

All in all, Bruce celebrated life and love with a wholesomeness she hadn't known existed. He didn't judge or condemn. He accepted and encouraged.

She hadn't known a man like him existed, much less that she'd ever meet him.

There was a lot of work still to be done before the church could open its doors to the membership. Construction was a messy business, so Cyn always had a reason to be there, helping out.

She'd been at Bruce's home since noon, but everyone had been so busy, she hadn't had much of a chance to talk to him. Sometimes it felt as if he avoided her.

But other times, when she had his undivided attention, she felt special. Like an average woman, with average problems and an average life. It was strange, and she was cautious about getting too close. But in the end, she knew she didn't really have a choice. She already cared far more for him than was wise.

She was sweeping up a pile of drywall chunks and dust, lost in thought, when she felt unwanted attention. Surreptitiously, she glanced toward the two rangy young men who had spoken with her earlier. They watched her with heated expressions and a lot of speculation, whispering, probably bragging. She'd been polite and they'd gotten the wrong idea.

Such infantile idiots.

Then Shay's laughter drew her gaze in another direction. Like a golden goddess, Shay stood in a ray of bright sunshine chatting with Luna Winston and discussing trim work. Cyn had met Luna a week ago, and she couldn't get over her. The woman changed her hair almost weekly, dressed in the most flamboyant clothing, and loved to laugh.

Shay held three pieces of crown molding, and she was very animated in her comparisons. Today, Luna had reddish hair that caught and held the sunlight as she tried to talk Shay into a different piece. Several men were eyeing them with prurient interest.

"If Bryan caught them, he'd be bashing heads."

A smile already forming, Cyn turned to Bruce. "I think Joe Winston would have something to say about it, too."

"Naw. Joe just acts, he doesn't talk about it."

Cyn laughed. "That's probably true."

Bruce glared at the men, cleared his throat loudly, and with sheepish expressions, they began storing their tools.

Bruce might be the original "nice guy," but no one wanted to get on his bad side. He didn't instill fear or issue physical threats. He didn't exude menace the way Joe Winston did, and he didn't have that aura of danger like his brother. But because he was so respected, no one messed with him.

It was one of the reasons Cyn found herself falling head over heels for him. "Sometimes guys are just idiots."

Still watching the men, Bruce said in distraction, "It's hard to blame them for doing what comes naturally."

"Oh?" She'd gotten used to the sometimes silly, sometimes profound things that came out of Bruce's mouth. "And that is?"

"Appreciating the sight of a beautiful woman." The men were forgotten as he faced her, then touched the tip of her nose. "There's a reason God made you so different from us, and it sure wasn't to discourage interest."

Pretending disgust, Cyn pulled in her chin. "Too bad He didn't give you a few more brains to go with the eyesight, because even a doofus knows it's rude to stare."

Bruce accepted her insult with a smile. "They'll learn eventually."

Cyn picked up her dustpan and walked toward the garbage can, aware of Bruce following on her heels. "I was thinking about that," she told him. "Men watching women, I mean."

"Oh?"

They were now out of hearing range of the others, and Cyn leaned the broom against the brick wall. "Some guys were watching me —"

"Who?"

His sharp tone had her lifting her brows. "It doesn't matter who —"

"They made you uneasy or you wouldn't have noticed." His gaze scanned the area. "Who was it?"

Though it was entirely foreign to her, Cyn appreciated his protective nature. Still, she'd sooner put up with a groping, never mind a simple stare, than have Bruce arguing with his friends and neighbors on her behalf. "Will you let me finish?"

She could tell he didn't want to, but he subsided. "Go on."

Now that she had his attention, she felt self-conscious. "It, well, it still makes me wonder if they somehow know me."

The bright afternoon sun added golden flecks to his brown eyes as he stared at her. "You've worked with us almost every single day. Of course they know you."

"I don't mean that."

Dark brows lowered in grim warning. "Then what?"

Her temper sparked. "I have to spell it out?"

Stubbornness could be his middle name. "Yes, I think you do."

Cyn gave up. "I always wonder if they know I was a hooker, if they can somehow see the things I've done, like the reverend said —"

Bruce turned away with a muffled curse.

Surprised, Cyn blinked. Bruce *never* cursed. "What was that?"

He whipped back around to face off with her. "You're beautiful. Stunning, in fact. My brother just pointed it out to me, as if I didn't already know it. And yes, Cyn, you're sexy."

His ire left her breathless. "You sound awfully mad about it."

Ready to explode, Bruce jutted his chin toward her. "You're also smart, and you have a great smile and the work ethic of a mule. No non-blind man with a pulse is going to be able to ignore you. Not because they know your private business, but because you're you, a very noticeable woman."

Trying for a little aplomb, Cyn propped her shoulder against a tree. For early May, the weather was unseasonably warm and today she wore only a T-shirt with jeans. "Your sweet-talking abilities could use some work."

His face went blank. "What?"

"Shouting compliments at a woman is a new approach, but hey, I'm up for new things."

Bruce appeared confused for a second, then he scrubbed his hands over his face and groaned. "Okay." His arms fell to his sides and he said, "I admit, I overdid it. It's been a rough day. But I want you to like yourself, and to realize that other people like you, too."

He could be so darn sweet. "Well, if *someone* would let me finish."

He pretended to zip his lips, making her laugh.

"That's what I was trying to tell you before you did your Tarzan impression. I saw those men staring at me and felt exposed, but then I saw more men staring at Shay and Luna, and I just knew they weren't thinking dirty thoughts about them."

"Depends on what your idea of *dirty* is. If you think they're exempt from male attention, you're wrong."

Cyn nodded. "They were admiring the women, because they're so attractive. And I thought, well, maybe they were just looking at me the same way."

Very slowly, Bruce's expression changed until he looked downright smug. "Eureka! I think she has it."

Cyn playfully punched him in the chest. "Smart-ass."

He caught her fist and tugged her closer. "Want to take a ride with me?"

His voice was low, somehow intimate and, to her hopeful ears, suggestive. "To where?"

"We need more window blocks. A box got dropped and several pieces were broken. It's about an hour's drive."

Her heartbeat sped up. "I'd love that."

"Julie and I were going to have dinner, too. There's a really wonderful Italian restaurant near the building supply store."

Her brain sputtered, then stalled. No, he hadn't just done that to her, hadn't made her think . . .

"Julie?" Had she really thought he was sweet? Well, he was a jerk. Her mouth felt too tight to form a smile. Why did she have to continue being a gullible idiot around him?

"She's got some errands to run, too."

At that moment, Julie called Bruce's name and then started toward them.

She was smiling, as usual.

She wore a dowdy, very proper outfit, as usual.

She picked her way across the debris-filled yard with prim determination.

Cyn knew it was wrong to dislike the woman, but she couldn't seem to help herself.

Julie shamed her by gifting her with a bright smile. "Hello, Cyn. How have you been?"

Cyn blushed — and tugged her hand away from Bruce. "Great. And yourself?"

"I just broke the engagement to my fiancé."

Cyn's mouth fell open. Talk about dropping a bomb. "You were engaged?"

"Yes, but that's over now." She beamed at Bruce. "Thank heavens."

Bruce nodded in satisfaction. "So you finally did it, huh?"

"Yes, and I feel much better. You were so right about that."

"Wonderful." He took both her hands. "We can celebrate at dinner."

No way did Cyn want to be part of their little party. She waited in strained silence.

She felt invisible. She felt mean — until Julie declined.

"Thank you, but no. I've decided to put off my errands for now. I want to make some new plans, have some fun."

"Celebrate in your own way?"

"Exactly."

Julie leaned forward and hugged Bruce, and damn him, he hugged her right back. Her head fit into the hollow of his shoulder and his big hands moved over her back.

Cyn's eyes nearly crossed.

"You've been such a good friend," Julie told him. "Thank you."

"My pleasure."

Cyn wanted to puke. "Look, I've got work to do —"

Julie didn't take offense. She pushed back from Bruce, and her smile now made her *almost* look pretty. "Then I'll let you get back to it. Have fun today." And she was off.

Bruce, the sap, smiled after her. But just before Cyn could march off in a huff of annoyance, he turned to her as if that whole private exchange hadn't occurred. His smile strained, he said, "Looks like it's just us, then."

Cyn seriously considered hitting him with her broom. Not that she'd ever expected Bruce to get moony-eyed over her, but damn it, he'd let her think . . . Or had he? He was so nice to everyone, *always* smiling, *always* welcoming. He made a great preacher.

While she was just learning how to make it in normal society.

"I should stick around and help Shay." It'd be less fun, but safer for her heart. "It wouldn't be right to go off and leave her alone."

"Shay is never alone, you know that. And I already spoke to her about it."

He'd asked Shay before he even asked her? "Oh, really?"

As obtuse as a man could be, he grinned. "She sends you off with her blessing."

"Well." Cyn was back to feeling mean. "As long as it's okay with Shay, how could I possibly refuse?"

Bruce eyed her warily. "Why are you looking at me like that?"

"Like what?"

"Like you want to take my head off. Don't you want to take a drive?"

Damn it, she did. But more than that, she wanted to know if he had something serious going with Julie Rose. And deep in her heart, she knew it didn't matter either way. "I don't know."

He suddenly turned resolute. "Come with me. I won't take no for an answer. It'll be fun. And now that I don't have to worry about Julie, I'll be better company."

"Why would you worry about Julie?"

He took Cyn's broom and started her toward the house. "She wasn't happy."

"Why not?"

They stepped into the kitchen. "Her uncle wanted her to marry, but she's not ready, and she definitely wasn't in love with her fiancé." Bruce leaned back against the sink while Cyn washed her hands. "Don't you think people should be in love before they get married?"

She shrugged. "I never figured on getting married, so I never gave it much thought."

"You don't want to marry someday?"

She'd made it a point not to daydream about the impossible. As a kid, she'd wanted to fly. As a hooker, she'd wanted to win the lottery. Wishing had never done her much good. "Do you?"

He showed no hesitation. "Yes." He looked at her mouth, sending a shiver of excitement down her spine. "The idea of spending my life with the right woman, having children and setting up house, is very appealing."

Oh. That did sound so nice . . .

Then, as if he realized what he was doing and what they were discussing, Bruce shook his head. "Tell me you'll keep me company."

Cyn was still reeling over his impassioned "right woman" speech, so she said without thinking, "Yeah, okay," then she stared at him, appalled at herself and wanting to renege.

He didn't give her a chance. "Great. Let's get going." He pulled her away from the sink before she'd even finished drying her hands. She grabbed her windbreaker and readjusted her purse.

She still kept it on her at all times, and more than one person had remarked on it. Sooner or later, someone would realize she had something of value inside.

Maybe it was time to open a savings account. Maybe it was time to take the next step toward blending into normal society. Her salary from Mary was small, but it was still a salary.

Before long, they were alone in Bruce's station wagon, suffering through a heavy silence and driving along the road that would lead right out of Visitation.

Bruce allowed Cyn to brood for all of

five minutes. "Why don't you like Julie?"

She continued to gaze out the side window. "Who says I don't?"

So much antagonism laced her words that Bruce had to fight a smile. Cyn was jealous, and he wasn't above enjoying the possessive show of emotion. It meant she cared, that she was starting to trust him.

At least, that's what he chose to believe.

He was considering whether or not he should reassure her, when she spied the bank, and straightened in her seat. "Do you use that bank?"

Bruce blinked twice to clear his head. His brain had been so far away from finances that it took him a moment to make the switch. "Yes." What was she up to now? "I think I mentioned that it's the only one. Most everyone in Visitation uses it."

"I'd like to open an account."

"Okay." He frowned in thought as he considered what would have to be done. "What type of account?"

"Savings." She bit her lip, then with a look of nonchalance, she opened her purse and dumped it on the seat between them.

"Cyn?"

"I want to show you something. Hang on."

Bruce glanced at the hodgepodge of items on the seat. Because her purse never left her, he'd expected . . . he didn't know what he'd expected. A photo of a loved one. A remarkable memento of some sort. Not a brush and dental floss, candy and lotion.

Then Cyn yanked at the lining on the bottom of her bag, tore it free, and removed a stack of one-hundred-dollar bills. Bruce quickly pulled off to the side of the road before he wrecked.

"How much?" he asked with a dry throat.

"Twenty-five hundred dollars." Her gaze was direct, beseeching. "It's mine. I earned it. I saved for years . . ."

Bruce thought of how easily she could have been mugged, how easily she could have been hurt if anyone had known —

His temper shot through the roof and before he could even think of reining himself in, he shoved the car in PARK and shouted, "Are you out of your mind?"

Her eyes went glassy and hard. "No. That's why I saved it."

"And you carry it around your neck, just waiting for someone to rob you blind?"

"Where, exactly, do you think I should have left it?"

"A *bank?*"

"Stop yelling at me!" She angrily gathered up her belongings and dropped them back in her purse, along with the money.

"I'm sorry," Bruce said, in only slightly less-provoked tones. "It's dangerous to have that much cash on you, especially in the life you've led."

"I had no choice. You know damn good and well I couldn't put it in a bank, because opening an account required ID."

With an effort, Bruce got a handle on his anger. It was born mostly of fear anyway, and he knew, from here on out, she'd be okay. He'd see to it.

He made a sudden decision. "We'll go to the bank first."

"I thought you needed glass block."

"I do. But if we stop at the bank first, we can find out what you'll need. With any luck, we can get it taken care of in a day or two." He glanced at her, saw she was still peeved, and sighed. "You don't have a driver's license, do you?"

"You know the answer to that."

"You'll probably need a photo ID to open the account. We can get that in the city. Do you have a birth certificate, social security card, or —"

"Both."

"Really?"

She lifted one shoulder, still not looking at him. "I was taking Driver's Ed right before I ran off. I had to have them for that."

And she'd had the good sense to take them with her. Amazing. "Does Mary expect you home any certain time tonight?"

Now Cyn eyed him. "She doesn't keep tabs on me. As long as I'm there to tend the horses in the morning, she won't know or care when I get back. Why?"

"It's possible this could take all day. And no, I'm not complaining."

A very female smile curling her lips, Cyn opened her door and climbed out. "Then get a move on."

Framed by the open door, Bruce stared at her. Her now raggedy purse was again slung around her neck. Her jeans were snug, her T-shirt loose, and for once she hadn't braided her hair.

Bruce seldom lost his temper with women, but then Cyn seemed to bring out all his emotions, from worry to fear to heated awareness. With a grin, he got out of the car to follow her. Bryan was right. She needed to know how he felt about her.

He'd tell her today — after he got her to tell him how she felt first.

Chapter Seven

It was nearing eight o'clock when they finished their business and headed back toward Visitation. They were both quiet — not an uneasy quiet, but one of pure contentment. As usual, Cyn had removed her sandals and stretched out her legs. Her head was back against the seat, her body relaxed. Bruce reached across the seat and took her hand. Cyn didn't object; after a searching look, she laced her fingers in his.

They'd spent a good part of the day getting her account set up before driving into the city. All through the shopping and dinner, she was like a proud peahen, and it pleased Bruce to know that something so simple could make her so happy. What others took for granted, Cyn cherished.

Before dinner, they'd picked up the supplies he needed and stored them in the back of the car. After dinner, at his urging, Cyn had done some of her own shopping. She'd bought new socks and gloves and a fat pillow. The one Mary had supplied was too flat, she said.

Bruce pictured her cuddling into that

fluffy pillow at night, and he wanted to kiss her. Later, he reminded himself. When they were alone.

While they were in the mall, Bruce noticed her gazing toward the bookstore, and he insisted they go in. This bookstore was enormous compared to the scant book section offered at their local strip mall in Visitation. There was a wider variety, more color, more displays.

Cyn was like a kid in a candy store, perusing the aisles for almost an hour.

He bought a new mystery, but to his surprise, Cyn chose a cookbook. She didn't have a kitchen, but she said she didn't care. Bruce vowed to invite her over that weekend to prepare dinner with him.

The sun had turned deep red, hidden behind the tall trees and giving the area the peaceful shadows of dusk, when he rounded a sharp bend in the road. It might not be wise to test his restraint, but still Bruce said, "Want to come to my place for coffee?"

Her fingers tightened in his, and her eyes grew alert to nuances in the offer.

"Unless you're too tired," he added.

"No." She shook her head. Her voice was soft, uncertain. "I'm not too tired."

Her words, said in that special low,

mellow tone, sank into him. "You had a good time?"

"I had the best time."

Bruce glanced between her and the road. He wouldn't rush her, he vowed, but he wanted her to have more good times. He wanted her whole life to be filled with fun. "Maybe we could take in a movie sometime?"

Her lips parted — and something moved in the road. Bruce jerked his attention back to his driving just in time to see Jamie Creed step away from a tree.

No. Dread immediately swamped him. Jamie only showed himself when something wasn't right.

He didn't socialize.

He didn't indulge friendships.

He only tried to help others when he felt he had no choice — when someone was in danger.

Tension gripped him, making his shoulders rigid, his eyes narrow. Bruce released Cyn's hand and slowed the car. "Prepare yourself," he muttered. "You're about to meet the one and only Jamie Creed."

"What . . . ?" Cyn twisted in her seat, spotted Jamie on Bruce's side of the road, and went still with fascination. "It's him," she breathed.

Bruce didn't question her recognition. In her dreams, maybe by God's design, she'd seen Visitation and she'd seen Jamie. Somehow, Bruce was sure the two were tied together. He brought the car to the side of the road.

As if she thought Jamie might disappear, Cyn refused to blink. "What do you suppose he wants?"

Bruce understood her apprehension. Jamie was strong and healthy, but he looked like a cross between a human and a wraith, if such a thing were possible. He was there, but so motionless, so self-contained, that he might have been a figment of the collective imagination.

Since the last time Bruce saw him, Jamie's beard had gotten bushier, his hair longer, his clothes more ragged. Jamie didn't concern himself with style or the opinions of others. Bruce had no idea what he did concern himself with, other than offering cryptic information when he could.

Bruce rolled down his window. "Jamie," he said by way of greeting.

Jamie's fathomless black eyes never left Cyn. His expression seemed more severe than ever in his concentration. His mouth was flat. He circled the car toward her.

Alarmed, Bruce hastily opened his door and got out, following Jamie. "Hey, are you okay, Jamie? Is something wrong?"

Jamie didn't answer.

Cyn, too, released her seat belt and opened her door. She stood there, her lips caught in her teeth, her breaths uneven. Waiting.

Bruce almost ran into Jamie when the man stopped dead, not more than two feet from Cyn.

Bruce gathered his wits. "Jamie, this is Cyn Potter. Cyn, Jamie Creed."

"Hello," Jamie said in his gentlest voice. He searched her face, slowly nodded in satisfaction. "You came."

Cyn shrugged. "You wanted me to?"

Jamie's piercing gaze moved over her from head to toes. "It was a solution."

Feeling very much like an outsider, Bruce raised his voice and asked, "A solution to what?"

Jamie remembered Bruce and looked at him over his shoulder. In an absurdly matter-of-fact tone, Jamie replied, "She's in trouble."

"No," Cyn corrected. "Things are finally going right since I came here." Her hands twisted together. "I have a job. I have a savings account."

Jamie softened more. "I'm sorry, but you need to see Scott."

"Scott who?"

"Why?" Bruce asked at almost the same time. "What's the law have to do with Cyn?" The second he asked that question, he saw Cyn go pale.

"The law?"

Jamie took her hands, tilted his face to look at her. He was silent for a lifetime before he continued in his explanations. "Scott's a good man. The deputy of Visitation. Go with Bruce. Talk to Scott."

For the very first time, Bruce understood how the other men felt when dealing with Jamie, especially with a woman involved. Jamie was so much larger than life, so purposeful and yet so obscure, that mortal men faded when near him.

A frantic pulse fluttered in Cyn's throat. Bruce could see the wide-eyed fascination in her unusual eyes as she stared at Jamie —

"It's her eyes that distinguish her," Jamie remarked, as if he'd known Bruce's every thought. "They give her away. Take her to see Scott."

"You keep saying that," Bruce barked.

"I have to make sure you're listening," Jamie told him. "Scott wants to see her."

Bruce had just about had enough. *"Why?"*

Jamie released Cyn, moved back a step, but still stared at her, keeping her pinned in place with the force of his attention. "Things aren't what you thought they were."

Bemused, Cyn looked between Bruce and Jamie. With a helpless, near hysterical laugh, she asked, "What does that mean?"

"I'm sorry, but you didn't kill him."

She staggered back with a raw cry, coming up hard against the side of the car. *"No."* She shook her head hard, then lurched back forward, driven by anger. "You can't know anything about that!"

Jamie wasn't deterred by her distress. "You hurt him, but you didn't kill him."

Her hands knotted into fists. Her voice was a rasping, horrified whisper. "You don't even know me."

As if much struck, Jamie said, "You're afraid of me." He locked his hands behind his back, bent his head and paced. More to himself than anyone else, he said, "I didn't think you would be."

Ignoring Jamie and his strange mutterings, Bruce moved to stand in front of Cyn. Not once since he'd met her had he seen her this upset. She faced the world with brash bravado, not panicked fear.

"Who did you think you killed?"

Her back stiffened, her face white and pinched with uncertainty. "No one."

"The man her mother moved in," Jamie answered. "Only he didn't die."

Cyn covered her mouth and looked ready to faint.

"Damn it, Jamie, you're scaring her."

Without changing expressions, Jamie managed to look annoyed. "She should be afraid. You should be afraid for her." Jamie stopped pacing and speared Bruce with his ebony gaze. "It's up to you to protect her."

Oddly enough, that statement calmed Bruce. He *would* protect her, he'd —

"Oh, no. No way." In a sudden burst of anger, Cyn pushed her way past Bruce. "No, damn you. You don't know what you're talking about, so don't you dare stick that responsibility on Bruce."

Brows raised, Jamie glanced at Bruce, who remained silent, and then shrugged. "He wants the responsibility."

Cyn whipped around to face Bruce. She looked horrified by that possibility. *"No."*

It nettled him, but Bruce had to admit the truth. "Jamie's always right, Cyn."

That brought a touch of surprise to Jamie's normally enigmatic features. "Thank you."

Bruce shrugged. "No problem."

"Damn it," Cyn yelled, sending birds to take flight in screeching excitement. "Don't you understand? You can't pretend this is nothing."

"I'm not pretending anything." Bruce decided she'd have to trust him now, not later. "I'm not going to let anything happen to you, Cyn."

She backed up two steps, then two more. "You're a good man, Bruce." Her voice was raw with determination. "I'm not about to let you get involved in my problems. If Palmer is alive, then he knows I tried to kill him."

"He knows," Jamie said.

Cyn fried Jamie with a killing look. "You're egging him on."

Unconcerned, Jamie explained, "It is what it is. Bruce isn't walking away."

"No, I'm not." Bruce understood that Palmer could be out for revenge, and no way was he going to let him hurt Cyn. Not again.

Jamie seemed mostly unmoved by the drama unfolding in front of him. "Don't run. You've nowhere to go."

Bruce hadn't realized she was thinking of running until Jamie said it, then he noticed that she'd backed up a good distance from him. He gave her a hard stare. "Try it, and I'll just catch you."

She shook her head. "No."

"Afraid so."

She gazed at Jamie with a look so lost, it made Bruce's stomach cramp. "I don't know what to do," she whispered.

Jamie gazed back. "Go with Bruce to see Scott." Then he added with philosophical insouciance, "You have no choice."

By small degrees, Cyn wilted. Her shoulders slumped, her spine bowed. She covered her face and if Bruce hadn't been so attuned to her, if he hadn't been hurting for her, he wouldn't have heard her whispered words.

"I never do."

He reached her in three long strides. "You listen to me, Cynthia Potter."

She dropped her hands.

"It's different now." Bruce pulled her against his chest. "I'm with you."

Her laugh was watery with suppressed tears. "Great. That only makes it worse."

Bruce didn't think about his reaction, he simply gave in to it. Sinking his fingers into the thick, warm silk of her hair, he tipped her head back and kissed her hard.

She didn't fight him. She crawled closer, as close as two people could get. She bit his bottom lip, licked his tongue. Her hands locked around his neck as if she'd never let him go, when moments before she'd tried to deny him.

Knowing it was the wrong time and place, and his motivations were skewed, Bruce gently eased her away.

"Bruce?" she whispered against his mouth.

He pressed her head to his shoulder. "Take a few deep breaths. Get yourself together. And then let's go see Scott."

"I don't want to."

"But you will?"

She stepped away from him. "Do I have a choice?"

He shook his head.

"Then I guess I have to trust Jamie, don't I?"

That wasn't what Bruce wanted to hear. He needed her to trust *him,* but he was willing to fight one battle at a time.

She smoothed her hair back, composing herself and donning a ridiculously cheerful smile. Bruce shook his head. "Forget it."

"What?"

"You don't have to buck up for Jamie, honey. He's already gone."

"No way!" Cyn jerked around, searched the area, and blinked in disbelief. Just as

Bruce had suspected, there was no sign of Jamie Creed. "Was he really here at all?"

"Oh yeah, he was here." Bruce took her hand and led her back to the car. He glanced at his watch. "It's getting late, but with any luck, Scott will still be at the station. I'd like to see him tonight, so we can get this out of the way."

"And then?"

"We'll take it one day at a time."

Bruce called ahead to make certain Scott was at the station. Cyn sat tucked as tight to the passenger door as she could get, barely listening as he spoke to Scott in hushed tones. Still, she realized from Bruce's side of the conversation that Scott wasn't too keen on having Jamie call the shots.

She was even less keen about it. How could he know what she'd done to Palmer? How could he know that Palmer was alive? Her stomach cramped and churned and her eyes burned. All this time, she'd thought him dead.

She hated being a murderess. She hated even more for Palmer to be alive.

Just moments before, she'd been so stupidly content. Her life had seemed to be on a definite upswing, but now —

Bruce caught her elbow and pulled her toward him. "Stop it, Cyn."

Feeling lethargic, sick at heart, she asked without much interest, "Stop what?"

"Expecting the worse. You heard Jamie. He said for me to take care of you, and I will."

"I'm taking care of myself, just like I always have."

"With my help." He gave her a pat. "Jamie said so."

It was almost ironic that the one man who seemed to give credence to Jamie's dire predictions was a man of strong faith. "Jamie also told you that I tried to kill a man."

Bruce sighed, then tugged on her until she was up against his side. "I know you have a past, honey. I know you were mistreated. If you lashed out at someone —"

"At Palmer." Why was he calling her "honey"? Sincere endearments were new to her, so she wasn't quite sure what it meant.

"You had good reason."

He sounded so insanely sure of that. She closed her eyes and concentrated on breathing. "If Jamie's right, then Palmer isn't dead. I've spent my life doing stupid things, avoiding notice, hiding, for no good reason at all."

"You were a runaway."

She laughed at the absurdity of it all. "No one would have looked for me. No one cared that I was gone, unless Palmer wanted me back just so he could dole out retribution. But mad as he must have been that I hit him and got away, he couldn't have done much about it. He didn't have money or resources."

"The school might have gotten involved after you dropped out of sight. Who knows? But don't think about that right now, okay? What matters is the present. Whatever reason Jamie has for wanting us to check in with Scott, it must be important. And I trust Jamie."

Strangely enough, she did, too. But she was scared. More scared than she'd been in years. So many times she'd lied to herself, claiming to have no fear because fear, like tears, was a waste of time.

She knew the truth. "I hate being such a coward."

Bruce pulled into the station and shut off the engine. In the next instant, he had her hauled into his arms. "You, Cynthia Potter, are about the bravest woman I know."

"Knock it off, Bruce. I'm not stupid."

"Not stupid, and not a coward. You're incredible. Believe me."

"And you," she said, her voice muffled against his shoulder, "are a nut." She pushed back. "A nut in rose-colored glasses."

"I'm a realist."

"And I'm a whore. Before that, I tried to kill a guy. I thought I *had* killed him and I was so glad. Nothing incredible about that."

"You were a kid acting out of desperation, and you're no longer a hooker. Now you're Shay's assistant —"

She said, "Ha!"

"Okay, Shay's helper, then. And her friend. You're also the caretaker for two horses, and you baby them shamelessly." He leaned forward and kissed her brow. "You're a good woman. Quit trying to convince me otherwise."

Cyn sat there a moment, frustrated, feeling unworthy and hating herself for it. "Why don't you kiss me again, like you did two weeks ago?"

He looked blank-brained, wary, and she warmed to her topic. She was anxious, upset, and he made a good target for her churning emotions. "You started to back on the road, but then you pulled away.

Why all these brotherly pecks, Bruce? Why the damn handholding and placating, when we both want more?"

Bruce released her and settled back into his seat. "The way I kissed you on the road . . . I don't know. That was adrenaline, I guess."

"Felt like lust to me."

"And that business in the loft . . ." He shook his head. "It was a mistake."

"Well, I know that, but you keep insisting that I'm things I'm not."

He studied her face. "You're young. Only twenty-two."

Where had that complaint come from? "So? I've lived enough to be three times that."

His half-smile made him look more appealing than ever. "You accuse me of wearing rose-colored glasses, when you're the one in blinders. You see things your own way, in any way that suits you. I'm thirty-five, Cyn. A grown man when most would consider you little more than a kid."

"That's just plain stupid."

"I'm also well used to women who are confused about who they are and what they want from life, thanks to tragic backgrounds or personal disappointments."

"Give me a break." Exasperation rolled

over her. "In other words, you think I might just see you as some grand savior, and I'm confusing my feelings because of it?"

Rather than react to her antagonism, he seemed to focus on one small thing she'd said. "What are your feelings?"

Cyn pinched her mouth shut. No way was she going to open her heart to him while he sat there, all sanctimonious and full of grave understanding, telling her what she thought and felt. "Never mind."

"Cyn . . ."

"Come on. Let's get this little visit with the law over with."

Cyn wanted to get back to her loft, where she could curl up on her narrow bed and console herself — as she'd done many times in the past. She didn't need Bruce Kelly and his bleeding-heart favors. She didn't need him looking out for her. She sure as hell didn't need his perfunctory kisses that didn't mean a damn thing.

She could take care of herself and Bruce would only get in her way. Things were looking good, and she wouldn't let bad news change that.

Unfortunately, the second Scott Royal made her acquaintance, things went downhill.

* * *

Bruce scowled at Scott. "She's wanted for what?"

"Stealing a trucker's wallet. He called it in, even gave a description of her."

Cyn blinked, chuckled nervously, then began to howl with laughter. When Bruce and Scott stared at her, she only roared that much louder.

Bruce went to her, gripped her shoulder. "Cyn, stop that."

"Don't you get it?" She hiccuped around an enormous smile. "It's *nothing*."

"Theft is hardly considered nothing, Ms. Potter."

Cyn waved that off. "It's a big, fat lie, made up by some pathetic bozo from a dining lot. And here I'd thought it was —"

Bruce cut her off before she could make any confessions she might later regret. "Can I get you a drink of water? A Coke?"

She drew in a shuddering breath and tamped down on her absurd mirth. "Naw, I'm okay. Just relieved."

Bruce turned back to Scott. "You're sure it's Cyn? A swiped wallet could be blamed on anyone."

"I don't think so, Bruce. The guy described her as . . ." he cleared his throat, "well, attractive."

Cyn made a face. "Please, I'm going to blush."

"He also specified long, dark hair and the strangest, lightest blue eyes he'd ever seen. If it wasn't for the eyes . . ."

Cyn started laughing again. "Good old Jamie told me that it was my eyes that would give me away."

"Well, you can forget it," Bruce insisted. "I was there, and she didn't steal the guy's wallet."

"You were there?" Scott looked more than a little skeptical.

"Yes. It's how I met her. He was hassling her, giving her a hard time, and I intervened."

"And you're one hundred percent sure she didn't lift his wallet? Maybe before you got involved." Scott, the epitome of patience most of the time, kept looking between Cyn's smile and Bruce's frown.

"It wasn't like that at all," Bruce insisted. "The trucker was manhandling her, claiming she owed him."

"Money?" Scott asked, more intrigued by the moment.

Cyn piped up, saying, "Sex, actually."

Scott propped his hands on his hips and surveyed her. "And naturally, you refused?"

"That's right. But then Bruce showed up and being the incredible, generous man that he is —"

"Cyn," Bruce warned.

"— he gave the guy cash just to shut him up and send him on his way."

"And I watched him put the money in his wallet." Bruce moved to stand in front of Cyn. She was in a strange, defensive mood, and she wasn't helping the situation at all. "I was still standing there when he stuck his wallet in his back pocket. I saw him do it. He probably dropped it somewhere else later that day, but Cyn definitely didn't take it."

With Bruce blocking his view of Cyn, Scott paced away. He ran a hand through his sandy brown hair, rolled his shoulders as if vexed, and then sighed. "I still need to do a check. It's procedure. If you two can sit tight for a few minutes, I'll run her name and see what we come up with."

Cyn turned to stone.

Bruce glanced at his watch. "It's getting late."

"Tell me about it. I've been here twelve hours already."

"Where's the sheriff?"

With a wry look of disgust, Scott said, "Off on a fishing trip. As usual." He shook his head. "The man wants to retire and he's making no bones about it."

"Maybe you should take his job."

Scott turned his appalled frown on Bruce. "Not on your life. I have my hands full as it is. No way do I want his paperwork added to the pile."

The station was small, with cells in the basement and desks on the first floor. Scott led them to an empty, quiet room that could have been used for interrogations or regular meetings. Crime in Visitation was nearly nonexistent. But that didn't mean Scott was incompetent. On the contrary, the man knew his job.

"You'll be more comfortable here." Scott hesitated, then said, "Coffee?"

Cyn ignored him to roam the room, so Bruce nodded. "Sure. Thank you."

"I'll have someone bring it to you. And if you need anything else, let me know. This might take a few minutes."

Bruce was relieved to have the privacy of the closed room, but that same privacy only made it harder for him to keep his hands off Cyn. She was scared and trying to hide it with sarcasm.

"This is just great," she complained. "My one legitimate claim was that I'd never been arrested."

Leaning back on the edge of a long table, Bruce watched her. "You're not arrested now."

"I'm sitting in a sheriff's station, in an interrogation room. Feels the same." She flopped down into a chair, put her elbows on the table and propped her head on her hands.

"You know what I think?" Bruce pulled a chair up close to her. "I think you should be relieved it's just a misunderstanding, considering you were thinking the worst."

"The day isn't over."

"Such an optimist." He shook his head at her.

She lowered her hands to glare at him. "Jamie did say I was in danger. I hardly think this is what he had in mind."

"No, probably not." Bruce dug out his cell phone. "And in fact, I think I'll ask Bryan and Joe to run a check on this Palmer Oaks fellow. They should be able to track him down, find out where he's at and what he's been up to since you last saw him."

"Since he's not dead."

"Since you didn't kill him."

Aggrieved, Cyn lifted one shoulder as if to say *I don't care*. "Sure. Knock yourself out."

Bruce hadn't waited for her permission. The second Bryan answered, he explained the situation. It was actually a pretty amazing tale to retell, and to Bryan's credit, he didn't falter. He did question Bruce's motives, though.

"Yeah, I know what I said earlier, but this changes things."

"What did you say earlier?" Cyn asked.

Bruce covered the phone. "That I didn't want him poking around in your past."

She stiffened. "He would have?"

"If I'd asked him to, yeah." And then to Bryan, "No, I don't need you here. Thanks. And tell Shay not to make a big deal of it. The fewer people who know, the better."

Hearing that, Cyn softened, sending him a grateful look. What had she expected? For him to throw her to the wolves? To have her name bandied around the entire town?

She gave him a thumbs up, and Bruce winked back.

"So," he said to his brother, "you're pretty sure you can find this Palmer idiot for me? Yeah, I'm willing to bet he has a record. His kind always do." Bruce listened, grinned. "No, I'm not going after him. You know better than that. I'm serious. Bryan, I *don't* lie. If I wanted him, I'd tell you so. Swear."

Bruce meant what he said. He wouldn't seek Palmer out, but God help the fool if he came around Cyn again.

"I just want to know where he is, Bryan, to make sure he's nowhere near Cyn."

Bruce didn't go into his meeting with Jamie and the warnings. Bryan didn't put much stock in Jamie's insights, regardless of having experienced them firsthand.

"All right. Get back to me as soon as you can. And if you think Joe can help, fine. Just tell him to keep it quiet. Yeah, I know, an unnecessary warning."

Bruce hung up just as the coffee arrived. Pretending a detachment from the situation, Cyn added a lot of sugar and creamer to her cup, then sipped while eyeing Bruce.

After the door was again closed, she said, "You're going to an awful lot of trouble for a woman who's too young for you."

The way her mind worked never ceased to amaze Bruce. "I didn't say you were too young for me."

She paused in mid-sip, then sent him an accusing frown. "You did, too. You said —"

"I said that twenty-two was awfully young. Too young to leap into a relationship. You have a lot going on in your life right now." He tasted his own coffee.

Cyn watched him. Bruce could see her calculating her next words, and he prepared himself.

"Who said anything about a relationship? I just asked you to kiss me."

She might not want a relationship, but he did. So how could he reassure her, without encouraging or discouraging her? Honesty seemed his best bet. "I'm a man who doesn't get involved unless I intend to stay involved."

"Give me a break, here. We're talking about kissing."

"Feels like a lot more to me." His gaze held hers, and he saw her reciprocal awareness of that truth. His voice went low and deep. "I'm not at all sure I can kiss you without wanting more."

"More?"

He took a breath. "Like everything."

"Oh."

"So, we're back to square one. Unless you want to answer my question now."

After everything he'd just admitted, she needed to take a second to catch her breath. She fidgeted in her chair, smoothed her hair, and finally cleared her throat. "Which question's that?"

"What are your feelings for me?"

Very slowly, her tongue came out to moisten her bottom lip. Bruce felt that warm, damp lick as if it had been against his own mouth. His nostrils flared, his body warmed and his abdomen grew taut. It was insane the effect she had on him. Insane, but undeniable.

"I like you."

He suppressed a groan. "And?"

"I think you're handsome and sexy."

Humor saved him. He grinned. "That's an observation, Cyn, not a feeling."

Her shoulders straightened in defiance. "Okay, you turn me on."

He hoped so, because she definitely did it for him. But her past couldn't be dismissed, so he tilted his head in contemplation, and pressed her further. "You told me when I kissed you that you hadn't known a kiss could be so nice."

"Yeah, so?" She stared at his mouth. "Maybe you're just a good kisser."

Determined to make some headway, Bruce scooted his chair closer to hers. He didn't lighten his tone, didn't remove the seriousness from his question. "Have you ever been turned on before, Cyn? Seriously turned on?"

She actually blushed. "I was a hooker."

"Who didn't like kissing," he reminded her.

Disgruntled, she finally understood. "Okay, so for me it was a business. It's hard to feel anything when you just want to get the guy off so he'll pay you. And they were strangers, mostly pathetic, not exactly a young girl's dream, if you know what I mean."

Her words tore through him, leaving lacerated emotions in the wake. Bruce had to fight the awful, possessive urges because as much as it galled him, he couldn't protect her from her past. He *could* protect her from the present. And he would.

"You're different," she continued stubbornly. "I do want you. Physically, I mean."

Bruce hoped that was true, but he knew enough about abuse not to trust surface claims. He gentled his voice, took her hands in his. "Are you sure it is physical? Are you sure it's not just because I provide a sense of comfort, or acceptance?"

He could tell by her expression that she wasn't sure at all.

Back to square one. "That's what I thought. I want you, Cyn. Never doubt that." His hand lifted to her cheek, downy soft and warmed from their discussion. "I think you're desirable, inside and out. But I'd be an unconscionable bastard if I took advantage of you now."

As she often did when she felt defensive, she tucked in her chin and gave him such a sultry look, a slow burn started in his belly. "Maybe I want you to take advantage of me."

It wasn't easy, but Bruce fought temptation. "Not yet, honey." And before she could get too upset about that, he voiced a niggling question. "You thought you had killed Palmer. Will you tell me what happened?"

"Why? He's alive, so obviously I failed."

"I care about you. I need to know what happened in case any trouble shows up."

"I don't want you involved."

"That's tough, because I am, and there's nothing you can do about it except make sure I'm informed, so I can better handle the situation."

She looked rebellious, before she gave up and shrugged with feigned indifference.

Bruce felt the trembling in her fingers and saw the wariness in her gaze. He knew this wouldn't be easy for her, and if he could, he would have spared her. But in case Palmer did show up, he had to know what had happened.

"He tried coming into my room."

"Your bedroom?"

"Yeah." She nodded, her gaze averted. "He'd been different all day, and I could practically feel him building up to something."

Bruce swallowed, squeezed her hand tighter. His throat felt tight, but he forced the question out. "Rape?"

She rubbed her forehead. "Yeah, I think so. He'd been in my room before, and it was awful, but this was different. He'd been weird all day. Full of . . . sick anticipation. It turned my stomach and I . . ."

Bruce put his forehead to hers and whispered. "Tell me."

"I couldn't take it." She swallowed, bit her lips. "I wasn't stupid even then, so I knew what he wanted to do and I knew I couldn't let him. I waited, and when he opened my door, I bashed him over the head with a lamp."

"I see."

"I doubt that." She gave a near-hysterical laugh. "Whatever you're picturing, add a lot more blood." She shuddered, and for only a moment, the pain suffered by a young, frightened child filled her eyes. "It was . . . everywhere."

Bruce held her closer to his heart. "You

struck him in the head?" At her nod, he explained, "Head wounds often bleed a lot. They can look worse than they are."

"Well, this one looked pretty damn bad. I hit him more than once." She stared at him, refusing to look away. "I hit him, and even though part of me wanted to stop, I kept hitting him. It was like I couldn't help myself. Like I was someone else. Then I realized he wasn't moving. He wasn't even breathing."

"And you thought he was dead." It made sense. She'd been a kid, on the run.

She pressed away from him and pushed to her feet. With her arms wrapped around herself, she paced away. "I never thought to check the obituaries or anything. I just got away, as far and as fast as I could."

Bruce stood and followed her to the other side of the room. Cyn was such a paradox of emotions, so cocky and proud most of the time, but so small and hurt whenever she discussed her past.

He took her shoulders, turned her to face him. "And now, thanks to the vagaries of fate, you're here with me."

"Probably thanks to Jamie Creed."

"As I said, the fates." Bruce smiled. "Will you trust me, Cyn? Please? Because more than anything else, I want your trust."

She drew a deep breath, pinched her eyes shut in indecision, then nodded. Her lashes lifted and Bruce got lost in the blue depths of her eyes. "I don't want to. I don't want you involved."

His chest tightened, in anger, in remorse. "Cyn —"

"But I do trust you. I have almost from the first."

He'd just finished explaining to her all the reasons why he couldn't kiss her again, why they couldn't get physically involved yet.

He was all hot air.

A hypocrite of the worst kind.

A man with no backbone at all — at least when it came to Cyn.

He didn't mean to do it. He didn't even remember moving. But when Scott opened the door, it was to find Bruce holding Cyn tight, his arms wrapped around her while he kissed her like a man on his honeymoon.

Chapter Eight

Scott cleared his throat loudly, and they jumped apart. Cyn felt her face flush, more because of how she knew Bruce would feel than any discomfort on her part.

When Bruce kissed, he did so like a starving man, which suited her just fine. Her lips were still tingling, her heart racing, when Bruce cleared his throat.

"Any news?"

After a long look of dawning understanding, Scott closed the door, crossed his arms over his chest and leaned back against the wall. "Am I interrupting?"

Bruce scowled and stepped in front of Cyn. She had to tiptoe to see over his shoulder. "Don't be obnoxious, Scott."

"Wouldn't think of it." Scott grinned, noticed Cyn peering at him, and lost his amusement. "You both might want to sit down."

"Look," Bruce said, "I've known her a few weeks now. It's not like —"

Scott shook his head, disregarding that. "Your business is your own."

"Of course it is." Bruce tried to look

stern, but Cyn was willing to bet he didn't get caught making out very often.

Then the look on Scott's face registered.

Cyn stiffened. "What is it?"

His gaze lifted and he shook his head. "Miss Potter, I'm sorry. I have some bad news."

Cyn's mouth went dry. "The trucker . . . ?"

"Forget that. He found his wallet and dropped the complaint."

She didn't feel an ounce of relief, not with Scott's expression so concerned.

"Then . . ." Bruce frowned. "That's good news, right?"

Visibly troubled, Scott pulled out a seat. His eyes, when he looked at Cyn, were gentle and kind. "There's a new . . . problem."

Together, Cyn and Bruce took seats opposite Scott. Sensing the worst, Cyn asked, "What sort of problem?"

"I'm sorry, but there's no easy way to put this." He braced himself. "Your mother is gone."

Confused, Cyn laughed. "Gone where?"

Bruce's hand touched her shoulder. "Cyn, sweetheart, he's trying to tell you that she's *gone*."

Cyn looked from one man to the other. "Dead?"

Scott rubbed his face. “I’m sorry.”

Aware of a deep silence, of Bruce pulling her closer and Scott standing in front of her, Cyn asked, “But . . . how?”

Scott appeared more troubled by the moment. “She was murdered.”

Murdered.

Unmoving, Cyn stared at the deputy. As his words sank in, her vision began to narrow, growing darker and tighter. In the back of her mind, somewhere far away, she could hear both men asking her if she was okay, but it wouldn’t quite register.

He’d said her mother was gone. Forever.

“Cyn.” Bruce pulled her from her chair and shook her until she gasped. Then he held her so close that his heartbeat drummed with hers and his warmth seeped past her clothes, into the coldest part of her soul.

Certain that she’d misunderstood, Cyn shook her head. “That doesn’t make any sense.”

Scott was miserable. “I’m sorry for springing it on you like that.”

“How did you discover this?” Bruce wanted to know.

“I ran her name.” Scott paced in restless acceptance of his job. “She was listed as a runaway through NCIC.”

Cyn flattened one palm on Bruce's chest and eased herself away. If she didn't want him responsible for her problems, then she'd better start speaking for herself right now. She started to talk, sounded like a sick frog, and tried again. "NCIC?"

"National Crime Information Center." Scott rubbed the back of his neck. "It's eerie that you would show up here now, right after your mother . . ." He glanced at Cyn and looked away. "After a murder's been committed."

"How . . . how did it happen?" In every scenario ever enacted in her mind, not once had Cyn ever considered that her mother might be gone. She'd pictured her full of regret, wanting her daughter back and sorry for the way she'd treated her. She envisioned her old, sick and needy, wanting Cyn to care for her. She'd even thought of her still obnoxious and uncaring.

But never dead.

She hadn't thought she would care, but . . . she did.

"Please, sit back down and I'll tell you what I know."

More coffee was fetched, and both men treated Cyn with kid gloves, making her uncomfortable. She wasn't breakable. And she couldn't even claim to be all that hurt.

Her mother hadn't loved her, hadn't been close to her at all — regardless of the many times Cyn had wished otherwise.

"It's not eerie," Cyn said to no one in particular, while sipping at an especially sweet cup of coffee. Bruce had really laced in the sugar. "Remember, Jamie sent me here."

Scott wasn't happy with that reminder. "I go by facts, Miss Potter, not Jamie Creed's predictions."

"And the facts are?"

"Someone entered your mother's house, likely someone she knows because it wasn't a break-in, and that person . . . strangled her."

"When?"

Scott blinked at her dispassionate question, then glanced at his papers. "Only a few days ago. Last Friday. Because you were a runaway, listed with NCIC, I ran a check and found the connection between the names."

Bruce put his arm around Cyn. "But there is no connection. Cyn had nothing to do with it. She's been here, with me."

"That's the weirdest part, and why her name came up." Scott tugged at his collar. "There was a note on the table, supposedly from Miss Potter."

Cyn's mind went blank. "Miss Potter? But that's . . ."

"You."

Her heart almost stopped. "I didn't do it."

Bruce squeezed her fingers. "He already knows that, honey." And then to Scott: "Isn't that right?"

"It is." Scott leaned toward Cyn. "The detective I spoke with said that although the handwriting was similar, it wasn't yours. Someone forged the note from you."

It seemed too absurd for words. "How would anyone know my handwriting?"

Scott shook his head. "I don't know, but isn't that a good reason to go see Detective Orsen, to maybe find out?"

Her eyes closed. Oh God, she'd been so dumb, believing things were over, that she was safe from her past. Why did it have to come back now, when she'd just gotten comfortable with the present?

"Tell us what you know," Bruce requested.

"Arlene Potter didn't show up to work. I'm guessing that wasn't an uncommon occurrence, because the owner of the bar where she worked sent someone after her." Here Scott paused. "Apparently she had a drinking problem?"

"For as long as I can remember."

He nodded in acceptance of that. "Her boss thought she was still in bed, but when he sent the bouncer after her, he found her on the kitchen floor. She'd been there a day. The note — signed by you — was on the kitchen table."

Cyn went over it in her head, but nothing made sense. "Why would anyone want to frame me for murder?"

"I don't know. But you're wanted for having possible information regarding the case." Scott held up a hand. "Now, that doesn't mean you have to go back to Benworth if you don't want to. But it'd be helpful if you could find the time to answer the detective's questions."

Bruce turned to Cyn. "Benworth, Indiana? I've never heard of it. That's where you're from?"

"Home sweet home." Her mouth trembled with the effort to smile. "Our little house wasn't that far from a pig farm. You could smell them cooking in the summer sun. It was rank."

Scott appeared pained with his current duty. "I'm sorry to ask, Miss Potter —"

"Call me Cyn, okay? No one calls me Miss Potter." She wrinkled her nose. "It makes me sound like a retired schoolteacher."

Bruce hugged her. "Julie might take issue with that image."

She elbowed him, but she smiled, too.

"Cyn, the detective wants to know if you'll be visiting. They'll hold your mother's body if there's any hope of new evidence."

"I don't have any evidence. I don't know anything about it at all. I haven't seen my mother — I haven't even seen Benworth — in five years."

Scott wasn't discouraged. "It's amazing what a detective might be able to uncover with the right questions. You just never know. It'd be real helpful if you'd go back there, give them a chance to pick your brain." Cajoling, he added, "Just for a few days."

"It's a long drive," she complained, giving herself time to work up her nerve. The last thing she wanted to do was to return to Benworth and all the awful memories. Just the thought of it had her stomach in knots.

Scott agreed. "Probably about fifteen hours, give or take. That is, if you drive."

"I'll take the bus."

"No." Bruce shook his head. "We'll fly

up and rent a car."

Wide-eyed with incredulity and affront, Cyn rounded on him. "I don't think so." She didn't dare look at him too long, or she'd be begging him to come with her. "The bus is good enough for me, and besides, you have responsibilities here."

"It isn't up for debate, Cyn."

Her mouth fell open, then snapped shut. "The hell it isn't! You're not my keeper."

"I'm going. Period." He stood and turned his back on her to walk Scott to the door. "You can tell the detective that we'll be on our way tomorrow."

Things were happening too quickly. Everything was out of her control and she didn't know how to deal with it. "I can't leave that soon! I have work to do with Shay, and the horses to think of . . ."

Bruce waved that off. "Forget it. I'll find someone to care for the horses until we return. Mary's not going to fire you over a family emergency. She adores you. And Shay will just have to do without you for a time. Trust me, she can handle it."

He'd taken all of her excuses before she could even voice them!

Scott let out a sigh of relief. "Thanks. I'll call the detective right now. Be right back."

Fuming, Cyn stared at Bruce's back and

knew that even though he was a "nice" guy, she'd never be able to handle him when he was in protective mode. And he seemed to be in that damned mode all the time around her.

"Fine." She stood and stalked up to face him. "But if you get to make demands, then I get one, too."

Somehow, he managed to look even taller than his six feet, two inches. And for once, he exuded the menace so typical of his brother. But the menace wasn't directed at her. It was for her benefit.

How could she not love him for that?

Heart racing, she said, "I'm coming home with you tonight."

Bruce gave her a very long look, but she didn't back down. Tonight, she needed someone. She needed Bruce, damn it, and for once in her miserable life, she was willing to admit it.

Very slowly, he nodded. "Okay. We'll stop and you can check on the horses first."

Cyn hadn't realized how badly she dreaded the thought of being alone until Bruce agreed. All the vinegar drained from her attitude and she slumped, boneless and worn out, back into her chair — and she barely noticed Bruce's smile of triumph.

* * *

Bruce had known how Mary would react when Cyn told her of her loss. She was understanding, hugging Cyn, which made Cyn nearly cross-eyed with discomfort, and telling her not to worry, that she'd see to the horses until Cyn returned. Even now, almost half an hour later, Cyn looked mute with disbelief.

For certain, she wasn't used to people caring about her. But she was in Visitation now, a part of the town, so she might as well begin to accept things.

Bruce had made some decisions along those lines, and tonight he'd get the ball rolling.

His home was dark and empty when he led Cyn inside. She started to veer to the kitchen, but he caught her arm and turned her toward the stairs.

The pall of bleakness left her, only to be replaced with confusion. "What are you doing?"

"Taking you to bed."

Her eyebrows lifted. "Really?"

Smiling at the obvious assumption she'd made, Bruce said, "You don't want to be alone tonight. No one would."

Predictably, her spine stiffened and that stubborn chin pulled in so she could look down her nose at him. It was such a cute gesture, at least to him. She was so tiny, so delicate, but she tried to appear more imposing.

"I'm used to being alone."

"But you're not. Alone, that is. I'm here, and I want you next to me."

Her steps faltered. "What the hell does that mean?"

He steered her into his bedroom. He didn't bother with the lights; he didn't need them, and Cyn, so bristly in her struggle for independence, might relax more if she didn't have to keep up appearances.

Stopping in the middle of the floor, Bruce cupped his hands around her neck and put a kiss on her forehead. "I need to hold you. I care about you and I don't like what you're going through. Have you ever slept with a man? And no, don't get sarcastic. You know what I mean. Have you ever spent the night with a man holding you?"

"No."

Just that one tiny, hurt word. "I haven't slept with a woman in years and years, either. Not since I was seventeen and I slipped off to Desiree's boathouse. Dad was so furious the next day, he took away my license for a month."

He could see Cyn's wide eyes glistening in the darkness, with only the scant moonlight filtering in through the windows.

"You haven't had sex since you were seventeen?"

"I had sex after that, I just didn't spend the night with anyone. Actually, I miss holding women more than the sex, if you want the truth. I miss the closeness of a woman's soft, fragrant body." His hands began a slow massage, meant to help her relax. "Can I hold you tonight, Cyn?"

Her swallow was audible, and a sign of her nervousness. She may have been free with her body, but he asked for her emotions, and that wasn't something familiar to her.

"Yeah. I guess. It's gonna be weird, though."

Relief, and anticipation, made him tremble. "Do you want to borrow a shirt to sleep in? You didn't get anything from the loft."

"If you insist."

Using his thumbs, he tipped her chin up and lightly kissed her mouth. "I do. I may have strong moral beliefs, but I'm still a man, and you're too much temptation."

He left her stammering behind him to

fetch a long T-shirt from his bureau. When he turned back around, she'd seated herself on the side of the bed.

He caught her arm and urged her to the hall bathroom. He flipped on the light and she shrank back, her face averted. "You've had my tongue in your mouth," Bruce told her deliberately, "so I don't suppose you'll mind using my toothbrush. You can clean up, change in here, then I'll take my turn."

She locked onto his face, her own a study in dazed bafflement. "You get stranger by the minute, Bruce, you know that?"

He almost laughed. He was a man on a mission — nothing strange about that. "Ten minutes, okay? I'll call and get us a flight for the morning."

He trotted back down to the kitchen, where Cyn couldn't hear him on the phone. He dialed Bryan first, but after four rings, he decided his brother must be otherwise occupied and he hung up. He glanced at his watch. It was late, but he doubted Joe would mind.

Luna answered on the second ring. "Hello?"

"Hi Luna. It's Bruce. I'm sorry to call so late."

He could hear some rustling as Luna

asked, "Is anything wrong?"

"Maybe. Is Joe around?"

"Sure, just a sec."

Joe came immediately on the line, sounding drowsy, his voice deep with sleep. "What's up?"

Watching the stairs for Cyn, Bruce explained about the imminent trip. "What do you think?"

"I think it's a setup of some kind and you should be damn careful."

"Me, too."

"Bryan told me about this Palmer Oaks creep. But murder? That's taking it to a whole different level. I'll make some calls in the morning, but this trip . . . I'd feel better if you had backup with you."

"There's a detective on the case."

"Not that kind of backup."

Bruce hated to ask. "Then what kind?"

"My kind."

The way Joe said that, as if arguments were useless . . . Still, Bruce immediately objected. "No, I can't do that, Joe."

"I'm not asking, I'm telling you. You don't want to risk the girl, now do you?"

"No."

"Good. I'll make the flight arrangements. You can settle up with me later. I'll call you back in just a few minutes to tell you when to be at the airport." The line went dead.

Bruce stared at the phone. And he considered Bryan tough! Thinking of Bryan, Bruce knew his brother would probably agree with Joe, and at the same time be annoyed that he wasn't the one tailing them. His head began to pound with all the complications. But he'd do what he had to do to ensure Cyn's safety.

Cyn appeared at the top of the stairs. "Everything okay?"

"Oh, yeah." Bruce put the receiver back in the cradle. "I'll know about our flights in a few minutes. If the phone rings, I'll get it, okay?"

"Hey, I don't grab up other people's phones. No problem."

Bruce stared up at her. She was bare except for the large white T-shirt swallowing her slender body. Her legs were as beautiful as the rest of her, shapely and slim and long for a woman so petite. And her breasts . . . even in the dim light at the top of the stairs, he could see her dark nipples, now stiffened, pressing against the fabric.

God give him strength.

He started up the stairs to her, and she backed up. That stalled him for only a moment before he continued on up. He stepped past her. "I'll only be a moment." He closed the bathroom door behind him, then leaned on the door, giving himself a second to recover from the sight of her.

In record time, he had washed up and brushed his teeth. When he entered the bedroom, Cyn was again sitting on the bed. Her long hair hung down to her elbows. She had her knees pressed together, her small feet not quite touching the floor.

Young, Bruce reminded himself. Wounded and untrusting and in need of solace — solace that only he would give her. Now and forever.

"Get under the covers."

Without a word, she did as he ordered. Her movements were stiff, and she pulled the sheet up to her chin, realized what she did, and pushed it back to her waist. Her pose became practiced, meant to deceive him about her uncertainty. But he knew her. Maybe better than she knew herself at this point.

Bruce stood there, just looking at her with her looking back, neither of them speaking, until the phone rang. He picked up the bedside receiver. "Bruce here."

"Plane takes off at eight, so you need to be at the airport at six. Sorry, it was the only direct flight I could get on such short notice." Joe gave him the airline and flight number. "If you see me, though I doubt you will, ignore me."

Bruce had so many questions, but with Cyn watching him, he couldn't ask.

Joe must have realized that. "I'll be wearing a hat, glasses . . . don't worry. I'm not exactly a master of disguise, but Cyn doesn't know me well enough to pick me out of a crowd. I already rented us both cars. Yours is an Escort, mine is a Durango. I'll be right behind you at all times."

"I appreciate it."

"Hey, I'll enjoy it." Then Bruce heard him say to Luna, "Yes, I'll miss you, honey. Don't doubt it."

Bruce grinned. "I owe you."

"Paybacks are hell, but I'll be kind. Get some sleep."

Without looking at Cyn, he hung up the phone and walked to his dresser. He kicked off his shoes, sat on the foot of the bed to remove his socks. He could actually feel Cyn's gaze on his back, burning with curiosity, anxiety, and expectation.

He stood, still with his back to her, and pulled off his shirt. Purposely taking his time, he folded the shirt and placed it atop the dresser.

Cyn caught her breath. The mattress squeaked.

More tense by the moment, Bruce unsnapped his jeans, dragged the zipper down over a rapidly engorging erection and pushed them down his hips.

Cyn's small, cool hands touched his heated back. "Bruce?"

It wasn't easy, but he stayed on course, folding the jeans, putting them atop the shirt. Finally, wearing only snug boxers that couldn't hide his interest, he turned to face her. "I need to set the alarm. We have to be at the airport at six. As it is, we won't get much sleep."

Her face was flushed, her heavy lashes at half-mast.

She didn't say a word, just turned on the bed to keep him in her sights as he walked to the nightstand and adjusted the alarm clock. His body throbbing, Bruce turned out the light and crawled beneath the covers.

Cyn still knelt in the middle of the bed.

"Come here, honey."

She hesitated.

"I want to hold you, remember?"

Seconds ticked by while the tension in the air thickened. "Oh Bruce, I don't think I can."

The trembling of her voice nearly did him in. He sat up, pulled her to him, and it was as close to heaven as he'd ever been.

Her mouth sought his, and Bruce didn't deny her. While kissing her, accepting her tongue and giving her his own, he lowered her to her back on the mattress, half covering her with his chest.

"I don't know what's happening," she admitted in a small, tight voice.

"You want me," Bruce told her, "and I'm glad."

She huffed in exasperation. "Duh. I *know* that. I meant with you."

He smoothed back her hair, kissed her cheek, her throat, her ear. God, he'd forgotten how sweet and small a woman's ears were, how exciting it was to hear a shuddered breath, feel the bite of nails on his shoulders.

He loved her. He knew that now, and no way could he expect her to sleep when her whole body was trembling and warmed with desire.

"Tell me you trust me, honey."

Her head was arched back, her mouth open. "Yeah, sure. Bruce? Don't stop, please."

"No, I won't." At least, he wouldn't stop

until she was satisfied. His own satisfaction would wait for the right moment, when she wasn't fraught with emotional conflict.

When he knew she accepted him completely, for all the right reasons.

He kissed the very top of her breast and they both groaned. She was so incredibly soft.

Cyn reached for him, but he caught her hands. "No. Listen to me, Cyn."

Instead of replying, she tried to get her hands free, her hips lifting into his, her breath accelerated.

Bruce stretched her arms up over her head. She tried to pull free. "Cyn, answer me."

She moaned. "I never suspected you were a sadist, Bruce Kelly. Shut up and let me —"

"No." He held her gently, but firmly. "You don't need to do anything for me."

Her eyes snapped open, peering at him in amazement. "I *want* —"

"No." He wouldn't be able to stand it if she touched him, and beyond that, he didn't want her to think she had to use what she knew to bring him pleasure.

Right before his eyes, she seemed to shrink with shame. "I'm clean, if that's what you're worried about. I've always been careful and I had regular checkups at the clinic —"

"Shhh. It's not that at all." Cyn was too smart to have ever done differently. With complete honesty, he said, "Touching you, tasting you, is all I need."

Embarrassment fled. "Oh, for the love of —"

"I mean it, Cyn. Promise me." Too many times in her young life she'd been forced by circumstances to only consider a man's physical response.

Tonight, it was her response he wanted.

To encourage the right answer, he locked her wrists together in one of his hands, and cupped her breast. Her nipple pressed into his palm and he rubbed over it with his thumb, circling, flicking.

Her breath hitched, her back arched. "All right."

Bruce smiled at her quick compliance. "Relax. Let me enjoy you."

A broken groan, then: "You're the boss."

He knew better than that, but for right now, he'd take her at her word. "Let's get rid of this shirt, okay?" He didn't wait, but caught the hem and pulled it upward and over her head. It tangled around her arms, and Bruce decided he liked that. It'd help discourage her from getting too grabby, and possibly save his rapidly dwindling control.

"Don't move."

"I won't, if you do."

Time and again, she delighted him. "How's this?" He bent and drew her left nipple into the heat of his mouth. His tongue curled around her, he tugged, suckled.

"Great. Fabulous. Ama— *ah*."

Heat pounded beneath his skin, leaving him feverish with need. He gorged himself on the taste and texture of her body. While sucking at her nipple, he touched her everywhere. Her breasts were full and soft, a handful and then some. Her nipples were very sensitive and he took turns until they were both wet and stiff and the lightest touch wrought a moan from deep inside her.

"I'm dying," she whispered.

He was, too. He couldn't wait to feel the heat of her, and moved his hand — slowly, in case she wanted to object, down her belly, lower, lower. She grew tense with anticipation, her breath held, until his fingers slipped beneath her panties, pressed through her crisp curls and he found her wet, slick.

"Beautiful."

She gave a soft sob, writhing against his hand, lifting to increase the pressure. In a raw whisper, she pleaded, "Fuck me, Bruce."

His whole body shuddered and he had to grit his teeth. Her language was coarse, but that only told him that she was too far gone to measure her words or consider his vocation. And he was so damn glad. He'd gotten her there, and that had been his intent.

He wanted her to be totally natural. He wanted her to think of him only as a man, because at the moment, that was all he could be.

A man — who claimed this one special woman.

He circled her soft, slippery opening, pushed one finger deep, carefully inside. More wetness bathed his hand and it excited him unbearably. He opened his mouth on her throat, sucking her skin in against his teeth, knowing he marked her as his own and not caring. She was his.

Soon she'd know it, and not long after that, he'd tell the rest of the world.

Her hips moved in time to the rhythm he set with his thrusting finger, but it wasn't enough. Her breaths became choppy with growing, frustrated need. She whispered,

"Oh, please, please . . ." in a litany that fired his blood.

He added a second finger, working her while testing himself. Her nipples drew him again and he wallowed in the pleasure of having her in his mouth, exploring her with his tongue. She felt like a small, female furnace. Little tremors coursed through her hot body. Building sensations sent small jerks and shivers through her, making her groan, her movements rougher.

"Shhh," Bruce said, barely able to draw a breath himself. "I'll help you." Knowing what she needed, he kissed his way down her body, over her lush, swollen breasts, to her taut belly, her hipbones.

He eased her panties down to her knees.

She froze on him. "Oh no, Bruce, *no*." She forgot his instructions and caught her fingers in his hair, trying to pull him back up.

"Let me," he ordered. More than his next breath, he needed to taste her, all of her.

"But . . ." With tears in her voice, she fought with herself, then admitted in a breathless rush, "No one has ever . . . ever done that."

Oh God. He was glad, so glad. Bruce stared down at her body in the darkness, unable to see her clearly, but inhaling the spicy scent of her need. He nuzzled his nose against her pubic curls, filled his lungs with the delicious smell of woman, an aroma guaranteed to make a man wild.

Cyn waited in an agony of frozen suspense — and Bruce licked her, darting his tongue around his buried fingers, prodding, then up and over her engorged clitoris.

She cried out, wilting back on the bed, her hands still tight in his hair.

Gently, determined to have her climax, he teased her most sensitive flesh, drew her into his mouth, sucked softly, insistently, rubbing with the roughness of his tongue, rolling, nipping — and minutes later, a tearing moan escaped her as an orgasm raged through her body.

Bruce pressed himself hard against the mattress and fought his own release, but it was useless. He'd been celibate too long, wanted Cyn too much.

With a muffled groan, he gave up.

As the tension drained from his body, he held Cyn still with the weight of his shoulders, staying with her, pushing her, making her pleasure go on and on until she subsided in near soundless whimpers, her body limp, damp with sweat.

Bruce rested his cheek on her slender

thigh, his fingers still pressed deep inside her, absorbing the little aftershocks and tremors. He didn't want to leave her yet. Truthfully, he didn't want to leave her ever.

She gulped air. Little by little, her fingers loosened in his hair, began caressing, smoothing. Finally, after several minutes had passed, she whispered, "Holy cow, Bruce."

With a contented smile, he said, "You're wonderful."

He didn't want to move, but he had to clean up and they really did need to get some sleep. With a tender kiss to the inside of her knee, he pushed up to his elbows. "I'll be right back."

Idly, she flapped a limp hand at him. She sighed, sighed again, longer and deeper, and finally said, "Yeah. Whatever. I'm not going anywhere."

Bruce made fast work of it, took the time to don fresh boxers, and crawled back into bed beside her. Without making him ask, she curled into his side and put her arms around him. He knew she wanted to say something, and he just waited.

"What you did . . ."

He hugged her. "Gave me more pleasure than I've had in years."

She shook her head. "But you didn't . . ."

"Yeah. I did. I didn't mean to, but you're very special to me and I lost control."

He could actually feel her confusion before she laughed. "I will never understand you."

"Yes, you will. I'll see that you do." He settled into the mattress. "Now sleep. We've got a big day tomorrow."

That reminder made her shudder in regret. Bruce hugged her closer; he wanted her to remember that she was no longer alone. She'd never be alone again.

Seconds later, her breathing deepened and Bruce knew she was asleep.

Chapter Nine

Cyn fell silent as Bruce pulled the compact rental car to the curb in front of her mother's home. It was a blustery, overcast day and Cyn pulled her sweater closer around her.

After a brief meeting at the airport, Detective Darby Orsen requested they join her at the house to talk.

Bruce had wanted Cyn to eat first, but her stomach was too jumpy for that. He'd wanted her to nap too, as if she hadn't slept through the entire flight. She couldn't remember ever being so exhausted — or so uneasy.

It wasn't just the imminent stroll down memory lane, either. It was Bruce.

What did last night mean to him?

She had no idea, and it was driving her nuts. What he'd done . . . tending to her needs while ignoring his own, left her floundering in uncertainty. She knew of *no* man who gave so unselfishly. Especially where sex was concerned.

In general, men were pigs in bed. She saw it in the movies, heard it on the streets. As a hooker, she'd expected no less. With

Bruce . . . she hadn't known what to expect. Certainly, she hadn't expected what he'd done.

"Ready?"

Damn. She realized she'd just been sitting there, staring at the yellow tape around the ramshackle house. Weeds were high in the yard, filling up cracks in the concrete walk. Beer cans, cigarette packs, and various other debris were scattered everywhere.

Cyn nodded — but it was a lie. She was far from ready.

The detective had parked behind them and now she opened Cyn's door. She was a woman in her early fifties, tall and stout, a woman who looked very capable.

"I'm sorry," she said to Cyn. "I know this must be difficult for you."

"No, it's all right." Cyn took two steps toward the house, and then Bruce's hand slipped into hers. Strangely enough, that simple touch gave her the added strength she needed to get through the ordeal of visiting her own personal hell.

The detective wore plain clothes: gray slacks, a black cotton shirt. Her short brown hair was cut in a mannish style, but didn't detract from the understanding in her faded green eyes. She lifted the police tape and both Cyn and Bruce stepped under it.

"We've had it closed off, but I doubt it's kept everyone out. This neighborhood is rife with looters and every crime scene has to deal with the curious. Not that we expect to find much more here, but I wanted to give you the chance to take a look, to tell us if anything seemed different."

The detective opened the front door and stood back to let them enter.

The house was trashed, but Cyn had expected no less. Even if her personal situation hadn't been too ugly to involve friends, she'd always been too ashamed of how they lived to invite anyone over. Cigarette smoke and the sweet, sickening smell of old alcohol permeated the air.

"Where was she killed?"

At her dispassionate question, Orsen looked at her curiously. "The kitchen."

In silence, Cyn headed that way, aware of Bruce at her side, tall and unwavering in his support. Incredible, caring Bruce.

Stopping in the kitchen doorway, she watched as roaches scurried from the sink to disappear into the walls. Drawers had been emptied, leaving the floor filled with odds and ends. A chair was toppled, a cabinet door open.

The detective said, "The forged note from you was on the table."

"Wasn't that a dumb move?" Bruce wanted to know. "Any handwriting expert would be able to tell the writing apart."

Orsen shrugged. "The school still had records on Cyn, and her last papers before she went missing. We used those to compare the handwriting and yeah, it was clear right off that it was different. But I don't think it mattered in the scheme of things."

Cyn didn't care what it meant, but Bruce did. "What are you saying?"

"Someone wanted us to talk to her. That was the objective. And so we are, and Cynthia, we're hopeful you can tell us something."

Cyn shook her head. She felt as if a great void had opened up inside her, expanding, leaving her cold and empty.

The detective considered Cyn. "According to her neighbors, Arlene had no less than six boyfriends in the last year. But for a few months now, she was living alone."

"She must have hated that," Cyn said with a harsh laugh.

"We're checking into the men, but so far they all have alibis."

So, Palmer wasn't still in her life. Cyn

wasn't surprised to hear that he'd moved on. Even as a kid, she'd known that he'd lost interest in Arlene, and with Cyn gone, he had no reason to stay. Odds were, he'd been so pissed after his recovery, he'd probably wanted nothing to do with either of them.

Bruce asked, "Are you all right?"

Shrugging, Cyn said, "Except for the drawers being dumped, it looks about the same as it always did. We lived like swine and the house always stank." She turned to Detective Orsen. "What'd you expect me to say?"

Orsen leaned against the doorframe and crossed her arms over her chest. "I don't know, Cynthia. I was hoping you'd see something different."

Cyn shook her head. "Nope. All I see is that nothing changed after I left."

"Do you know of anyone who'd want your mother dead?"

"I used to wish her dead when I was a kid." She didn't care what they made of that. "But other than me, no."

Orsen pulled out a chair and sat. "I know you ran off five years ago. Some of the older neighbors told me that much."

"Yeah, well, did they tell you that Arlene Potter lacked any kind of maternal inclinations?" A simmering rage began to build inside her, but it wasn't as strong as the hurt. She couldn't breathe deep enough to remove the squeezing pain in her chest. "She was a drunk," Cyn said, "and a slut, and to be honest, I don't know why you care that she's dead."

Bruce's hand landed on her shoulder. "You care."

Her bottom lip began to quiver, and she shook her head. "No, I don't." She didn't.

Darby Orsen's eyes filled with sympathy. "I've worked through a lot of shitty cases, Cynthia. The stuff of nightmares. One thing I see time and again is that even the lousiest mother is still someone's mom. And losing her hurts."

"She was never a mother, not to me."

"And now you've lost your chance to find out why, to tell her how you feel, maybe even to give her hell and tell her that you hate her. And that probably makes it hurt worst of all."

Cyn couldn't breathe. She gulped air but it didn't help. Whirling away from Bruce and the detective, she dashed out of the kitchen, down the short hall, and burst onto the porch. Her knees wanted to give out, so she quickly plopped down on the top step.

Damn Arlene. Damn her. Tears clouded her vision, made her throat tight.

Bruce sat down silently beside her. He didn't say anything, he was just there.

"*Why?*" The word tore from Cyn's throat and she swiped angrily at the stupid tears rolling down her cheeks. Gasping, hating herself, she wailed, "Why didn't she love me?"

Ignoring a few nosy neighbors and Detective Orsen's quiet presence on the porch, Bruce pulled her into his lap. His voice sounded strained; his hold was tight. "She was blinded by drink and stupidity, or she'd have known what she was missing." He kissed her forehead, his touch lingering, healing. "It's her loss, baby. *Her* loss."

Cyn stared blindly at the scraggly bushes on the other side of the steps, wishing she were stronger, wishing it didn't hurt. Arlene deserved nothing from her, but the detective was right. You only had one mother, and now hers was gone forever.

She tried to focus on other things, blindly staring at the broken bricks beneath the porch, the split rails, the cracked, overturned clay pot that, to her memory, had never sported a flower.

The detective spoke quietly behind

them. "There has to be a connection to your mother's death and you, some reason you're being drawn in. Someone knew you both. Maybe before you left?"

A harsh laugh bubbled up. "Arlene never bothered herself with my school, so she didn't know anyone there. I didn't have friends, and she only had guys around, no females."

"An old boyfriend then?"

"Oh sure, we both knew her boyfriend at the time, but you said she's switched up a lot in the last year, so he was long gone before this happened."

Then something clicked. Cyn slowly sat up, her eyes not leaving that flowerpot. She wiped away the tears, forgetting her own embarrassment for the moment. "He had a key."

The detective moved down to the step beside Cyn. Her anticipation was a live thing, pulsing in the air. "Either that," she said in encouragement, "or your mother left the door unlocked. There was no forced entry."

"No one leaves their doors unlocked around here. It'd be suicide, and even at her drunkest, Arlene took care of herself."

"So how do you think he got in?"

Cyn pointed to the pot. "There was a

key hidden under there. For emergencies." She looked from Bruce up to Orsen. "No one ever touched it, and if you did, you damn sure put it back."

There was a pause, then the detective was off the step, hovering over the pot. "Damn. The rest of the yard is so trashed, no one noticed. But look, the weeds are grown up everywhere except where the pot had been sitting. That means it was tipped over recently." She leaned closer. "I can even see an impression of the key in the dirt."

With throbbing expectancy, Darby Orsen returned and crouched down next to Cyn. "Who hid the key there?"

Cyn swallowed down her own apprehension, took Bruce's hand, and stared directly at the detective. "Palmer Oaks."

Sweat beaded on his upper lip, slid down the middle of his back, and his breath came fast and low. With one hand, he held back the threadbare curtain from the grimy window.

With the other, he stroked himself, imagining, planning.

Jesus, she was sexier than ever, a woman made to be fucked hard and long. By him. Her tits were big and round, her legs so long they'd wrap around him and squeeze him tight.

The abandoned house across the street and two doors down from her mother's place afforded him the perfect position to see without being seen. Rats scratched and scuttled behind him. Bugs ran up the walls.

He didn't care about any of that.

He should have taken the little slut when he'd had the chance, but Arlene wouldn't have liked that. She was the lousiest excuse for a mother he'd ever seen, but she was also a jealous bitch, especially where her daughter was concerned.

So he'd waited, biding his time, making plans — and she'd escaped him. But not before almost destroying him.

Now things were falling into place again. He watched them on the porch, checking the stupid pot, doing just as he expected. He might have laughed if his need wasn't so great.

Oh, she'd get hers, he'd see to it. First he'd take what he wanted, what he'd wanted for far too long. And then he'd make her pay. She'd been away for five years.

Finally, her time had come.

Bruce answered the knock from room

service and accepted the tray of sandwiches and drinks. Cyn had to eat, whether she wanted to or not. Glancing at her, how she slouched in a chair staring at the television, he knew she'd try to refuse.

She'd been so distant, so withdrawn, since they'd left her mother's house. It was her house now, handed down from her grandparents to her mother, and now to her. But it was apparent that no one had done anything to it in a decade. Without upkeep, the house had fallen into disrepair that reflected the failed suburb.

Detective Orsen had offered to let her take any personal photographs or items of sentimental value, but Cyn had turned away as if repulsed by the idea. "The state can have it. Let them use it to bury her."

After that, she'd gone silent, but she couldn't close herself off from him. Bruce wouldn't allow it.

He understood her turmoil. Seeing the hellhole where she'd grown up filled him with disgust and rage, too. He saw it as a young girl might have, as a small, dank prison with no joy and no love. Without the simplest things that all children needed.

They'd gone through the rest of the house, including Cyn's room, just to see if anything clicked or offered additional clues. Cyn was surprised that her bedroom hadn't changed much. There were aged stains on the wall and floor that, judging by her expression, could have been dried blood from where she'd attacked Palmer. Even shards of dusty, broken glass still littered the floor, with the base of an old lamp resting on its side.

Knowing Cyn as he did, seeing her small, cramped room had pained him most of all. She was a bright, witty person, quick with a comeback and always ready to smile. She was cheerful when given the opportunity, and meticulous in the extreme. Mary had commented on how immaculate Cyn kept the horse stalls, how diligent she was in tending to the animals' needs.

Her loft was bright and cheery, dust- and clutter-free. When she worked at the church, she exuded boundless energy and attention to detail. She always did the best she could; Cyn would be able to do no less.

The Cyn Potter he knew was a direct contrast to what her childhood bedroom depicted, and Bruce knew that hadn't been her choice, but rather her lack of choices.

Tattered gray blankets were strewn across her bed, with faded sheets tacked up as makeshift curtains on her window. Peeling paint hung from the ceiling. Her furniture was no more than a metal bed frame and mattress, and a shabby dresser with one drawer missing.

Where other young girls were treated to ruffles and pink print wallpaper, Cyn had dealt with cockroaches and assault.

And she was still a caring, giving person.

Bruce put the tray on the dresser and sat down beside her. "Cyn?"

"Hmm?"

"Come to the table and let's eat."

"I'm not hungry."

"I don't care."

Her gaze snapped over to him, and slowly, her frown bloomed into a smile. "Worrying over my well-being, Lancelot?"

She hadn't called him names in a while. Bruce wasn't sure what that meant. "You haven't eaten since breakfast."

Dismissing him, she looked back to the television while patting her full breasts. "Trust me, I've got plenty of fat to keep me from starving."

Bruce considered her a long moment, decided he had nothing to lose, and leaned forward to take her mouth.

She stiffened, her mouth firm, her eyes open. He wasn't discouraged. He cupped one hand to her cheek, and continued to kiss her. Soft, teasing . . . and she melted.

Her arms came around him and she parted her lips.

Bruce pulled her down on the bed beneath him and sealed their mouths together. Her nails curled into his shoulder. He *really* liked that.

Smiling, he lifted his head. “Signs of life.” His thumbs brushed her temples. “Finally.”

She blinked slumberous eyes and frowned. “What?”

“Don’t shut me out, honey.” He kissed her nose, her chin. “I can’t bear it.”

With fury brightening her eyes, she accused, “You only kissed me to —”

“Get a response.” He considered kissing her again. “I always want a response when I kiss you. It’s no fun if I’m enjoying it all on my own.”

Her eyes narrowed.

“You were ignoring me, Cyn, pretending I wasn’t here. Conversation got me nowhere. But you need to eat, and we need to talk. At least a kiss got you out of your stupor.”

She erupted. “Get off!”

“No.”

“No?”

Her dramatic, exaggerated incredulity was amusing, and preferable to no emotion at all. Bruce shook his head. "I like touching you. You might be so tough that you don't need to be held, even after all that happened this afternoon. But I'm a preacher. We're notoriously wimpy. *I* need to be held."

Caught between her anger and the urge to defend him, she finally growled, "You are *not* a wimp."

She was so adorable. "Am too."

"Bull." She smacked his shoulder. "You're rock solid, and totally hunky, and what's more, you know it. From the beginning, I told you that you didn't look like a preacher. And when I saw you the first time without your shirt . . ." Words failed her for a few heartbeats, and then grudgingly, she admitted, "I almost swallowed my tongue."

"Yeah?"

She didn't appreciate his smile one bit. "You're just claiming you need to be held to make me cave."

Bruce nuzzled the softest part of her neck where it met her shoulder, and was rewarded with her small shiver. He could kiss her forever and it wouldn't be enough.

Against her skin, he whispered, "I'm

saying it because I want you to smile. I care for you, whether you feel the same about me or not."

She stiffened again.

"When you hurt, it hurts me, too." Bruce leaned back up to see her face. "And I am hurting, Cyn. For you. For what that young girl went through. At the same time, I am so damn proud of you."

Her hands quit shoving against him and instead rested on his shoulders. Suspicion had her brow puckering and her mouth tight. "Proud?"

"Very, very proud. Look at you, at who you are and all you went through to get there."

"I'm —"

His finger pressed over her mouth, shushing her. "We're done mentioning the whole hooker thing. That's in the past. You did what you did, and it's over. Now you're here, with me. There are problems to solve, issues to deal with, and I want to help you with those."

She wrapped her fingers around his wrist and drew his hand away. "Isn't there some other pathetic person you can go pester?"

A man could only take so much. Driven by a flood of anger, Bruce pushed himself off the bed. He stared down at her, refusing to be drawn in again by the uncertainty in her rebellious expression.

He turned away, snatched up the car keys from the nightstand, and stormed out of the room. If he stayed, he'd throttle the little fool. Pathetic? Is that what she thought? Is that how she still saw herself?

He stomped through the motel, across the parking lot, and just as he reached the rental car, a hand came out and grabbed his arm.

Fury rushing to the fore, Bruce turned, cocked back a fist — and almost punched Joe Winston in the nose.

To his credit, Joe didn't flinch. Behind a disguise of mirrored sunglasses and a trucker's hat, he gave a sinner's grin, slapped Bruce on the shoulder hard enough to dislocate his arm, and said, "Hey, killer. Let's talk in the car."

Bemused and rattled after that close call, Bruce got behind the wheel while Joe folded his large frame into the passenger seat.

The car faced the motel, so Bruce would be able to see Cyn if she tried to run out on him. Not that he thought she would, but he wouldn't underestimate her. She needed time to stew alone; being alone was familiar to her, much as he wished otherwise.

Again, Bruce tried to remind himself that she needed time to become accustomed to him —

"I'm not really used to being ignored."

Mentally castigating himself, Bruce turned to Joe. "Sorry." He blew out a long breath. "I've got a lot on my mind."

"No shit. I thought you were going to walk right past me. That is, until you decided to deck me instead."

Bruce locked his jaw. "Sorry about that."

"You've got fast reflexes." Admiration laced Joe's tone. "If it hadn't been me, well, someone would've been sorry for bugging you."

Bruce rolled his shoulders, trying to relieve his tension. "I'm jumpy because —"

"Yeah, I know." Joe spoke with quiet understanding. "No big deal."

"I almost hit you."

"Naw. I wouldn't let you do that." Joe rolled down his window and pulled off the cap, then ran a hand through his sweat-damp hair. "Hot today, isn't it?"

"I suppose so."

"Makes me wonder why some jackass came out of a house across from where Cyn's mother lived, wearing a knit cap and a jacket with the collar up."

Joe said it so casually that it took Bruce a moment to understand. His head jerked around. "Someone was watching her?"

"That's what my gut says."

"You don't know for sure?"

"I didn't notice anyone watching when we were at the house, but then I was back quite a bit so no one would notice *me*. Could be he was peeking out a window. A lot of the houses around there looked abandoned. It'd be easy to get inside one, and just as easy not to be seen."

Bruce felt himself practically swell with antagonism. "But you did see him?"

Joe nodded. "I was tailing you, but we hadn't gotten to the end of the street when I saw him in my rearview mirror. He came out in a hurry, got in a rusty blue Ford truck, and hung behind until you reached the motel."

Joe pulled a slip of paper from his front pocket. "I got the license number, and friends are running it now to see if it turns up any info."

"I should give that to the detective."

"I'll take care of it." Joe tucked the paper away again. "He didn't stop at the motel when you did, and I was caught trying to decide if I should follow him, or stick with you and Cyn, just in case."

"And you stuck with us?"

"Tough call, but yeah. I figured I can go back to where he was staying, see what I can turn up there. With any luck, I'll find him home and that'll be the end of that."

"Don't do anything crazy, Joe."

Joe winked. "I used to be a cop, remember? I know how it works. In fact, soon as I take a look around, I'll let your detective know and she can poke her nose in there, too." He replaced his cap. "I just wanted you to know you're on your own for a few hours, so don't let Cyn out of your sight." And with a knowing look, he warned, "No stalking off mad."

Disgusted, Bruce faced the windshield again. "I wasn't going to leave. I just needed some air and I didn't want her to have the car keys."

"Because you were afraid she would leave?"

"She's headstrong, and right now, she's hurting." Bruce rubbed his face tiredly. "We had a stupid argument."

"So apologize."

That made Bruce laugh. "She won't want to hear it."

Joe shrugged. "Then seduce her. Keep her naked in bed and stay there with her."

He winked. "Safest place for both of you to be."

Bruce stared at his hands where they gripped the steering wheel. That was pretty much Joe's solution to most problems. But he wasn't Joe. "I'm a preacher, remember?"

Snorting, Joe said, "Don't bullshit me. You're in love with her. You and Bryan are alike in that way."

"What way?"

"You're damned obvious. Hell, I can see it when you look at her. I can even hear it when you talk about her."

Joe's good humor rubbed Bruce's nerves raw. "You're the expert on love now?"

Joe grinned. "Having experienced it firsthand, yeah." He settled back in his seat. "Listen, it gets better. She'll drive you nuts at first, women can't help that. She'll run you through the wringer till you think you can't take it, then she'll love ya back and it'll be okay. You've got my word on that."

Bruce decided he'd do well *not* to discuss love with the notorious Joe Winston. "You're right. Somehow I'll get around her temper."

"Good, because I think this is going to get ugly."

The way Joe said that, with such conviction, had Bruce's protective instincts on red alert. "Was it Palmer Oaks?"

"Could be." Joe constantly scanned the area, especially paying attention to the cars coming and going on or near the lot. "Bryan called me about a half-hour ago."

"He found out something?"

"Yep." Hesitant, Joe rubbed his ear. "Seems Palmer was in prison — until three months ago."

Oh God. "He escaped?"

"They released him. He did some time for breaking and entering, but, if you can believe it, got marks for good behavior. So, our boy is definitely loose again. I have feelers out to see where he is now, but so far, nothing."

"Detective Orsen is checking into his whereabouts, too." Bruce explained about the key and Cyn's suspicions.

"Good. The more people on the job, the better our chance of avoiding disaster."

Disaster. Bruce hated the sound of that. He couldn't wait to get Cyn back home where she'd be safer. Except . . . staying in the loft, so far from the main house, how safe would she be?

Joe gripped his shoulder. "We fly out tomorrow morning, so unless something urgent comes up, I'll tell you whatever I find out back in Visitation."

Anxious to return to Cyn, Bruce nodded. "Thanks, Joe."

"No thanks necessary. Just keep your guard up. Especially on the way to the airport. I'll be behind you, but still . . . be careful." With that cryptic warning, Joe left the car.

More concerned than ever, Bruce glanced back at the motel, and found Cyn standing in front of the glass foyer doors. She watched Joe move away before looking back at Bruce. Their gazes caught and held.

On a sigh, Bruce got out of the car and started toward her. One way or another, he'd make her listen.

As he approached, Cyn crossed her arms under her breasts, lifted one brow in mocking inquiry, and shook her head as if he'd somehow vexed her.

Then, finally, she smiled.

The second Bruce stepped through the doors, Cyn said, "I thought you'd left."

"I'm not going anywhere without you."

She absorbed that promise, and nodded. "Okay, so you just went out for air. You wanna tell me why Joe Winston is here?"

Bruce stopped directly in front of her,

staring down with so much intense emotion, she almost blushed.

"You recognized him?"

What, did she look like a complete dolt? "It's a little hard to miss Joe."

"Really?"

Cyn rolled her eyes. Was he toying with her? "Bruce, the man is huge, and scary, and —"

"Joe's scary?"

She threw up her arms. Joe wasn't scary in the same way that Palmer was, or even in the way of Reverend Thorne. But the man looked dangerous and only the blind wouldn't see that. "Why — is — he — here?"

Bruce caught her arm and Cyn allowed him to lead her to the elevator. "Let's talk in the room, where we have privacy, okay?"

Cyn eyed him. He looked different. When he'd left, he was furious. Maybe because she'd put herself down. She hadn't even meant to do that, it was just habit. But Bruce didn't like it.

And that was, well, kind of nice.

Now, though, he looked . . . She wasn't sure. Protective. Determined. Alert.

She stared at his mouth and attempted a seductive tone. "Are you going to kiss me again in our room?"

"Maybe."

Well. He didn't sound overly enthusiastic either way. But after the nasty, childish way she'd treated him, she'd take what she could get. "Okay, then."

He kept her tucked to his side until he had their door open and had ushered her inside. He dropped the car keys, put the door card away, and faced her with grim resolve.

"Palmer Oaks was in prison, but he's out."

Ohmigod.

Blank for only a second, Cyn fabricated a sarcastic grin and gave Bruce her back. "I hope his cell mate had fun with him while he was there."

Gently, inexorably, Bruce pulled her around and right into his arms. His hand opened wide on the back of her head and eased her cheek to his chest. She loved his chest, how hard and warm it was, how she could feel the strong beat of his heart.

"Joe came along to trail us, to make sure whoever murdered your mother didn't get a chance to touch you. Not that I'm incompetent, or that I wouldn't die trying to protect you, but two sets of eyes are always better than one."

Cyn shoved him back hard, and he staggered in surprise. *Or that I wouldn't die trying . . .*

"Now what?"

How dense could a man be? She could handle the threat of Palmer much easier than the idea of Bruce being hurt. "You *idiot*."

Aggrieved, Bruce propped his hands on his hips. "One minute I'm Lancelot, now I'm an idiot?"

She thrust her face up to his and snarled, "What do you expect?" God, she didn't know if she could take much more of this. "I was ready to forgive you, but if you're going to talk stupid, then you can just forget it."

Bruce shook his head and walked to the room service tray to open the sandwiches. "Be as mad as you want, Cyn. Rant all you want. Yell loud enough for the entire motel to hear if it'll make you feel better. But Joe thinks someone followed us today, after we left the house. We know Palmer is out of jail. There's a lot going on, and you are *not* leaving my sight."

Derision seemed her only defense. "So now you're my guardian angel?"

"God knows, you need one."

A temper tantrum was not the way to reason with Bruce Kelly. The man was a rock of moral conviction and if he thought it was his duty to protect her, sniping at him wouldn't change his mind.

Cyn drew a breath to calm herself and then started over. "Look, Bruce, there's no reason to think Palmer wants anything to do with me now —"

"He's the biggest suspect. Detective Orsen said so."

"But . . ."

"Your mother was murdered, Cyn. And with that ridiculous note forging your name, you are most definitely involved. Probably as the next victim."

She curled her arms around her middle and shook her head.

Bruce took in her expression and narrowed his eyes. "Don't worry. I'm not going to let that happen." He took her arm, and because she was so muddled, so afraid for him, she let him lead her to the tiny round table tucked into the corner of the room.

She sat, and Bruce put half a cold-cut sandwich in front of her, along with chips and a cola. "Now eat."

She wanted to throw the stupid sandwich at his head. She stared at it while trying to think of some way to remove him from danger. Only one option came to her. "Make me a deal, Bruce."

While taking a big bite of his own sandwich, he eyed her. Chewing thoughtfully, he pulled out the chair across from her and sat. He swallowed and said, "What kind of deal?"

"I'll eat," she promised. "I'll let you stick close to my side. I'll be extra, extra careful. But I want your word that you won't put yourself at risk."

Bruce picked up a pickle spear and munched into it. "Will you quit insulting yourself, too?"

So now he was going to push? She should call it off — but she couldn't. "Sure." She only hoped she could remember that one. Old habits were hard to break.

Bruce pondered her, probably trying to judge her sincerity, until her integrity felt lacerated.

Finally, he said, "All right. But for the record, I never put myself at risk. And as long as you stay safe, I'd have no reason to anyway. So I'll give you my word — and we both know I never lie — if you'll give me yours."

Gritting her teeth, Cyn said, "I already did."

Bruce shook his head. "No, you don't understand."

He laid the half-eaten sandwich aside to fold his arms on the table and give her the benefit of his undivided scrutiny.

"Joe and Bryan have done this cloak-and-dagger stuff for much of their lives. They eat danger for lunch. They smell it when it gets too close. If either one of them . . ." He paused, thought about that, then added, "or if Jamie Creed, says you need to do something to be safe, swear to me you'll do it."

Of all the . . . "So now I not only have to take orders from you, but from your brother *and* Joe *and* Jamie?"

"That's right." He looked very resolute. "Luckily, we're all reasonable men."

Cyn jumped up from her chair. "Well, what about the rest of Visitation?" She laughed in disbelief and propped her hands on her hips, glaring at him. "Don't they get to boss me around, too?"

"No." He ate another chip. "Just us four men."

He was totally serious. Cyn blinked in bemused disgust. It would have been funny if she wasn't so damned afraid of Palmer. She'd tried to kill him, and Palmer wasn't a man given to forgiveness. Her mother had been strangled to death. What might he do to Bruce?

Once more, her life left her with no choice.

"Yes, sir, General Patton." With blatant

disgust, she saluted smartly. “I’ll follow orders to a tee.”

Bruce looked up. “Lancelot, idiot, and now Patton? Make up your mind, will you?” He stood, reached across the table to ease her back into her seat. “Now let’s eat, honey.” His fingers touched her cheek, drifted away. “I don’t know about you, but I’m starved.”

Chapter Ten

Bruce watched Cyn pace the room. She'd showered and changed into a slip-type nightgown guaranteed to make his imagination run wild, and now she was suffering insecurity of a most unusual kind. So far, he'd done very little of what she expected from men. Considering the men she'd known, he intended to keep it that way.

He'd gotten a room with only one bed, so she'd have no delusions on where she'd sleep — which would be right beside him. Or on him, or under him, spooned beside him . . . as long as they were touching, he didn't care how she got comfortable.

And he'd already turned off the lights. He cared deeply for the person Cyn was, but he was a man, and the sight of her tested him. Dim lights seemed his only recourse if he was to be able to play this through.

Only the television illuminated the room, and neither of them was watching it.

Without a word, he stood, stripped off his clothes without haste and with no modesty. He turned back the spread and blankets. "Come to bed, Cyn."

Glancing at him, she let her gaze linger on his chest for a thorough inspection, then went to the window and parted the heavy drapes to peer out at nothing in particular.

"Or," Bruce said, chagrined by her reaction, "we can take in the parking lot view." He came up behind her, put his hands on her shoulders and drew her back against his chest.

"Bruce?"

"Hmmm?"

"What are you going to do tonight?"

He smiled to himself and kissed her hair. "I'm waiting to see what you want me to do." She surely wasn't used to her wishes being a priority. How many times had she told him that she had no choice in things?

With him, it was always her choice. To a point.

"If you're tired, we'll sleep. If you're anxious, we can talk." His mouth grazed the side of her neck and his hand opened over her belly. "If you're aroused," he said, in a voice grown deeper with desire, "I'd be happy to give you relief."

Her hand covered his, her fingers lacing in his. "And if I want sex?"

"Consummation?"

"Yeah, the whole shebang." She tipped her head back to look at him upside down, and her eyes were dark and mysterious as only a woman's could be. "You inside me, both of us coming —"

"Soon," he interrupted, "but not tonight." He slipped his free hand, fingers spread wide, down her body, over her chest and onto her breasts, cupping the heavy weight, cuddling her, moving his thumb over her nipples. "I have my reasons, and I hope you'll trust me enough to wait."

Her mouth twitched even as her breathing deepened. "Until you're ready? Like a virgin on prom night?"

Until you're mine in every way known to man and God. But of course, he didn't say it. She had an odd habit of panicking anytime she thought they were getting too involved. She feared commitment, not because of how it'd bind her, but because she believed that she'd fail him somehow. It had taken him a while, but he'd finally come to that realization.

"Until I know you're ready — for me."

She reached back and her hand closed around his erection. Bruce sucked in a breath as his knees locked and his guts tightened. "You're all man, Bruce Kelly, but not so much that I can't handle it."

Humor saved his crumbling convictions. Chuckling, Bruce stepped back from her, forcing her to release him. Much more of that and he'd have had her on the floor — which was exactly what he didn't want to do.

She dropped the curtains and turned with him.

Bruce took her hands in his, still smiling. "Physically, we're meant for each other. It'll be nothing less than perfect." He back-stepped to the bed, taking Cyn with him. "It's your emotions that are wavering, honey. But I figure my charm is bound to win you over sooner or later."

Together they went down to the mattress, and Bruce covered her, relishing the soft, lush cushion of her small, sexy body.

"Exactly what do you want, Bruce?"

Everything. But he didn't tell her that, either. He kissed her nose, her fluttering eyelashes, and said, with great but inadequate sincerity, "You."

Burning with a mixture of rage and lust, he lowered the night goggles and cursed. Fucking whore. His hands shook so badly, he felt like he had a damn disease. He tossed the goggles onto the bed and dragged a forearm across his hot, sweaty face. He'd seen her there in the window, in the nicer motel across the street. And he'd seen the man with her, playing with her tits, licking her throat — doing the things *he* should be doing.

He'd kill them both. But not until he'd finished with Cyn. And he wouldn't finish for a long, long time.

Minutes from the airport, Joe's cell phone rang. After snooping in the empty house last night, then hooking up with Detective Orsen, who really was a crackerjack cop, he'd barely gotten to bed at all. He yawned before answering with a less than jovial, "Winston here."

In the old days, pre–wife and kids, he'd been accustomed to running on little sleep. Hell, he'd been accustomed to doing without a lot of stuff. Like sleep, comfort. Love. Now he missed those things. Shit. He was spoiled. And getting soft.

"Hey, Winston. Aren't you the bushy-tailed one this morning."

Joe grinned at the detective's wit. "Leave my tail out of this." He felt comfortable joking because Darby was a very happily married cop of twenty-plus years. He'd found that out after having coffee and pie with her in a diner. And they'd gone for the pie after Joe clued her in on the abandoned house not far from where Cyn's mother had been murdered.

Darby had been through it once before, right after the body was found. They'd checked the entire street and searched all the empty houses — which only proved what Joe had already known: that the fast-food wrappers, muddy footprints, and body fluids were fresh.

Darby and a forensics team had done their thing, and Darby was seasoned enough not to take offense at Joe's presence. Of course, that was probably because he was seasoned enough that he hadn't touched a damned thing, but instead had called her ASAP.

And since she knew he'd once been a cop — and she'd checked his files on that — she didn't mind the input, and the additional eyes, once Bruce and Cyn moved from her jurisdiction.

"Bad news, Winston."

"I'm ready."

"The blue truck was stolen, but it was found yesterday, dumped in a creek bed. The plate numbers don't do us a damn bit of good, but if we can get some good prints, they might match. Either way, we'll run what we get through the system. I'll keep you posted on that."

Very quietly, Joe cursed. The house had been so trashed and nasty, it'd be impossible to tell prints apart. And lifting a good print off a paper cup wasn't likely.

Hopefully there'd be something better in the truck. But if the bastard wasn't driving it anymore . . .

Joe could see Bruce and Cyn ahead of him. Cars, trucks, and a motorcycle crowded the highway, and he had no idea who to watch, so he'd watch everyone. "Someone's going to a lot of trouble," Joe told her. He might be out of the business, but that hadn't killed his instincts. And his instincts didn't like this worth a damn.

"Assuming it is the same guy, well hey, what's a little spying or a car heist after murder?"

"You have a point." One he didn't like.

"I'm calling Deputy Royal next. We'll catch the guy — don't worry too much."

"Are you going to take that advice?"

"No, I'm going to take a few antacids and get back to work."

Joe was still smiling when he disconnected the line. But the smile faded with the threat of danger so thick, and he called his wife, Luna, just to hear her voice, and just to know she was okay.

* * *

Cyn picked Joe out at the airport. Given the ferocious heat in his laser-blue eyes when she snatched the not-so-concealing newspaper out of his hand, he didn't like it that she recognized him. He was scary, but she wouldn't let him intimidate her, so she plucked the ridiculous hat from his head and laughed in his face.

Bruce shrugged at Joe's look of disgust directed his way, and then Joe's mouth twitched, before lifting into a wry smile. He really was a handsome devil, Cyn thought, but he had nothing on Bruce.

They returned the rental cars and got their boarding passes together, then sat down with pastry and coffee while waiting for their flight. Cyn was uneasy throughout it all, and finally Bruce put his arm around her and said, "Okay, what's wrong? Is Joe bothering you?"

After nearly choking, Joe cocked a brow over the edge of his coffee cup. "Me?" He pokered up in affront. "I haven't done a damn thing."

"You wouldn't have to," Cyn assured him, but she was worried and it had nothing to do with Joe Winston. "I don't know what it is. I feel like we're being watched."

Bruce sighed. "You are being watched. I keep telling you, you're beautiful, so men will look. Don't let it get to you."

Joe leaned forward. "There's a difference in being noticed and being tracked."

"Exactly."

Bruce immediately scanned the area.

Joe said, "Tell me again what he looks like."

For about the hundredth time, Cyn described what she remembered of Palmer. "Obese, rheumy blue eyes. His hair was thin then, so he might be bald now, but it was sort of a washed-out brown."

Joe worked his jaw. "In five years, people lose weight, lose hair, and you did say he might even be scarred now. I think I'll just keep an eye on everyone."

Bruce took her hand and by his tight hold, Cyn knew the picture of Palmer bothered him, too. "Bryan's getting a copy of his mug shot, which should be more recent. It'll give us something to go on."

Joe stared at one man, who quickly continued on his way, then another, who wisely turned his back to give his attention to his magazine.

When no one else was paying them any mind, Joe relaxed. "You do draw men like flies. Sorry, honey, but it's the truth."

Bruce hauled Cyn protectively into his side. "Joe."

Joe shrugged. "The girl's not blind, Bruce. She knows what she looks like."

"The girl," Cyn assured them both, "thinks it's no big deal. As long as Palmer isn't looking, then who cares?"

"Exactly," Bruce said.

She rested against his shoulder. "But man, I'll be glad to get back to Visitation."

"Me, too," Joe said. Then, just to tease Bruce, he added, "You think you'll have time to work up a sermon?"

"I've been with you," Bruce joked right back. "I've had plenty of fodder for thought."

They were all chuckling when the men became aware of the young suit across from them. He watched Cyn and made no bones about listening in on their conversation.

Both Bruce and Joe glared at the hapless man with vicious intent.

Cyn elbowed Joe, but that had no discernible effect on the big brute, so she turned her cannon on Bruce instead. "You're a preacher, for crying out loud. Preachers don't bully innocent people."

Bruce blinked. "I'm not."

"What would you call it?"

Joe said, "Minding his interests."

His interests, being her? Cyn considered the meaning behind that, and the young man wisely chose that moment to make a last-minute trip to the restroom. He no sooner left than an attendant announced they were seating for their flight.

"If he misses the plane, it'll be your fault," Cyn said to both Joe and Bruce.

Neither man, unfortunately, seemed too concerned about it.

"Hey."

In a rush, the suited man grabbed several paper towels and glanced to the side while drying his hands. Next to the sink, a scrubby, ragtag fellow lounged. He had longish hair and a really hideous hat with the brim pulled low to hide half of his face. His teeth were yellowed and patches of whiskers covered his jaw and chin.

Scary dude. But they'd just called his plane and he wanted to get to his seat, so he nodded, said, "Hello," and started out of the restroom.

"I saw you were talking to a friend of mine. Valerie."

"Who?" The passenger hesitated. First, he'd had the two guys glaring bullets at him, and now this loco. "I don't know any

Valerie." Again he started away, but a heavy hand snatched at the sleeve of his suit coat, stalling him.

"That wasn't her? She sat across from you. A real looker — long, dark hair." He winked. "Hot as a chili pepper."

Realization dawned. "Oh, yeah." So, he wasn't the only one noticing the babe. Why the hell did the two bruisers with her act like he'd committed a damn felony? No sin in looking. "I don't know her personally." And with a grin. "Hard to miss that one, though."

"I hear ya. She always was sweet on the eyes." He tipped his head, and his long hair fell past his shoulder. "Must be heading back to Iowa, I guess. I meant to stop and say hi, but I ran out of time and now she's already boarded."

"But . . . we're not going to Iowa. We're headed to North Carolina."

"North Carolina? What, like Raleigh?"

"That's my stop, but I heard her mention something about Visitation."

Fingers tightened on the sleeve of his coat. "Never heard of it."

Pulling away, he glanced out to the waiting area and saw that the line to board was just about gone. "It's a little town. The guy with her is a preacher of some sort.

That's all I know." He tugged on his arm. "Look, I gotta go."

"Oh, yeah, sure thing." Grubby fingers smoothed his sleeve, and he got another vile, yellow grin. "You take care, now. And since that wasn't Valerie . . . well, no need to mention that I was admiring her or anything."

"Trust me. The two with her would not like to hear it." He gave a hasty farewell and trotted to the attendant, who took his boarding pass. Once on the plane, he had to pass the woman again to gain his seat. After one quick peek, he kept his eyes on the aisle.

Hell, no — he wouldn't mention his conversation in the john. The last thing he wanted was a run-in with that group. The woman might be sweet, about the sweetest thing he'd seen in his lifetime, but the two with her were all the discouragement any guy needed.

Cyn strolled across the barn to the spacious stalls where Satin and Silver Bells were kept. Even before she reached them, the horses recognized her tread and greeted her by throwing back their heads and neighing.

"You're both too clever," Cyn accused,

and stopped in the middle of the stalls to greet her friends. She'd been back two days now, and still the horses celebrated her every visit as if she'd been gone a month instead of two days.

Silver Bells butted her head into Cyn's shoulder, almost knocking her over.

"Yeah, I'm happy to see you, too!" Cyn laughed and stroked the horse's muzzle.

Jealous, Satin stretched out her neck to lip Cyn's hair.

"Now stop that. I didn't have time to braid it." She freed her hair and stepped up close to Satin, charmed, as always, by the horses' antics.

Since her return from Benworth, she hadn't had too many reasons to smile. It seemed she and Bruce had done nothing but argue. He was overprotective to the point that he'd expected her to stay with him. In his house, and maybe even in his bed.

He might have lost all sense, but Cyn hadn't. Bruce was a preacher, and that meant he couldn't just move a woman in and pretend the town would understand. Bruce knew it was true, and frustration made him ridiculous.

At least, she assumed that was the reason for his absurd suggestion that she stay with someone else. As if Shay or Luna, regardless of their claims, wanted her underfoot. She was responsible for herself, not a kid who still needed protection.

And so she returned to the loft and her own lonely bed.

It was only right.

Still, she spent more time thinking of Bruce than sleeping. Odd, how quickly she'd gotten used to having him near. His body was big and hard, warm and comforting. With him, she slept in peace.

But she couldn't ignore the difference in their outlooks. Even while Bruce seemed to enjoy their time together, he held back from her, unwilling to go all the way because he saw that as a sin. He did as much as his moral conscience would allow, but for Cyn, it wasn't enough.

How much longer could she keep from pushing him? How much longer before she convinced him to do things he wasn't comfortable with?

She wanted to be a better person, and she'd start by honoring his decisions.

Unfortunately, she could only do that by staying away from him.

It hurt to know the truth, and Cyn sought to distract herself with the horses. "You want out to run, don't you? But I can't ride you both by myself and I'm not going to ask Bruce over. We'll just have to make do without him. I know, it won't be easy, but let's try. Maybe I can take turns riding you. What do you think of that idea?"

"I think it'd be better if we took them out together."

Cyn jerked around. She'd thought she was alone, or she wouldn't have been chatting with animals as if they understood her every word.

Julie Rose stood there, amazingly enough in slacks and flat shoes instead of a ladylike dress. Her shoulder-length hair wasn't pinned up as usual, but instead had been pulled into a loose ponytail.

It was the first time Cyn had ever seen her dressed so casually and the shock kept her tongue-tied for only a moment. "Julie. What are you doing here?" That sounded rude even to Cyn, and she made a face. "Sorry. Hi. You took me by surprise. I wasn't expecting anyone."

"I know. I hope you don't mind if I visit a bit." Smiling in that gentle, understanding way of hers, Julie approached Satin. "What a beautiful lady you are."

That won points with Cyn. "They're both gorgeous, aren't they?"

"Very." Unlike Cyn, Julie seemed to know exactly how to handle the animals. "I used to ride a lot before last summer. I miss it."

"You have horses?"

"Yes. My father kept a stable and I used to ride at least weekly, but since his passing" — she shook her head — "things aren't the same. My uncle is very different from my father. He has strange notions about what's ladylike and what isn't."

Fascinated, Cyn leaned on the stall door. "He objects to you riding?"

"No. He objects to me riding with the hands." Suddenly Julie's brown eyes twinkled and she laughed. "There were rumors of me having a torrid affair with Angelo, the trainer. Can you imagine?"

No, Cyn couldn't imagine Julie having an affair with anyone. Well, except maybe Bruce, because Julie, with her quiet grace and teacher's backbone, was far better suited to Bruce than Cyn would ever be. "Did you?"

"No." Julie didn't take offense at the question. "Angelo is only twenty-two, built like a Greek God, and I'm sure, very popular with the ladies. His only interest in me was friendship, brought about by our mutual love of the horses.

Still, it was fun while it lasted."

"What was?"

"Being thought of as a siren." Julie reached out to Silver Bells. "My uncle hated it, though, especially when it hit the papers and I wouldn't deny it."

Cyn's eyes widened. "Why would the papers care if you had an affair?"

"You don't know? I'm an heiress." She wrinkled her nose, looking very human, even vulnerable, for a blink of the eyes. "Daddy left me quite well off, but with my uncle in charge of my trust . . . well, I just don't care. In the big scheme of things, money means very little."

Spoken as only the rich could speak. To those without money, it meant a lot. But at the same time, it was kind of nice to forget her own problems for a time while chatting with Julie. "You broke things off with your fiancé?"

"He was handpicked by my uncle. And we got along well, or at least I thought so. I loved him, but I wasn't in love with him. Do you understand?"

Cyn shrugged. "I guess so." Other than Bruce, she'd never really felt love, so maybe the little nuances escaped her.

"Then I discovered that he had a paramour."

Cyn's eyebrows shot up. "Paramour? You mean he was cheating on you?"

"Yes. He promised it wouldn't happen again."

Cyn snorted.

"That was my reaction exactly! A cheater cheats, period. But my uncle thought I should forgive, I disagreed, and once again we're on bad terms." Julie quit stroking the horse to give Cyn all her attention. "I'm ashamed to say that I dumped my worries on Bruce."

"Hey, Bruce loves that kind of thing. He probably enjoyed handing out the advice."

"He was an enormous help." Julie straightened. "But enough of that. Would you like to ride? I'll confess, I'm hoping you'll agree. It's a beautiful day and now that I've left my fiancé and decided to leave my home, too, I'm happy, and a ride in the fresh air is the perfect way to enjoy my new freedom."

Cyn's head began to reel. "You left your home?"

"I've yet to tell my uncle, but yes, I've decided to relocate to Visitation. I've spent quit a bit of time subbing here, working specifically with some of the children who are struggling or falling behind. I've found it to be so . . . rewarding. I always wanted to make a difference to children, not just accept astronomical pay for babysitting, which is what my former position amounted to. Here, in Visitation, I've made a difference. I can feel it."

When she talked about kids, Julie got downright passionate. "Will your uncle have a fit?"

"Oh, to be sure. I imagine he'll cut off my funds first thing." Julie looked delighted by that possibility. "I can't wait to see his face when I tell him I don't care. He can take the money and stuff it."

Startled by that colorful sentiment, Cyn laughed.

Julie lifted her face to the sun and held out her arms. "I'm twenty-nine years old, and finally, I'll be free."

When she smiled like that, Cyn thought, Julie really was pretty. The sun glinted on her golden brown eyelashes, and the warmth of the day had brought fresh color to her pale complexion. Huh. The idea of Julie being attractive was almost as much of a surprise as her wearing slacks.

But one thing was certain — Julie truly cared about kids. And just that easily, Cyn decided she liked Julie Rose after all. "You any good at saddling up?" Cyn hadn't completely gotten the hang of it yet, and she usually had Bruce to help out.

Julie laughed. "Angelo taught me. I know what to do, but if we're using Western saddles, I may need help lifting the thing. I'm not exactly muscle-bound."

"All right, then." Cyn led the way to the tack room. "I'm not so great at riding yet, but I suppose I can keep from falling off."

Together, the two women prepared the horses, one at a time. They brushed Satin, then put on the saddle pad, the saddle itself, which probably weighed forty pounds, and finally the bridle. Silver Bells was next, and it took them a total of twenty minutes to prepare both horses.

It was indeed a chore, but they talked and laughed the entire time. It was odd, Cyn decided, but she was actually more at ease with stuffy, prim Julie than with Shay or Luna.

Shay was nice, nice enough that at times she seemed unreal. Nice enough that she constantly tried to give Cyn a handout. Be it work or contacts or whatever, Shay wanted to help, and it nettled Cyn that she was a person in need of assistance. She understood Shay's motives, and appreciated them, but she would rather have just been a friend, not a person who stood out as less than equal.

Luna was lovely, too, very warm and friendly. But she went out of her way to show understanding, to include Cyn. And once again, Cyn felt the difference, how she didn't quite measure up.

Julie was just Julie. She had no airs, said just what she thought, and she, like Cyn, was single.

As the horses trotted into the far pasture, Cyn ventured a touchy topic. "So. You and Bruce got something going on?"

The laugh erupted from Julie. "Oh, please. He's wildly infatuated with you. We're friends, and I love him as such. I want him happy. But we're not involved *that* way."

"You think Bruce is *un*happy?"

"Not at all. Bruce can certainly handle his own business, as I'm sure you can. I only meant that I hope you feel the same as he does. You'd make a lovely couple."

Cyn smirked. "Our backgrounds stretch the great divide."

"Opposites attract? But no, that wouldn't be correct, because you're really very similar."

"Wait," Cyn teased, "let me clean out my ears. I could've sworn you just said Bruce and I were alike."

Julie grinned. "Indeed. Both of you are

refreshing and ready with a smile, very open. I don't know if that's a good thing or not." She shrugged. "Love is a tricky business, I'm finding. Romantic love, anyway. Not that I'd know for sure since I've never been in love that way."

They continued on in silence for a time before Julie said, "Forgive my curiosity, but do you love him?"

Cyn chewed her lip, tried to work up some annoyance for Julie's prodding, but in the end, she felt like confessing. "Yeah."

"I thought so."

Cyn groaned. "But I shouldn't, and don't you dare tell him."

"I resent being labeled a tattletale."

Since Julie didn't really sound peeved, Cyn let that go. "Bruce is . . . he's one of the good guys, when I didn't think good guys existed."

"Why would you think they didn't?"

Cyn couldn't quite bring herself to burden Julie with her truths. "Colorful background?"

"I see." Julie nodded as if in complete understanding. "I'm sorry."

"It's done and over — no biggie."

"Is it? I mean, Bruce did hint, rather heavily, that I come visit you today. I had the feeling he didn't want you to be alone for some reason. And since I know you're not given to melodrama, he must be worried for your safety, not your frame of mind."

Cyn could do no more than stare at her. "You're scary."

"I listen when people talk, that's all. At first, I thought Bruce suggested it for my benefit, which suited me just fine. I have missed riding. But the more I thought about it . . . if I'm intruding, you have my apologies."

Cyn barely kept her seat on Satin's back. "Bruce really told you to come here?"

Shaking her head, Julie said, "It was as much what he didn't say as what he did. He asked if I was busy, and when I wasn't, he told me you'd be home alone all morning and that you enjoyed riding. And so here I am."

"What the hell does he think you can do that I can't?"

"I believe Bruce thinks it's a matter of safety in numbers."

Cyn recalled how Shay and Luna had stopped by yesterday, trying to talk her into shopping with them. Had Bruce twisted their arms?

Luckily, she'd already started a complete cleaning of the stalls and was knee-deep in manure, so she'd declined. She didn't want her company forced on anyone.

Later, Bruce had stopped by, too, as had Joe and Bryan. Damn him, how many babysitters did he think she needed?

"Should I go?" Julie asked. "Truly, I didn't realize it'd be a problem."

"No, it's not," Cyn said through her teeth. It wasn't Julie's fault Bruce had gone overboard.

When Satin sidestepped, Cyn made herself calm. "No problem at all. I'll just strangle Bruce later."

"I doubt you want to do that," Julie said, taking her literally. "Besides, it wouldn't be easy. His neck looks pretty thick."

"His head is thick, too."

Julie burst out laughing again. "See? You and Bruce are perfect. Most of the women who meet him are awed by him. He is a preacher, after all."

"And a hunk."

"There is that. But it takes second place to his calling, from what I can tell. Even the most down-to-earth women are tight-lipped and prissy when Bruce is in the room. But you . . . you just treat him like a man."

"That's because he *is* a man."

Julie grinned knowingly. "You see? He

has to love that attitude of yours."

"I worry about it," Cyn said. "I'd like to curb my tongue around him, but I haven't really had to do that in way too long." As an aside, she admitted, "I've been on my own since I was seventeen."

"Goodness!" Julie stared at her, then confessed back, "I've never been on my own." Her eyes brightened. "Until now."

"It's not all it's cracked up to be."

"You were a child, so your experiences would be far different from mine." Julie led her horse around a tall walnut tree, turning back toward the barn. Cyn followed.

"You're not a child any more, though. You're a young lady and Bruce watches you with so much . . . greed. It's wonderful to see. Someday, I hope a man looks at me that way."

Greed. That sounded kinda nice.

"Race you."

Drawn from her thoughts, Cyn barely had time to agree to the challenge when Julie nudged her mount into a gallop. They were a good distance from the barn, and the horses loved the chance to run full out.

They were both laughing like loons, and Cyn barely maintained her seat as they rounded the barn and pulled the horses up. She was winded, her heart raced, and she felt energized.

After dismounting, Julie said, "That was wonderful. I had so much fun."

Even with the annoying news of Bruce's interference, Cyn had to admit she'd had fun, too. "Come by anytime. The horses love it."

They walked the horses around the area for a few minutes to let them cool down, then, because it was a hot day, they treated them both to a brief shower with the hose.

Julie scraped off the excess water and sweat with a sweat scraper and Cyn picked the hooves to rid the animals of mud and stones. One more brushing, and the horses were turned loose in the pasture to laze in the sun. The women headed back for the barn and Cyn heard herself say, "You want to come up for some coffee or something?"

"Thank you, I'd love that."

They reached the interior ladder and headed up. The outside stairs might have been more convenient, but neither woman minded using the ladder. It was another way that they were in accord.

Julie reached the top rung first, and noticed the damage. "Oh my." She pulled herself up and waited for Cyn.

"What is it?" Cyn hoisted herself to the

loft floor and followed Julie's line of vision. She stared at the open door to her apartment. Through it, she could see that her bed had been trashed and clothes were strewn everywhere.

Julie touched her arm. "You're not this messy, are you?"

"No."

"I didn't think so."

Cyn took in the damage. Her books were destroyed. Mary's beautiful quilt was ripped. And her panty drawer had been pulled out onto the floor.

Someone had been in the loft. *Her* loft.

She pressed a hand to her middle, over the sick knot of dread twisting her stomach.

Already, Palmer Oaks had found her.

Now what?

Chapter Eleven

Ever the reasonable, responsible sort, Julie had made numerous phone calls before Cyn could stop her. Now there was so much confusion in her tiny living space, Cyn couldn't hear herself think. Bruce sat with her on the narrow, twin-size bed, and she knew he wasn't about to budge.

Both Bryan and Joe were perusing what was left of her books, which made her hot with humiliation and stiff with indignation. Deputy Scott Royal was on his phone, issuing orders, and Mary . . . poor Mary looked ill. The sanctity of her home had been invaded — thanks to Cyn. Her grandmother's beautiful quilt was destroyed — thanks to Cyn.

God, she was tired of it all.

"Anything missing?" Scott asked.

Cyn closed her eyes, but Julie answered for her. "Quite a few of her underthings have been taken."

Bruce remained silent, but Bryan said, "Her underthings?"

"Panties?" Joe asked at almost the same time.

"That's right." Julie pointed out the overturned drawer. "Cyn said this is where she kept them, but those, and a few of her bras, are gone."

Scott's jaw locked. "Anything else? Anything of value?"

"I don't have anything of value."

"Except yourself," Bruce told her quietly. "And, thank God, you were off riding with Julie when this happened."

They'd only been gone an hour or so. How had Palmer known Mary wasn't home? How did he even know where Cyn was? Like a damn ghost, she couldn't be rid of him, which meant she couldn't stay.

"I'm leaving," Cyn said to the room at large.

Bruce nodded. "Yes, you are."

Without a doubt, Cyn knew they were speaking of two different things. No way would Bruce want her off on her own again. She knew him too well for that.

One deep breath later, Cyn pushed to her feet and gave a grim smile to one and all. "I don't want to hear any arguments. I know you're all very kind people, but I'm outta here. This is more than I want to deal with, and if I'm gone, well then, old Palmer can't find me. It's a win-win situation."

Strangely enough, rather than arguing

with her as she'd expected, or even showing concern, everyone looked at Bruce.

Bruce stood, too. "Mary, I'm very sorry."

Mary waved that away. "I agree with Cyn. I can't abide a threat to her or my animals. The alarm is only activated in the evening. I never once thought of anyone trying to vandalize me in the bright light of day."

It wasn't about vandalism, but Cyn didn't want Mary to know that. She looked shaken enough already.

"From now on," Scott told Mary after disconnecting the phone, "leave the alarm on at all times. Just get used to shutting it down when you check the horses or let them out."

"Of course." Mary picked up the quilt, and gave Cyn a weak smile. "I think it can be repaired, so don't you worry. I'll go work on that now." Her hands were shaking. "If someone could let me know what you all decide . . . ?"

Bruce nodded. "I'll be up to talk to you in a little bit."

"Thank you." Mary left with Julie at her side.

Scott hung up the phone and put his

hands on his hips. Cyn could understand the appeal of a man in uniform, but right now, Scott just looked very imposing and stern.

"Detective Orsen says she's closing in on Palmer's trail. He was in Putnamville, a low-to-medium-security men's prison in western Indiana. They've got a huge over-crowding problem, so that might've played in with his early release. Anyone who's not considered an imminent danger to the community can complete some rehabilitation therapy and get out on parole. Thing is, he hasn't seen his parole officer in a month. Last they can figure, he was on his way to Tennessee, or so the rumors go. They haven't located him yet."

"I had some people working on it," Bryan said, still holding Cyn's book, *The Road to Recovery: After Child Abuse*, dangling from his hand. "A week ago, he was spotted in Memphis, then a few days later, in Knoxville."

Joe cursed softly. "A clear trail leading to North Carolina."

"It leads here," Cyn said. "This was Palmer, I know it. And that's why I can't stay."

"You sure as hell can't stay here alone in the loft," Bryan agreed.

Even men weren't that obtuse; Cyn knew they deliberately weren't getting it. "Listen up, fellas."

They all looked at her with various displays of macho disgruntlement and bull-headed determination.

"I'm packing what's left of my stuff. Closing out my savings account. And I'm skipping town. Today."

Again, the men looked at Bruce, and Bruce shook his head.

It made Cyn so furious, she nearly shouted, "*Get out.* All of you."

As if she hadn't given an order, as if she hadn't spoken at all, Bryan held up the book. "Why do you have this?"

Hiding her hurt with sneering derision, Cyn laughed. "Oh, you mean Bruce didn't tell you all about that while he was giving you your schedule?"

"What schedule?" Joe asked.

"The one that assigned you each times to watch out for me."

Joe straightened to his full, impressive height and crossed massive arms over his chest. "I don't take assignments from anyone, little girl, so get that out of your head."

Cyn wasn't put off by his aggressive stance. She crossed her arms, too, and leaned into his space. "You're telling me your visit yesterday had nothing to do with Bruce?"

"It had everything to do with Bruce. He was worried about you, and I didn't want him to be. So, I stopped by to check on you. End of story."

Oh, hell. Cyn swallowed down a wave of embarrassment. "And you?" she asked Bryan.

He shrugged, grinned at her. "Since you're so headstrong and insist on staying alone, Joe and I wanted to see how secure this place is. And it's not secure, not in any way."

"I figured that out, thanks."

"Bruce is my brother," Bryan continued, paying no mind to her sarcasm. "I don't want him suffering sleepless nights fretting over you."

Scott laughed. "You're all a bunch of women." But when he looked at Cyn again, all that stern intention was back, amplified by the soft command of his tone. "Only an idiot would go off alone. And Cyn, you're not an idiot." He took the book from Bryan and waved it under her nose. "You want some closure with this bastard? Running won't do it. You're going to have to stay put and let me handle it."

Bryan nodded. "That's right. We'll handle it."

Scott rolled his eyes and turned on Bryan. "I said *me,* not you. I'm the law, and in case you've forgotten — you're *not.*"

Joe looked at Bryan with a long face. "He doesn't want us to have any fun, does he?"

Scott's hair practically stood on end. "Joe . . ."

Joe slapped Scott on the back. "Accept your fate, bud. You're going to need our help. The sheriff sure as hell isn't any backup, and besides, Alyx is coming to visit again so I have a feeling you'll have your hands full."

Cyn watched in amazement as Scott blanched at the mention of Joe's sister. "Why's she coming this time?"

"Because I'm going to invite her." Then, in the blink of an eye, Joe managed to look somehow caring and concerned, instead of wickedly evil. "Now Cyn, what's with the books?"

Luckily, Bruce took pity on her. "All of you, out."

Scott all but growled, "Excuse me, but I am the damn deputy and I'm not done investigating."

Bruce shrugged, so grim and sober that he didn't look like the same man Cyn knew and loved. "Fine, then we'll go."

"Where to?" Bryan wanted to know, almost swelling with protectiveness.

"Not far," Bruce promised. His eyes were the darkest brown, full of intensity, his mouth flat. "I have some things to explain to Cyn, and a very important question to put to her, and we don't need an audience."

Oh, hell. Cyn didn't want to go with him. He looked angry and inflexible, not peaceful and compassionate. She'd rather face the other three, unpleasant as they were than be alone with Bruce in her current frame of mind.

But when she looked at Joe, ready to provoke him so she could continue her argument, he just grinned and elbowed Bryan, who also appeared very pleased.

Bryan said, "Do me proud now, you hear?"

What in the world were they blathering on about?

Bruce gave his brother a negligent wave. "Come on, honey." Holding tight to Cyn's hand, he tugged her out of the apartment and to the far end of the loft, where it still served for hay storage. He sat her on a bale, stared down at her, and then, to her surprise, he cupped her face and bent to kiss her.

Joe sat on the side of the bed the second

they were gone. Head in his hands, fingers knotted in his hair, he growled, "Jesus, do you believe this shit?"

Bryan had already started pacing. With Cyn out of the room, he didn't have to hide his rage any longer. He threw the book onto the bed beside Joe. "Fucking bastard. God, how I'd love to get my hands on him."

Scott worked his jaw. "Child abuse. I'd met her, spoken with her, but I hadn't realized . . ."

"And he took her panties," Joe pointed out. "Sick fuck isn't exactly subtle about his plans, is he?"

"He's not getting anywhere near her," Bryan vowed.

"No," Scott agreed. "Hopefully we'll get some prints off the door where he entered, but the rest of this . . . it's just so damn hard to get a good, clean print."

Joe pushed to his feet. "Detective Orsen had the same problem at the murder scene. She checked the note he left, the one where he forged Cyn's name, but there weren't any clean prints. He must've been wearing gloves."

"Was probably wearing them here, too, then," Scott said in disgust.

They were all brooding in impotent

anger when Cyn let out a shrill screech.

No one was alarmed. Joe chuckled. "I reckon he asked her, huh?"

Bryan was so pleased, he couldn't stop smiling. "She's had him running in circles. It's about time he put an end to it." He nodded in satisfaction. "Marrying her is the only thing he can do, since he wants to keep her close."

Scott's mouth tipped up on the left side. "She doesn't sound the least bit happy about it."

"Bruce'll convince her," Bryan said. "After all, he *is* my brother."

And Joe, tongue in cheek, shook his head and said, "Related to you. Poor bastard."

Bruce tried not to let her horrified expression get to him. "The sooner, the better, Cyn."

Eyes wide, face pale, she shook her head again. "No. No way."

"You're refusing my proposal?"

She stared at him, dumbfounded, then started to stand. Bruce gently pressed her back into her seat. "Someone is after you. You can't stay here alone and you know it. I can only keep you safe if you're with me, all the time, definitely at night. And I can only make that work if you marry me." She shook her head, prompting him to sigh. "Talk to me, Cyn."

She tried, nothing came out, and she swallowed before giving it another attempt. "You can't . . . can't want to marry me."

Bruce straightened to his full height and crossed his arms over his chest. "Why not?"

"Because . . . because . . ."

It wasn't fair, but as a desperate man, he couldn't be fair. He *had* to keep her safe from Palmer Oaks. "You don't love me?"

She drew back as if slapped.

"You can tell me if you don't." Bruce sat beside her and clasped her hand in his. "Have I ever talked to you about my mother? How she hated being a preacher's wife? No? Well, Dad raised Bryan and me on his own. You see, my mother met my dad when he was in the service, and she thought they'd travel a lot, see the world."

Little by little, Cyn thawed from her shock. "When did he become a preacher?"

"I don't know exactly, but he was still young. When he got the calling, left the military, and became a preacher."

"That's a big change of careers."

"Yes, it is, and my mother hated it. Dad's congregation supplied our house, so it was, by necessity, modest. We lived on a tight budget. But I was happy. Bryan was happy. We had a good life."

"Even without your mother?"

Bruce shrugged. "Truthfully, I can't recall ever really missing her. Dad gave us everything we needed."

"Do you see her still?"

He shook his head. "She'd never kept in touch, so I feel like I never really knew her." He lifted one shoulder. "She passed away with cancer. We didn't even find out until months after the funeral. No one notified us."

"Don't compare me with her, Bruce."

He smiled to himself. He'd take Cyn full of gumption, over Cyn shell-shocked and silent, any day. "Oh? So you don't mind my small house or my tight budget or the fact that I'm staying in Visitation? You don't find me . . . less than you've expected or wanted in a husband? Do I measure up?"

Cyn punched him in the arm, not hard enough to hurt, but enough to make her point. "You know none of that has anything to do with it. It's not about you."

"So it's Bryan? He is the touted black sheep in the family, I can't deny that, but basically he's harmless and Shay keeps him in line."

She gave him a leery look. "I like your brother a lot."

"You'll like Dad, too."

Disgruntled, she muttered, "Probably."

"Then marry me."

She covered her face with her hands. "You feel sorry for me."

Bruce appreciated the way she always spilled the truth, just throwing it out there so he could deal with it. It beat guessing games anytime. "True. There are times when my heart breaks thinking about what you went through as a child, and what you must be going through now. If I could, I'd spare you, but I can't. This is something we have to deal with."

"I hate pity."

"Then marry me, because I'll pity myself a lot if you leave and I never get to see you again."

Her disbelieving laugh dwindled into a rumbling growl. "We're not suited to each other! It's like . . . like you were born in a church with a star shining down on you, and I was born . . . I dunno. Under a rock or something."

"Cyn." He wanted to remonstrate with her, but she appeared so dejected with her shoulders slumped, her head in her hands, that he couldn't bring himself to do it.

"Are you talking to me or your hands?"

It took some coaxing, but she finally raised her face to see him. Her shoulders went back, her chin, for once, lifted. She met his gaze squarely. "I do love you, Bruce."

His heart sang, his knees went weak. He grinned so hugely that it hurt. "A marvelous start."

She put her small hand on his chest, over his heart. "I don't want you at risk just because of me."

God love her, she was so sweet, and so caring. He summoned up a look of insult. "Understand, Cyn. I'm a peaceful man. I'm a man who believes in giving second chances and showing understanding whenever possible." He lifted her hand and kissed her knuckles. "But I'm also a man who believes in protecting my own, and you're mine now."

She tried to pull back. Bruce wasn't about to let her.

"If Palmer comes near you, if he so much as looks at you, I'll take him apart."

Her eyes widened comically.

"Don't doubt it." Bruce held her gaze, making sure there were no misunderstandings. He said it, and he meant it. "Being a man of God doesn't make me a weakling, doesn't make me too stupid to know how to protect you."

"I never said . . ."

"I've been a preacher for years. But I've been a man, and Bryan's brother, all my life. I'm not incapable of beating a man to the ground if it becomes necessary."

Cyn's mouth opened, closed, and then she burst out laughing. "Amazing, incredible Bruce." She wiped tears of sadness, and of mirth, from her eyes. "What am I going to do with you?"

"I have a suggestion. First, say yes. Then marry me and move in with me, make love with me every night, give me a few babies, and grow old with me."

Her expression sobered, and she closed her eyes. "I want that more than I've ever wanted anything."

Bruce didn't intend to give her time to rethink it, to list all the ways she considered it an unfair union. She was the one woman for him, and he'd make her realize it. "Great. Then I'll take that as a yes."

"But . . . !"

He yelled out, "She said yes," and all three men clomped out of the apartment and came across the loft toward them, issuing congratulations, hugging Cyn, pounding on Bruce.

"See," Joe said. "Alyx does have a reason to visit. A wedding."

Scott groaned.

Cyn turned her face into Bruce's chest and just hid. He knew she was hiding, and she knew that he knew. Still he just held her close with one arm while accepting accolades and handshakes with the other. She was so small and soft, so utterly female, and she'd never had the luxury of just enjoying life. He'd give her that luxury, and so much more. He'd give her respect and caring and pleasure.

He'd make her happy — with herself, and with him.

He had rushed her, after all, but this time, neither of them had a choice. Her safety was at stake, and Bruce would do whatever was necessary to make sure the ugliness left her life.

Everyone ended up at Joe's for dinner. Luna was in her element, breezing in and out of the kitchen, serving everyone in the dining room, and somehow making the event very casual and warm. Willow had already left the table to do homework, and Austin had run off to watch television.

They were terrific kids, well loved, full of energy, and not afraid of making a mistake

— or what the repercussions would be if they did. Everyone at the table treated them with . . . respect. It seemed an odd sentiment to apply to children, but it was true. People listened to them, asked their opinions, and teased them with good-natured affection. And Willow and Austin felt safe to tease back.

At one point, Willow had interrupted the adults to ask a question. Austin had spilled his milk. And no one went ballistic. No one yelled or . . . hit.

If Cyn ever had kids, she'd want them to feel just as secure.

And then it hit her like a ton of bricks. She might. As a married woman, it'd be possible to have babies, just as Bruce had said.

Kids. With Bruce. Cyn's heart felt so full and heavy it almost hurt. He was marrying her for all the wrong reasons. She had determined not to be selfish anymore, but just this one time, just once more, she couldn't deny herself.

She was so buried in deep, disturbing thought, she barely kept up with the conversations flowing around her. Bruce kept smiling at her as if he'd won the damn lottery, which made no sense at all. She looked at him, at his strong profile, at the integrity of his face and the caring in his brown eyes, and she wanted to burst into tears.

Shay let out a loud laugh. "Yoohoo, Cyn? He'll be yours soon enough, honey, but we need to make arrangements first. Stop daydreaming and give us permission to help before I pop."

Bruce turned his head and smiled at her. Again. He leaned close, keeping her attention trapped in his acceptance, his apparent happiness over the progression of events. "Luna and Shay would like to give us a hand with this wedding business. What do you say?"

Ugh. She looked at both women, and damn it, they looked happy, too. She was being a complete pill, and she had to stop. She also had to accept their help because she didn't know squat about organizing a wedding.

She cleared her throat while toying with her fork. "Shay, you said you and Bryan got married here, at the lake?"

"Yes, and it was beautiful."

Luna jumped in before Cyn could ask. "We'd love it if you had the ceremony here. The weather is perfect and I'm sure we have a free weekend sometime soon."

"Soon?" Cyn tried to sound enthusiastic.

"The sooner the better," Bruce told her

with such a look of naked hunger, she felt a slow heat unfurl in her belly. One good thing would come of marriage: he couldn't deny her anymore.

His brother reached across the table to punch Bruce in the shoulder. "She might want a big wedding, you know, and that does take time."

Bruce frowned. "Do you?"

God, no. She shook her head. "As small as possible, please."

"Is there anyone you'd like to invite?"

She half laughed, saw everyone looking at her, and shook her head. "No." She had no friends, no family.

Bruce looked around the table. "Just about everyone I want to attend is here, except Dad, Scott, and Alyx, so we'll have to check with them. But are the rest of you free?"

A round of affirmations followed.

"There you go." Bruce took Cyn's hand. "Do you have a preference on a date?"

She forced a smile that felt more like a grimace. "Um, well, we'll need time to do . . . stuff, right? I mean, aren't there required blood tests or something?"

Joe shook his head. "As a newly married man, I can assure you not much is needed in North Carolina."

"Just ID," Bryan explained. "Like a driver's license or a birth certificate."

Bruce said, "We have both."

"And forty bucks for the certificate," Joe added. "There's no waiting period, no age requirement, no tests or proof of residency."

Bryan bobbed his eyebrows. "They make it easy to get hitched here."

Luna jumped up from the table. "Let me grab the schedule and I'll tell you what we have open."

Wide eyes fraught with uncertainty, Cyn waited until Luna returned with a triumphant smile. "This coming weekend is the annual fishing competition. We'll be swamped. But the next Sunday is free. We could do an afternoon affair, maybe right after church service. What do you think?"

Everyone stared at Cyn. "Uh . . . great."

Bruce hugged her. "We need to find you a dress."

Agog, Cyn said, "I don't need —"

Shay protested. "No way, Bruce! You're not supposed to see her gown before the wedding. Luna and I can take her shopping." She turned to Cyn. "That is, if you don't mind."

They were all so nice, so generous. She nodded. "Thanks. Sounds like fun."

Bryan said, "Pick a day, ladies, and I'll drive you."

When Luna started to object, Joe said quietly, "No, honey. You can't go off on your own. Remember the threat."

Yeah, can't forget that. It was the whole reason for the wedding. But Cyn only thought it, she didn't say it out loud. Bruce was marrying her, everyone appeared thrilled with the idea, and she was through moping.

She straightened in her seat and accepted Bryan's offer. "That'd be great. You can carry packages — like our own personal mule."

Rather than take offense, Bryan nodded. "Exactly."

Shay clapped her hands together. "We'll have everything organized in no time at all."

Bryan raised his glass in a toast. "To happy-ever-after."

Cyn did smile then. Damn, if it wasn't for Palmer forcing it all, she really would be the happiest woman in the world. And who said she couldn't make it work? She'd molded her life however necessary, and somehow, she'd mold this into the happy-ever-after Bryan had just predicted.

She lifted her glass. "Hear, hear."

* * *

The next few days went by in a whirlwind. Cyn was installed in Bryan and Shay's guest room until the day of the wedding. She hated to impose, but like a kid, Shay was excited to have company. She kept Cyn up late with girl talk until Bryan would take Shay off to bed. It wasn't tough to figure out why Bryan refused to sleep alone. The heat in his eyes and the flush on Shay's cheeks always told the story.

Cyn only hoped that Bruce would want her as much. So far, he'd called a halt before they actually made love. She didn't know what to think of that, or why he denied himself. Didn't he want her? Was he so damn giving that he'd only been thinking of her, while disregarding his own needs?

Surely once they married, he'd quit his bedroom games. If he didn't, she just might resort to raping him.

With Bryan playing watchdog, they drove into the city to shop. Shay tried to steer her toward one of the more expensive boutiques, but Cyn won out, and the ladies landed in an upscale secondhand shop.

Cyn wasn't really surprised that Shay was as comfortable with used clothing as she was with designer duds. Luna kept pulling outrageous pieces off the rack, and Shay kept gravitating to the more extravagant gowns.

Cyn was pushed and prodded into trying on at least a dozen dresses before she found "the one." It was simply beautiful, a satin halter with beaded lace appliqués, a tulle skirt, and a corset bodice that made her waist look tiny and showed off her cleavage in what Shay termed a *tasteful tease*.

Admiring the dress from every angle, Cyn did a circle in front of the mirror before turning back to her audience. She bit her lip, waited — until Shay and Luna sighed their approval.

"Stunning." Luna looked near tears. "It doesn't even need to be altered."

"You look like Snow White with your dark hair and pale eyes."

Luna agreed. "Cyn, you have to get this dress. It's prefect for you."

Cyn peeked at the price tag, saw Shay ready to offer, and said quickly, "I'll take it."

It was too expensive, but she could afford this one extravagance for such a life-altering occasion. With the other women encouraging her, she also bought a beautiful rhinestone-and-pearl bun wrap made to look like flowers and vines in her hair. She didn't want a veil, but the delicate headpiece was too beautiful to resist.

By the time they found nylons and a garter, a bracelet and earrings, Cyn felt like a princess. And the fact that they'd accomplished it all in one day left Luna and Shay boggled. They probably didn't realize that for Cyn, shopping was a special treat and she wasn't hard to please. Like a kid in a candy store for the first time, everything looked good to her.

Bryan was a sport, getting them all ice cream that afternoon when they took a break, and only yawning a few times while they also picked out shoes.

Halfway through the day, while they were choosing a few simple flower arrangements, Cyn worked up her nerve to broach a touchy subject. "Shay? Luna?"

Shay gave up her scrutiny of the white sweetheart roses and Luna quit fingering the long ribbons that'd make up Cyn's bouquet. Cyn cleared her throat. "You know my mother is gone."

Sympathy welled up in suffocating proportions and Cyn dodged the hugs that started her way.

"The thing is," she said quickly, turning her back so she wouldn't see their pity, "I don't have any close female friends, either."

Shay took umbrage at that. "You have us."

"Yeah," Luna seconded. "And last time I looked, I wasn't chopped liver."

They were nuts, and fun. Cyn fought off tears. Damn, getting married was making her emotional. "True. And Julie's cool, too."

"Cool?" Luna smiled. "If you say so. I like her. I respect her. But I never thought of her as cool."

Cyn hadn't, either, until they'd spent the morning together. Julie was one of those ladies who had hidden depth. "The thing is, I don't have a special friend, you know, the type you ask to do special things."

Both ladies stared at her, making Cyn want to shrivel. She was so bad at this stuff. But then, she'd never had any practice. Making friends was harder than she'd realized.

She cleared her throat again. "I'm going to ask Julie, too, and I hope she says yes, but . . . would you two mind standing up with her as matrons of honor or whatever the heck it's called? I know that's not how it's really done, but then, this isn't a big, fancy event and I just thought if you all wouldn't mind —"

Cyn got snatched into the tight group hug she'd avoided only moments before, along with some shrill girl shrieks and a little dancing and jiggling and carrying on.

Never in her life had Cyn done the "girl" thing, and she thought it was pretty damn silly. Everyone in the florist shop was staring at them, and sort of smiling in tolerance.

Shay said, "I'd love to!"

And Luna added, "Me, too! And I know Julie will be thrilled."

And then, before she knew it, Cyn found herself bouncing with them, laughing, too, full of excitement — until Bryan came barreling around the corner with muscles tensed and murder in his eyes.

He pulled up short when he saw the women all squeezed together and going in circles and he rolled his eyes. Lips tight, he pointed a finger at Shay, started to speak, tried again, and finally drew a deep breath instead. "Okay, so no one is attacking you?"

Biting back a grin, Shay lifted her shoulders in apology. "No."

"This is" — he flapped a hand at them — "girl stuff?"

Luna raised her chin. "That's right. And

you're not a girl, so go away."

He narrowed his eyes, shook his head, and said something too low for the women to hear. With a nod to Cyn, he groused, "Sorry for the interruption." He stalked off, mumbling to himself, and Luna, with one quick look at Shay, fell into berserk laughter again.

"Get used to it, honey," Shay told Cyn. "Men are like that, always on guard and always hovering."

Luna managed to stifle her hilarity enough to say, "Joe is the absolute worst, but I wouldn't have him any other way. The kids feel cherished, and truthfully? So do I."

"Same here," Shay agreed.

Because Bruce was just as bad, or just as good, according to your perspective, Cyn didn't need the warning. The man was making the ultimate sacrifice for her. She knew all about overprotective men. "Joe and Bryan will stand up with Bruce?"

"Bruce asked yesterday," Luna told her. "I know Joe will pretend otherwise, because he hates suits, but he'll be honored."

"And Scott will have his hands full with Alyx. She does love to bedevil him." Shay grinned. "One of these days, Alyx is going to let Scott think he caught her, when she's been the one doing all the chasing."

"Poor Scott just doesn't know it," Luna agreed. "She's a female version of Joe, and I swear, if that isn't enough to curl your hair, then I don't know what is."

"I want Jamie to come, too," Cyn told them, but both women gave helpless shrugs.

"Unless we see him between now and then, there's no way to invite him. He doesn't have a phone and the mailman doesn't exactly scale the mountain to drop off correspondence."

"You can wish it," Luna added, "but you won't know if he's coming until he shows up. That's just Jamie's way."

Cyn decided that was good enough. She turned back to the floral clerk. "I want a small bouquet with a few sweetheart roses."

"And baby's breath," Luna added.

"And forget-me-nots, for tradition," Shay insisted. "Ohh, maybe in pale blue to match your eyes!"

Bowing to their better judgement, Cyn asked, "And rose boutonnieres?"

"Perfect," Luna said, and hooked her arm through Cyn's. "Now let's wrap this up. I need to buy a dress for a wedding."

Chapter Twelve

It was a beautiful, sunny day with a light breeze coming in off the lake and the scent of wildflowers in the air. Julie, Shay, and Luna wore simple sheaths of pale, frosty blue, and they were all radiant.

But Cyn, now his wife, was more beautiful than anything Bruce had ever seen. She had her thick hair piled up on top of her head with some sparkly, delicate thing entwined in her dark locks. The dress left her creamy shoulders and upper breasts on display, and at the moment, even her ears were turning him on.

He'd asked his dad to keep the vows simple and fast, to spare Cyn. She alternated between looking totally lost and afraid, and glowing with joy. After picking out her dress, she'd confided that not once, ever, had she attended a ceremony. No birthday parties, no graduations, no weddings and no funerals. She'd been a hooker, but she didn't like being center stage. She'd gleefully engage in a fight with a trucker, but she didn't like special attention.

And so his dad had kept it short and sweet, and Cyn, right on cue, had whispered, "I do." Now she was married, bound to him for all of his life. Bruce couldn't be happier. Or more aroused.

The past few weeks had served as prolonged foreplay and he was so primed, so hungry to have her, that he shook every time he looked her way. And he couldn't stop looking. She smiled and his heart raced. She laughed and he wanted to throw her over his shoulder and —

Joe whacked him on the back. "Get a grip, man. You're embarrassing me."

It wasn't easy, but Bruce drummed up a modicum of control. He was on a bench near the house, watching his wife — *his wife* — talk with Joe's children, Austin and Willow. Someday, they'd have kids, too. Cyn would make an incredible mother —

Bryan laughed. "Give up. He's a goner."

"He's been celibate too long," Joe said. "I told you it wasn't healthy."

Bryan sat down so close, Bruce had to scoot over an inch. Only he couldn't, because Joe was there. They hemmed him in, and Bruce knew they were anxious to rib him over his newly married bliss.

"Yeah, well, his celibacy will be over in

. . .” Bryan glanced at his watch, “ . . . oh, two or three hours.”

Bruce stared at him. “No, I won’t make it that long.”

And both Joe and Bryan roared with laughter.

“All right,” Bryan said, “I’ll take pity on you.”

He stood and called the single men to line up for the ritual removing of the garter.

Bruce got dragged to his feet reluctantly. “I don’t want all you yahoos staring at her legs.”

“Tough,” Joe told him, and then got distracted with Scott. “Look at him, the poor sap. He looks like a turkey on Thanksgiving Day.”

Bryan laughed. “That’s because Alyx is ready to pounce.”

Bruce stared at Alyx Winston. Like his wife, Alyx had long, dark hair, only Alyx had left hers loose and now it danced in the breeze. She’d worn a beautiful, light green, sheer summer dress that landed just at her knees and she’d already removed her shoes to stand barefoot, feet planted apart, in the warm grass. And she did, indeed, look ready to tackle Scott.

To Bruce’s mind, Alyx resembled a female warrior. Not that she was brawny, far from it, but her attitude was that of a conquering Amazon, and she put real grit in everything she did.

As she looked at Scott, Bruce smiled in amusement. "She is rather concentrated on him, isn't she?"

Bryan nodded. "The woman's a terror."

"She never terrorized you," Joe reminded him.

Bryan shrugged. "She was never really after me."

Scott, who was doing his manly best to ignore Alyx, stood next to Joe's ten-year-old son, Austin, and behind them both was Jamie Creed. Bruce had no idea how Jamie had known about the wedding, but he was glad he'd shown up because Cyn would have been upset otherwise.

Even Bryan and Bruce's father joined the bachelors.

Bruce went to his radiant wife, knelt on one knee, lifted her skirt, and, ignoring the cheers, slid her garter down. Just doing that, and with Joe and Bryan heckling him, had him at the end of his fuse. He needed to get her alone, and soon.

Bruce looked out in the crowd, aimed for his father just for the fun of it, and shot the garter.

Unfortunately, it smacked Scott right in the forehead. He groaned and pretended to reel while Austin tried laughingly to keep him upright. Scott scooped the boy up and they both went down in the grass.

Alyx hurried over with false sympathy and a seductive, "Poor baby," that had Scott rigid in only a heartbeat. But he wasn't fast enough to remove himself. Alyx was already on her knees and easing his head in her lap. Scott's only defense seemed to be playing dead. It didn't deter Alyx, but the moment Cyn prepared to throw the bouquet, Alyx dropped his head with a *thunk* and pushed back to her feet.

There were only three available females in the group. Because Willow was only fifteen, and because Julie was totally disinterested in giving up her newfound freedom, the two of them chatted a few feet away while Alyx stood with her hands on her hips, ready to nab the prize. Cyn turned her back, closed her eyes, and pitched the flowers into the air.

Grinning, Alyx reached up. But just as the bouquet would have landed in her arms, Scott, who was still on the ground, grabbed her ankle and sent her toppling into his lap. Out of sheer instinct, Julie caught the flowers against her chest.

That brought hilarity to everyone but Alyx, who tried to yell, but couldn't — not with Scott kissing her.

Bruce looked at all his wacky friends, laughed with the sheer joy of it, and returned to his wife.

"Hello."

She was breathless, flushed. Stunning. "Hi."

In such a short time, she had become the most important person in his world. Bruce cupped her face and stared down at her, wishing she could understand what she meant to him, how much joy she'd brought to him. "I think that finishes all the ridiculous rituals and now I can finally get you alone."

"Finally," Cyn agreed, and her eyes were sparkling in anticipation.

Julie approached them to hand Cyn back her bouquet. "I think brides like to keep these things."

Bruce hugged Julie into his other side. "So what do you think? Has your romantic future been given a nudge by fate?" He nodded at the bouquet that Cyn now held.

Julie said, "No," at the same time that Jamie said, "Yes."

With a comical look on her face, Julie reiterated, "*No.* I don't believe in that nonsense."

Jamie shrugged. "Catching flowers has nothing to do with it. Things are happening for you. Your life is about to take a drastic turn." And with a frown: "You should use caution."

Julie prissed up real quick. "Yes, thank you. I'm sure you mean well, Jamie, but you sound just like my uncle, wanting me to be circumspect in all I do." She smoothed her hair back with haughty disdain. "But now is the time for me to embrace life, not retreat from it."

"Sometimes retreat is a good thing."

Julie wasn't convinced. "I, ah, I'll just go help Shay put the presents in the car." She nodded to Jamie. "It was lovely seeing you again."

He returned her nod with a very empty look that somehow managed to convey smirking tolerance.

Julie dismissed him. "Bruce, Cyn, congratulations."

Cyn hugged her. "Thank you. For everything."

Jamie pulled Bruce to the side. "It's not over."

Bruce wasn't surprised. "I know. He'll come, but we'll be prepared."

"For the threat, yes," Jamie said, "but I think it's your wife you need to be prepared for."

"She is unpredictable."

Jamie frowned a moment, considered the situation, then shook his head in helpless confusion. "She loves you very much. It was always clear to me that you'd take care of her."

"But?"

"I don't know. Sooner or later I'll figure it out."

Bruce took his hand. "Thank you. We appreciate your concern and your effort. If for any reason you want to talk, about Cyn and what's happening with her, or about yourself, your life here, I'm always available."

Suddenly wary, Jamie released Bruce's hand and backed up a few steps. "I need to go." He bumped into Cyn, and an expression of resignation crossed his features.

"Jamie." Cyn faced him with huge eyes, hesitated, then she launched herself against him and squeezed him tight.

Jamie turned stiff with alarm. He had no idea how to react to Cyn's affection, or how to free himself from her hold, and Bruce couldn't help but smile. The man wasn't used to human contact.

It was just like Cyn to realize that, and to remedy the situation.

Jamie tolerated the embrace for all of five seconds before he caught Cyn's arms, peeled her loose, and set her beside her husband.

It was impossible to tell if his beard-covered cheeks were ruddy with embarrassment, or if he'd just had too much sun. But for once, his fathomless eyes weren't blank.

Jamie harrumphed and gathered his thoughts while appearing ready to flee. "Listen to me."

Cyn smiled. "We're listening."

"The threat still exists. Until I tell you otherwise, it's there. Don't be fooled."

Bruce put his arm around Cyn. "I'm not going to let anyone hurt her."

"I understand that. And it's good that you're married. But . . ." Jamie seemed almost pained in his inability to verbalize his worries. "Something's not right."

"Okay," Bruce told him gently. "We'll be very careful, and if you have any news for us, please let us know."

Jamie agreed, glanced at Cyn with wary regard, and bid his farewells. For once, he didn't vanish. He just turned and wandered off, his hands in his pockets, his head down in deep thought.

No one said a word to him, but Bruce noticed that the ladies were tracking him with compassionate gazes. Not only that, but both Bryan and Joe watched him with concern, too.

They cared about Jamie, despite their claims to the contrary. And for the first time, Bruce wondered if, in fact, it wasn't Jamie who suffered the most risk — for always trying to help them all.

Cyn stood behind Bruce, watching him stack the gifts they'd received around the bedroom. When he finished that, he removed his suit coat and hung it in the closet, dropped his cufflinks on the dresser, sat to remove his shoes.

And not once did he look at her.

When he stood again to unbutton his snowy white shirt — keeping his back to her — Cyn thought to herself, *Not this time.*

Her heart beat too fast and her stomach was fluttering with excitement. "I need help with my dress."

Bruce went still for a heartbeat before shrugging out of his shirt. "Just a moment."

Cyn moved up behind him, slid her arms

around his waist, and pressed her cheek to his bare shoulder. His skin was hot and sleek all over. "Let's go to bed."

Every muscle in his body tensed. "I need a shower. It was warm outside and —"

"Help me undress first, and I'll shower with you."

She felt his chest and back expand on a deeply drawn breath. Too much cheerfulness colored his tone as he faced her. "All right. The gown is beautiful, and perfect for you, but I can see it'll be tricky to undo."

Cyn turned. "Not all that tricky at all. It just looks like a row of tiny buttons, but there's a long zipper underneath."

Bruce hesitated. "I see." His hands didn't touch her.

"The zipper, Bruce? It won't open itself."

But it wasn't the zipper he touched. Cyn felt his mouth, warm and damp, pressing to her nape. His tongue came out, tasting her skin, and she quickened. Heated breath brushed the damp spot he'd left behind, and she shivered, leaning into him.

"I have to tell you something, honey."

Alarmed, Cyn started to pull away, but Bruce caught her rib cage, just below her breasts, and kept her pinned against him.

He nuzzled her ear, lightly bit her throat, and said, "I'm not going to last. I already know it."

Smiling in satisfaction, Cyn reached back and put her hands on his hard thighs. "That's all right. We have all night."

He shook his head. "You really don't understand, but you will. Eventually." His tongue dipped into her ear, teased, and Cyn wanted to melt on the spot. "You know what I kept thinking about all day?"

Her heart pounded. "Tell me."

"Slipping my hands into this bodice and freeing your breasts. At times, I swear I could almost feel your nipples on my palms. It made me nuts, especially with everyone watching me." His tongue left a damp path from her ear to the top of her shoulder. "I think I'll do that now."

Lost in the soft murmur of words, in the feel of his mouth teasing her flesh, she was startled when Bruce's hands slid up and over her breasts, to the top of the bodice where his fingertips teased a few moments.

"Bruce . . ."

He worked his fingers beneath the stiff material. "Shhh. I don't want to rip your dress. Relax back against me."

Her plans for seducing her husband flew the coop; she relaxed back as instructed.

Hot, rough fingertips touched her nipples, already stiff and aching, and she could feel his smile on her throat. "I love your breasts, Cyn." With his left hand, he pinched her nipple just enough to make her groan. "You like that."

She swallowed, then said, "Duh." But her heart wasn't in the sarcastic response, and Bruce knew it.

Laughing, he eased her forward and worked the back zipper halfway down. It loosened the bodice enough that her breasts were completely free, yet held up by the bunched material beneath them.

Keeping her turned away from him, he whispered, "Perfect," and went back to flicking, plucking, and rolling her nipples until Cyn thought she might scream.

"That's enough."

"No." He held her locked into place against him with one arm snug around her waist. His fingers caught her nipple and tugged.

Cyn's back arched. The pleasure was exquisite and acute and she wanted him, now. It was so easy for him to make her hot, when she hadn't even realized such a thing was possible. Sex to her had been a means to an end, a function to perform. But with Bruce, it was nothing like that. It was . . . more personal. Pure, raw pleasure. And addictive, because every time he touched her, she wanted more.

But she needed to touch him, too. She viewed his body differently from all the men who'd come before him. Bruce wasn't a chore; he was a craving.

Just as her hand began climbing his thigh toward the rock-hard cock that pressed into her bottom, he snagged her dress and hoisted the hem high. Cyn started to object, but his teeth closed carefully over her shoulder and the mingling of pleasure with the twinge of apprehension heightened her need. "Bruce?"

Wet, open-mouthed kisses left her skin sizzling as Bruce whispered, "Hold your dress up for me, Cyn."

She didn't even think of arguing. She bunched the material in her fists and lifted it as high as she could.

"Now, brace your feet apart." And in a growl: "I want to touch you."

The words alone almost put her over the top. She was inching her legs open when his hard thigh insinuated its way between her knees and nudged her legs far apart.

Using his left hand, he kept her nipple captive with a steady pressure between his finger and thumb. With the other, he dipped into her panties and found her wide-open sex.

Cyn's head fell back; she braced her shoulders on his chest. "How do you always do this to me?"

His fingertips parted her, but he didn't press in. "I'm the one man meant for you, sweetheart. Remember that. What we have is special because we're special together."

"Together?" She found the breath to huff. "You're always the one doing —"

His finger pressed in, fast and deep and Cyn cried out as her hips shot forward, her thoughts and grievances obliterated.

Bruce seemed in no hurry. For long minutes, he indulged foreplay, making love to her with his hand, using his mouth, his fingers, his entire body to push her to the brink. It was their wedding day, a day she'd expected to luxuriate in the bed with him.

And instead he brought her to a screaming climax while standing and half dressed.

Cyn slumped into him, limp and sweaty, her mind a blank slate, her bones useless. Bruce held her, continuing to kiss her throat and ear and jawline until she'd finally regained her breath.

When cognizance returned and she went rigid, Bruce asked, "You okay?"

She wrenched herself free and turned toward him, her mouth open to blast him, and just that quickly, Bruce toppled her to the bed. Stunned immobile, she watched as Bruce came down over her.

Her breasts were offered up by the taut restriction of the gown and Bruce eyed her rosy, stiffened nipples for only a heartbeat before closing his mouth over one and suckling.

"You're ruining my dress," Cyn tried to grouch, but the words sounded more like a wail. She was still so sensitive, still in the aftermath of a fabulous orgasm.

It didn't matter anyway, because Bruce paid no attention to her complaint. Maybe because her fingers were laced in his hair, holding him close to her breast. Maybe because her legs had opened so that he could settle between. Maybe because her hips were lifting in rhythmic invitation.

She was so alive with sensations from her release, that in only moments she was ready, even anxious, again.

"I can't believe you're mine," Bruce whispered.

But was he hers? *Not yet.* Before the day ended, Cyn vowed things would be different. She'd take him, and then some. "I want you, Bruce."

"You have me. Forever." He took her mouth hungrily to seal that promise, while stroking his fingers over her cheek, her throat, and her breasts again.

Suddenly he sat up and Cyn, hungry for him, opened her eyes to see him unfastening his trousers.

Finally. She tried to help, but he said, "Let's get you out of this dress." He flipped her onto her stomach and went to work on her zipper, pulling it all the way down to the bottom of her spine.

Now that they were married, Cyn had wanted this time to involve both of them. She wanted to touch him, too, to taste him everywhere and explore his body. But Bruce seemed bound and determined to hold her off.

Utilizing great care for the delicate material, he stripped the gown off her, leaving her in panties and garter-top nylons. He turned her to her back again and simply stared at her, from head to toes, his gaze growing more heated by the moment.

Then he touched her, letting his hands explore everywhere at once — soft, teasing touches, then firm caresses and gentle coaxing. Through it all, he fended her off, refusing to let her touch him at all.

Finally, he couldn't take it anymore, either, and stood to push his pants and boxers off.

It was late afternoon. Turning off the lights would do him no good. The drapes in his bedroom weren't thick enough to block out the daylight. Lying on her back on the bed, Cyn got her first good look at her husband, and he was magnificent.

The dark blond hair on his head contrasted sharply with his dark lashes and brows, and the darker body hair on his chest and thighs. His stomach was flat, his muscles clearly defined.

And he was her husband. A man with a heart of pure gold and a body to make women swoon.

Cyn considered removing her stockings and underwear, but then Bruce returned with a condom in hand.

"Sorry. This is going to be fast and furious," he said as he rolled on the protection. "I'd have preferred otherwise, but it's just not possible."

"It doesn't matter."

He shook his head and laughed, stripped her panties down and off, and came between her legs. "Put your arms around me, sweetheart. Hold me."

She was already doing it. Her legs, too. She wanted to hold him tight so he couldn't ever pull away from her again.

Bruce took her mouth, his tongue stroking hers, and Cyn felt the hard, hot length of his erection pushing inside her. She was wet enough that he eased right in, deeper and deeper, and she clamped down with a shuddering moan, thrilled to have him finally, to possess every part of him.

When he was fully seated, they groaned in unison. Bruce went still for a moment, eyes closed, face relaxed as he luxuriated in the sensation of being completely joined. Then his muscles twitched, his breath caught, and with a growl, he began thrusting — hard, heavy strokes, fast and deep, and Cyn loved it.

In no time at all, Bruce threw back his head and clenched his jaw tight. His chest heaved, the muscles in his shoulders and arms bunched, and Cyn knew he was coming.

Through a haze of pleasure and love, she watched him, amazed that seeing a man so out of control, so lost in release, was such a turn-on.

By small degrees his body lowered to hers. He kept his face turned into her throat while gulping air, and he was still inside her.

Cyn opened her hands wide and ran

them up and down his broad back. His skin was damp now with sweat, hot from exertion.

She loved him so much. "You can sleep if you want."

His lashes tickled her neck as he slowly opened his eyes. "Not likely." He stirred enough to roll to his back, but he brought Cyn with him, curling her into his side with her head on his shoulder. "It's going to take me a little time to get used to having you."

"Yeah?"

Eyes closed, he nodded. "I've thought about making love to you from the moment I first saw you. And no, it wasn't just your looks, though I can't deny I love seeing you in those pale nylons."

"Kinky."

"I'm getting there." He sighed out a long breath. "Of course, it'd be the same if you weren't wearing nylons. You, Mrs. Kelly, are just so unique, so full of spirit, that I can't be around you without indulging a few lecherous thoughts."

Mrs. Kelly. Wow, she liked the sound of that. She laughed and tangled her fingers in his chest hair. "Now we need a shower. We're both sweaty."

He patted her hip and started to rise.

"Right. I'll go first."

Cyn snagged him back with her hold on his chest hair. "I don't think so."

He glanced down at her.

"We'll shower together."

Very slowly, Bruce's eyes darkened as he looked down at her. He held her wrist so she couldn't pull on his chest hair. "My shower is awfully small, Cyn. I don't think we'll both fit."

Cyn pushed him flat and crawled atop him. "We will. And this time, you'll give me my turn."

He eyed her breasts, just inches above his face. "Your turn at what?"

"At pleasuring you."

His eyes narrowed. "You don't need to do that."

"But I —"

He rolled her to her back, patted her thigh, and pushed off the bed in a rush. "Stay put. I'll make it quick and then you can take a turn."

Cyn watched him leave, almost choking on her hurt. Damn him, why did he hold her at arm's length? Did her expertise with sexual matters disgust him? For certain, he'd never let her show him any expertise. He treated her like an ignorant virgin, as if screwing was permissible, but anything more was dirty.

Well, it was time Bruce Kelly realized just how dirty she wanted to be with him. If being herself repulsed him, then he'd have to tell her outright.

She left the bed and stood in front of the dresser mirror, removing the pins from her hair until the dark mass cascaded down her back.

As she headed to the bathroom, she heard the shower running, heard Bruce splashing around. She stepped into the tiny bathroom, drew the shower curtain back, and found Bruce soaping up one underarm.

Cyn plastered on a smile, and stepped in with him. Bruce's soap hit the tub floor.

He couldn't do this, Bruce thought as he watched Cyn step gloriously naked beneath the shower spray, soaking her long, dark hair until it hung around her round, pale breasts and trickled down her smooth belly into her pubic curls.

There were a hundred different ways he wanted to ravish her — raunchy, hot scenarios that crowded his brain at every opportunity. He wanted her on her back, he wanted her astride him. He wanted her on her knees . . . He squeezed his eyes shut, trying to obliterate that provoking image.

Cyn needed to know that he respected her, that she was precious to him. As his wife, she was by far the most important person in his world. He didn't want to treat her like an experienced woman because her past didn't matter to him. She didn't need to use her sexuality to keep him.

But if she insisted on flaunting herself in front of him . . . He was only a man, a man deeply in love with his wife.

Water trickled off her still-rosy nipples and gathered like tears on her lush lashes. "Don't worry, Bruce," she said, "I won't hurt you."

Smiling pained him, but then he was already so hard again, moving was an effort. "I'll be finished in just a moment," he said. But he didn't move. The soap was between her feet, and no way could he bend down there without kissing her, without enjoying the delicious scent of her.

Cyn did the unexpected. She turned her back to him, then bent for the soap.

Lord have mercy, the things this one particular woman did to him. He couldn't take his eyes off her heart-shaped rear, and then his hands were on her, stroking her wet hips.

Cyn straightened and slowly turned toward him. "I'll finish your bath for you."

He should have objected. He should have left the shower. Instead, he stood there while she worked the soap between her hands until she had a good, frothy collection of suds. She put the soap in the wall dish and, with a siren's smile, placed her hands on his shoulders.

His shoulders weren't sexual, for crying out loud, but his erection bobbed in disagreement, feeling the slick, smoothing motion of her small hands as surely as if she clasped him. Her palms moved down over his own nipples, back and forth once, making his breath catch, then down, down.

She went to one knee and lathered his right thigh.

Bruce closed his eyes and leaned back on the tiled shower wall. Maybe if he didn't watch her, he could handle this. Then again . . . maybe not.

She was quite thorough, rubbing her small, soft hands over every inch of his body, except for where he wanted her touch the most.

Her breasts were slick against his back while she washed his shoulders, the backs of his thighs and between them. She came so close to touching him that his control faltered and he nearly grabbed her.

Then she was on her knees in front of him again, paying extra attention to his abdomen, his navel, down his hips to his legs and feet.

He felt her breath.

Bruce swallowed and opened his eyes just as her fingers closed firmly around him. One hand held the base of his erect penis while the other cuddled his testicles. The showerhead sprayed over them both, but the warm water barely penetrated his senses, not when competing with her warm breath and warmer touch.

"Relax, Bruce."

His hand knotted a fistful of her slippery wet hair. "You don't have to do this."

She looked up at him, her eyes big and beseeching, her lips parted. "I want to."

His resistance crumpled. Rather than holding her away, he drew her forward until her lips touched the head of his penis. Her tongue came out, licking daintily, again and again, until he labored for breath and his testicles were tight with the need to ejaculate. And just when he knew he couldn't bear it anymore, she swallowed his length, drawing him into the wet heat of her mouth, her clever tongue moving over him, around the sensitive head, driving him insane while pushing him toward release.

Bruce rumbled out a long groan, and he held her there with his sex in her mouth, her lips tight around him, and he felt himself ready to come. "That's enough," he growled shakily.

But she didn't pull back.

He fought it, saying in a rush, "Cyn, honey, you have to stop."

She hummed out a disagreement, then clasped his thighs so he couldn't escape her.

Bruce pressed his back hard against the wall, needing the support. He locked his knees, cradled her head in his hands — and came like a wild man. It was so powerful that he could barely stay upright. His hips jerked, his entire body shuddered, and his shout was loud and raw with emotion, edgy with lust.

When Cyn released him, he slowly sank down until he was sitting, his head back, his limbs loose and his heart still racing. Cyn turned, put the stopper in the tub, and switched the shower so that the tub began to fill.

On her knees, she faced Bruce. And waited.

He got his eyes opened, saw the uncertainty in her gaze, and opened his arms to her. "Come here, you."

She scuttled up against his chest and Bruce stretched out his legs, holding her to his pounding heart while the water level rose.

After that, after what she'd done and what he'd enjoyed more than any man had a right to, he decided anything was fair game. They soaked while he regained his breath. But when he was ready again, he took his turn bathing her, then rinsed and dried them both and carried her back to bed.

It was a night meant for sexual exploration and excesses in the extreme. Bruce felt tireless, mostly because Cyn was an open, generous lover. She took, but she also gave, and she enjoyed anything that brought Bruce enjoyment. They skipped dinner, and until four in the morning, they skipped sleep.

But exhaustion finally won out, and when Bruce rolled to his back, he heard the soft, metered breathing of deep sleep. He looked at Cyn, at the wild tangle of her midnight hair and the even rise and fall of her breasts, and contentment settled on him, lulling him to sleep as well.

He turned on his side, pulled her up

against him, and dozed off with the knowledge that she was his, now and always. Nothing and no one, especially Palmer Oaks, would change that.

He wouldn't let it change.

Chapter Thirteen

Cyn woke to an empty bed, and it panicked her. Before she could even get her eyes open, she'd been reaching for Bruce — but he wasn't there. She bolted upright, her gaze searching the empty room.

Then her memory kicked in, and she sank back against her pillows with a pained frown. Last night had been . . . not what Bruce was expecting.

Heck, it hadn't even been what she'd planned. She wanted him to stop holding back, sure, but wow, had he gone overboard.

Bruce on the loose was something, all right. Wicked and naturally sensual. Exciting and inexhaustible. Provocative and daring. His stamina amazed her. Of course, he'd been celibate a long time, so maybe that contributed to last night's marathon. She wouldn't be dumb enough to make any more of it than that.

She'd forced the issue, sabotaging him in the shower, taking advantage of him when he was naked and unable to run off. Cyn grinned, because she knew Bruce would never run away from her. He might take control of the situation, but he wouldn't flee. He was a most remarkable preacher, and an equally remarkable man.

Sure, she'd gotten things started, but Bruce had certainly joined in after that, and the night had been *incredible*.

Here she'd thought she knew everything about sex. Ha! She knew the moves necessary to finish the deed. But she hadn't known about all the moves in between, all the touching and kissing and whispered words that made it so much more special. With Bruce, the moves didn't matter. He could have stood her on her head and she'd have loved it because it wasn't what she did, but rather that she did it with Bruce.

She sat up and shoved her hair out of her face, considering what to do next. Bright sunlight streamed in through the windows. It was late morning, or maybe even early afternoon, so no wonder Bruce wasn't still in bed with her.

God, let that be the only reason.

Please don't let it be that she'd repulsed him with her sexuality, that she'd encouraged him to do things he now regretted.

Bruce was a man of religion, and she'd debauched him — and gotten debauched

— quite thoroughly. It wasn't what he was used to, and maybe, even though he'd succumbed, it wasn't what he wanted. Had he hoped for a meek little wife who'd be content to have sex in the dark, beneath the covers? He *had* kept the lights off before yesterday.

But damn it, he'd married an ex-hooker. Preacher or not, he knew what he was getting into, and she wouldn't apologize for wanting him.

Slipping naked from the bed, Cyn was amazed at how unsteady she felt. Like a drunk with a hangover. She almost laughed. Even as a lady of the night, she hadn't spent so many hours in the sack.

She stretched her lethargic body awake, then found one of Bruce's T-shirts to slip on over her head. Filled with uncertainty and a twinge of belligerence, she went in search of her husband.

The house was small, so he wasn't hard to locate. She didn't call out, just peeked in each room until she finally found him in the back of the house, where the glass block wall was now complete. He wore only unfastened jeans and held a steaming cup of coffee while staring off into space, at nothing in particular that Cyn could tell.

His back was broad, and as he sipped his coffee, muscles flexed and moved, making her heartbeat accelerate.

He was so engrossed in his thoughts that he hadn't heard her enter the room. For a while, Cyn soaked in the sight of him, her heart full and her eyes burning. Sunlight flooded the room and played around his big body, gilding his skin and making his fair hair appear lighter.

"Bruce."

He looked over his shoulder, his smile soft and . . . loving. "Good morning, sweetheart."

He didn't look or sound disgusted with her. Just the opposite. Cyn cautiously brightened. "Morning."

That was it. Nothing more. Bruce simply stared at her, not at her body, but at her face. She fidgeted and pushed her hair behind her ears. "I slept like a log. You should've woke me."

His unrelenting gaze warmed and his smile lifted. "I liked the idea that I wore you out."

Oh boy, the way he said that, like a typical macho guy reveling in his bedroom skills, which maybe he was. "Yeah, well. That you did." Feeling brazen, she stepped forward and covered his hand with her own to bring the coffee cup to her lips. "Mmm. Good."

"Want me to get you a cup?"

She tucked in her chin, looking at him with sultry insinuation. "I'll just share yours."

"Okay."

Damn it, he could be so enigmatic when he chose. "So. What are you doing in here all by yourself?"

"Thinking."

"About what?"

He gave a casual shrug, while she stayed on pins and needles.

"The room is nearly complete." He peered around the empty space with that secretive, serene smile. "Another week or so and it'll all be done. Soon we'll be able to have services here instead of the bank's meeting room."

"That's all you were thinking?"

He handed her the cup for another drink. "No. I was also thinking that we need to get your driver's license. You'd like that, wouldn't you? I don't want you to be dependent on me, or anyone else, for a ride. There'll be times when we'll need two cars, so once you pass the test, we'll get something. Probably used. Maybe a truck." He crossed his arms and went back to perusing the glass block. "I could use a truck."

Cyn thought about throwing the steaming mug at his head. "Anything else on your mind?"

"Yes." He glanced at her. "I was saying my morning prayers."

And she'd intruded. Well, hell. Having a preacher for a husband would take some getting used to. She should probably start learning what she could about him. "You say your prayers in here?"

"Here, the kitchen, the backyard. God doesn't care where." Bruce took the mug and sat it on a worktable. "He just likes to hear from me."

Bruce made them sound like old pals, and given Bruce's vocation, she supposed he might feel that way. "Does He now?"

"As much as I like hearing from Him." Bruce looped his arms around her waist and bent to kiss the tip of her nose.

"And so you were in here, chatting with God?"

Bruce stared at her face, studying her features in minute detail. His voice dropped to a soft, velvety whisper. "I wanted to thank Him for my many blessings."

The burning of her eyes increased. She

would not cry like some ninny just because Bruce was happy. He was a devout and wonderful person who always looked to the bright side. Knowing that prompted her to say, "You're such a good man, Bruce."

"I'm a fortunate man, in many, many ways." He made a grand gesture toward the glass blocks. "It's a beautiful, sunny day, and my very own church is almost complete."

"It is shaping up. Everyone will like it."

His thumb moved to her bottom lip with a teasing, gentle touch. "Good friends surround me, and I enjoy good health."

"All things you deserve."

He smiled. "And I've been given the greatest gift of all."

"What's that?"

He laughed, tweaked her chin. "You."

"Me?"

He slowly nodded. "God's given me a lot. But best of all, He's given me you." He took her mouth in a long, toe-curling, stomach-tightening kiss, and in a husky rumble: "I'll be thanking Him every day for the rest of my life."

When the kiss ended, Cyn dropped her forehead to his chest. "Last night. You didn't think I was too . . ." No proper word came to her so she temporized with, "maybe . . . *raunchy?*"

Bruce squeezed her tight enough to make her squeak. "You were open and loving. Just what I wanted and needed and I reveled in every minute of it."

"We had the lights on the whole time."

"Mmmm. The sight of you inspires me." His nose rubbed against her hair, inhaling her scent. "We're married. There's no reason to hide in the dark."

"You turned the lights off every other —"

He pressed a finger to her lips. "You tempt me, Cyn, more than you realize. If I'd seen you any of those other times, I wouldn't have been able to hold back."

So he hadn't wanted to hold back — but he had anyway? "You didn't want to go all the way because we weren't married?"

"In part." He took her arm and together they went to the kitchen. "Even being careful, consummation runs the risk of pregnancy, and to me, that's not something that should be chanced out of matrimony. Also, it's the ultimate physical joining, something that should be very special."

"It *was* special."

Satisfaction darkening his eyes, he nodded. "Actually, for the most part, I was being an idiot. I wanted to treat you like a *lady* so you wouldn't get confused about how I feel. I wanted you to know that I respect you, and that your needs and wishes come first."

Incredulous, Cyn said, "Holding out on me was your way of being kind?" She laughed. "God help me if you ever set out to make me suffer."

Wearing an unrepentant grin, Bruce said, "Hey, I suffered, too. I've never wanted anything or anyone as much as I want you. Always. Every time I even think of you."

"Yeah? That's nice to know."

Bruce chastised her with a look. "Don't be so smug, young lady. After last night, I realized my whole plan was stupid. You're smart enough to know the difference between being used and being desired, regardless of what we do, or don't do, in bed."

"Yeah, I am." But she hadn't been smart enough to understand his motives until now.

Bruce glanced at his watch. "About one o'clock, we'll go get your temps and you can practice driving."

"Why wait till one?" That was at least a few hours away.

Bruce caught her around the hips, lifted her, and threw her over his shoulder. With

Cyn laughing, he started up the steps. "Because right now, I want you. Again." His hand landed on her bare bottom. "Like I said, you're smart — smart enough to know you can't prance around in one of my shirts without turning me on."

Cyn's laughter changed to a groan as Bruce's clever fingers began to stroke her thighs. He was so strong that he bounded up the steps without effort. He dropped her on the mattress and shucked off his jeans.

Sunbeams shone like beacons on the bedding, and Cyn, without shyness or reserve, sat up to remove the shirt and toss it to the floor. She shook her hair back.

His eyes on her belly, Bruce paused beside the bed. "I changed my mind."

He was hard, so Cyn knew he hadn't changed his mind about joining her in the bed. "About what?"

"We'll make it two o'clock." And then he came over her, holding her face and kissing her with passion, but also with love.

And Cyn said her own quick prayer — that it wouldn't end. Ever.

Her prayers seemed to be answered when nearly two whole weeks passed in a blissful fog. There was no sight of Palmer, and Cyn hoped for the best. Did Palmer know that she'd married? Had he given up on getting his revenge and left North Carolina for good? If Palmer stayed well out of her life, she could be the happiest woman alive.

But no one was willing to take the chance that he was still hanging around. Between Joe and Bryan, their home was secured with alarms and security cameras. The cameras were small enough that the townspeople didn't even notice them. It wouldn't do to scare people away from the church.

Cyn felt cautiously safe, especially when nothing more happened. And even though she was never left alone, she was so happy she couldn't contain herself. There had never before been a time in her life when everything seemed to go right.

Between loving and laughing, she'd kept her job with Mary and got to visit with the horses twice a day. Bruce always accompanied her, but he seemed to enjoy the animals as much as she did, and Mary was thrilled that Cyn was able to keep her job.

When they weren't doing that, she and Bruce worked hard on the church to finish it in time for Sunday services. Bruce was extra busy with last-minute details, but he took time every evening to help her practice driving. She now felt confident and comfortable behind the wheel, enough to take the test scheduled for tomorrow. Bruce was a patient teacher, but then, she was a cautious driver, so she hadn't given him too many gray hairs.

He'd surprised her a week ago with the addition of a large bookcase in the TV room. It took up one entire wall and Bruce had already put her books there. But he'd gone one step further and also added many other books. The shelves were nearly filled with cookbooks, books on gardening and home decorating, novels of mystery, romance and history. It was like owning her own library, and more than anything else material, it made Cyn feel as if she'd finally found a true home.

With a cookbook opened on the counter, she scraped potatoes over the sink in preparation of a roast dinner with all the trimmings. Bruce came in behind her, kissed the back of her neck, and gave her a hug.

Cyn turned to face him, caught sight of the envelope on top of the stack, and tried to grab it.

All she managed to do was make Bruce drop the mail. Giving her an odd look, he stooped to pick it up, and there it was, right in plain sight.

Bruce picked up the padded envelope. “Adult college classes?”

It took a lot to make Cyn blush, and that did it. She dried her hands on a dishtowel and snatched the envelope out of Bruce’s hand. “It’s nothing. I was just checking to see what colleges were within driving distance for me.”

As Bruce stood again, his too-astute gaze never left Cyn’s face. She was learning that when it came to her, very little passed Bruce’s notice. “You’d like to go to college?”

More heat rushed to her face. Damn it, she felt foolish, even though she knew Bruce would understand. “I need to get my GED first. But yeah, I think I’d like that.” And then in a rush, she added, “I don’t want to go full-time or anything. But maybe start with a few classes.” And finally she admitted, “I just want to be better educated.”

“It’s not because you feel inferior?”

“No,” she lied. But that definitely played into it. Most of Bruce’s friends, now her friends, too, were so much more sophisticated and knowledgeable about current issues, politics and everything else. Cyn knew how to survive on very little, but what use was that to a preacher's wife? She wanted him to be proud of her. She wanted him to have reasons to be proud.

Bruce didn't look convinced. "You're one of the smartest people I know, Cyn. Intelligence isn't always measured by what you've learned in a book. You're well read, reasonable, and you have loads of common sense."

God, it made her uncomfortable whenever he lauded her so-called positive traits.

"But all that aside, I think more education is always a good thing."

Cyn fretted the envelope, folding and unfolding it. "I don't know for sure what it'll cost, but I think what Mary pays me will cover it."

"We'll sit down and go over our budget once the church is open. How's that?"

"I don't want your money. You've done enough —"

Before she could blink, Bruce had jumped up, his face going dark with anger. "It's not my money, it's *our* money. We're married, which means we share a partnership in every sense of the word. That includes all things financial. And as for what I've done, I found myself a wife who suits me perfectly. That's all."

"But —"

"No buts. I mean it, Cyn. Don't push me on this."

Cyn still had her savings, and she made a stipend from Mary. Somehow, she'd managed with that, but she nodded to Bruce anyway. "Fine."

"Great."

He all but crackled with annoyance. Her mouth twitched in a smile. "You're not very good at arguing."

Eyes darkening, he leaned forward and kissed her hard, then, against her lips, he whispered, "Maybe that's because I know of better ways for us to spend our time."

Cyn pressed both hands to his chest. The envelope she held crumpled even more. "Oh no, you don't. I'm making dinner. The roast has been cooking for an hour and I've got to get the potatoes on soon."

Bruce looked past her to the stove, sniffed the air with appreciation, and finally gave up. "Smells great." He kissed her again, a soft, quick peck. "After dinner, then."

She patted his chest and grinned cheekily. "I'll hold you to that." She returned the envelope to Bruce, saying, "I'll look at this later," then went back to the sink while Bruce bent to pick up the rest of the mail.

Cyn had just turned on the burner beneath the pot of potatoes when she felt the stillness in the air. A cold finger of dread tickled up her spine. Heart hammering, stomach tight, she turned to Bruce.

He was standing right behind her, staring at the small package. Something was wrong. Very wrong.

A surge of anger ripped through her. She would not let anything threaten her happiness with Bruce. "What is it?"

He held the package with his fingertips on the uppermost right-hand corner. "I don't know." His voice was deep and distracted with worry. "It's addressed to you, but doesn't have a return address."

One last kernel of hope remained. "Then maybe it's nothing. An advertisement or a sample or something."

"No, it's not from a company. The address is handwritten. And it was mailed from North Carolina." His eyes lifted from the package to lock on Cyn's.

Breathing became more difficult, but in a voice flat and devoid of emotion, she said what they both were thinking. "Then he's still here."

Bruce didn't agree or disagree. He set

the package on the table and stalked to the phone. "Don't touch it. Maybe he left fingerprints this time. We'll call Scott and he can open it."

Dread bloomed inside her, vying with the anger. "We don't know what it is. It could be something I don't want Scott to see. What if Palmer has sent something nasty and degrading —"

Bruce held the phone with one hand and pulled her into his side with the other. He started to speak to Cyn, but didn't have a chance. "Yeah, Scott. It's Bruce."

Cyn squeezed her eyes shut. Palmer was never going to let her be free to live her life without looking over her shoulder. She'd known it all along, but hadn't wanted to accept the truth.

Bruce spoke with Scott, quickly explaining and saying that he could bring the package to the station if Scott thought it was necessary.

To Cyn's surprise, Scott offered to come to them instead. "We'll be here," Bruce promised. He hesitated, half smiled in weary amusement and said, "Sure. Bring Alyx along. We haven't seen her since the wedding."

He finished the call and hung up. He caught Cyn's shoulders and gently caressed. "Now, listen up. You are not the villain in this, honey. It doesn't matter what Palmer might send you — he's a cretin and everyone knows it. Understand?"

One thought crowded out all others, burning inside her, making her rage expand. "He took so much pleasure in humiliating me."

"And that makes him an animal. It does not detract from who you are."

For a man who'd run a safe house, Bruce could be so naïve. "You can't know."

"No, I can't. My life has been blessed. I should feel guilty because of that, but I don't. It afforded me an opportunity to help others."

Sneering, hurting, Cyn said, "Like me."

"Oh, sweetheart, if you only knew." He drew her close and hugged her. "There's never been anyone like you. If you were the same as the others, I'd have done what I could to help you, but I wouldn't have married you."

"You had no choice."

"No, *you* had no choice. I was bound and determined to have my way, to have you, and I did. Now, please trust me when I tell you that, for those who know you and care about you, Palmer can't affect the way they feel. He can only expose himself further."

Yes, little by little, Palmer got closer to her. Pretty soon, he'd get too close, and then . . . "Sooner or later, something is going to happen."

"I don't want you to worry."

Cyn pushed away from Bruce with a laugh. "Oh, I'm not worrying. I've had enough. I'm sick to death of it. If Palmer wants to play games, then he'd better be prepared to lose."

Bruce went rigid with alarm. "You are not to go anywhere near him."

"How's that even possible? If that package is from him, and he's in North Carolina, then he could well be right here, still, in Visitation. He's tracking me, and it's not like Visitation is a crowded city with plenty of places to hide." She paced the kitchen, scenarios playing out in her mind. "Sooner or later, we're bound to find each other."

"Stop it!" Bruce caught her arm, but Cyn jerked away.

"No, you stop!" She was too afraid, for herself and what she had with Bruce, to be reasonable. "Do I look like a damn coward to you? Do you expect me to sit at the table and wring my hands? Do you expect me to pray for my safety?" She poked a thumb into her chest. "I've written my own fate since I was seventeen and I'll damn well write this. Palmer thinks he wants revenge? Ha! If I ever find him, I'll —"

Bruce erupted with a combination of fear and rage. He grabbed Cyn's shoulders in his big, hard hands and shook her until her teeth rattled. "You will do nothing! You'll avoid him at all costs, do you hear me, Cynthia Kelly? If I have to stay on top of you to keep you safe, then that's what I'll do. You're my wife. *My wife.* I've only just found you and I'm not about to lose you now."

Cyn stared at Bruce in horrified wonder. He was livid. He was shouting, when Bruce never shouted. His face was mottled red, his eyes burning with his rage.

As they stared at each other, a feral growl exploded from deep in his chest. In the next instant, he'd hauled her into his arms, kissing her hard, his mouth grinding down on hers, his tongue invading. His hands were all over her back, down her spine to her buttocks where he pulled her tight into his body.

Cyn moaned, not in discomfort but in fast-rising desire. It hit her like a tsunami, drowning her, bruising her defiance with the power of it.

And a knock sounded on the kitchen door.

Bruce moved away from her so fast she nearly collapsed. He turned his back on her, both hands in his hair, his shoulders taut, his biceps bunched.

Wow. Touching her mouth, Cyn glanced at the door. Through the glass, she saw Scott, looking chagrined, and Alyx Winston, grinning like a magpie.

She'd forgotten all about them. But geez, they'd made quick time. And good thing, otherwise they might have found her and Bruce sprawled out on the kitchen table.

Bruce was no help. He still had his back to her, breathing hard. Poor baby. He wasn't used to such excess of emotion. Neither was she, but she liked it.

Plastering on a smile, Cyn went to the door and opened it. "Hey, there. Dinner's almost ready. Maybe you two will join us."

Alyx hooked her arm through Scott's and dragged him in. "We'd love to." And then to Bruce, "A passionate preacher! Will wonders never cease."

"Shut up, Alyx," Scott said, and she only laughed.

What the heck, Cyn laughed, too. She'd meant what she said. Let Palmer try his worst. She'd be ready for him.

Chapter Fourteen

A thorny bush scratched his back, and rocks dug into the soles of his feet. He was sick and tired of holing up in the mountains, but at least no one looked for him there. You could hide forever and never be found.

But he'd prepared for everything. He had enough food, the nights were warm, and a natural spring made it easy to clean the sweat off his body when he started feeling fastidious. The entire area was his toilet, so he wanted for nothing.

Except Cyn.

He snickered, settling deeper onto the bed of fallen leaves and mossy ground. Around him, a few insects buzzed and somewhere off in the distance, an animal howled.

Just thinking of Cyn's reaction when she opened the package made him nearly giddy with excitement. He hoped she felt threatened. He hoped it scared her good.

Stupid bitch, writing all that stuff about him. And marrying a preacher. He snorted. It was sacrilege, a crime against humanity. She'd pay for that, too. So many ways he'd make her pay.

And God, thinking of that always made him throb with anticipation. She was such a whore, beckoning him even though she wasn't near and he couldn't see her or smell her or . . . he shuddered, *touch* her.

With powerful binoculars, he could watch her from a safe distance away. These days, a sinner could buy anything from the Internet — night goggles, tiny cameras, anything. Not that he was a sinner. No. She corrupted him. She made him do things.

He rubbed his tired eyes and tried to sleep, but he couldn't. He needed her. She was like a burning in his veins that could only be cooled by having her. He'd been on fire since the first time he'd seen her. Once he got her, he'd take her into the mountains with him and tie her to a tree and do anything and everything to her that he'd ever imagined.

His guts twisted and predictably, he got a boner that throbbed and ached until he loosened his pants and closed his fist around himself. He shouldn't waste himself this way, but damn her, she was elusive. She'd somehow conned that preacher into marrying her, and that made the preacher damned, too.

He'd get her. His hand moved faster, picturing Cyn helpless in front of him, begging, crying. His eyes closed, his jaw slackened, and his lips parted. Oh yeah, he'd get her. Very soon now. Very soon.

The guttural howl of a human echoed around the mountain, more sinister than any animal's could be.

Bruce was ashamed of himself for losing his control, and for blasting Cyn with his temper. He wanted to protect her, not hurt her. She needed his reassurance and understanding, not abusive shouting. At the moment, she wouldn't even look at him.

Her attitude kept his anger on the ragged edge. He'd been wrong to shake her, and he'd apologize later. But how dare she even think about putting herself at risk?

Scott caught his attention when he pulled out a plastic bag and a large, tweezer-type tool. "Let's open it first, then I'll put it in the bag and get it tested. It'll probably take a few days." Alyx hung over his shoulder, Cyn sat at the table, somehow distant and quietly aggressive, paying them no mind.

Bruce let her stew. With both Scott and Alyx in the kitchen, he couldn't say what he had on his mind anyway. "What can I do to help?"

Scott asked, "Get a table knife. Something we can use to work out the folds in the wrapper without touching it."

Together, Bruce and Scott got one end of the package opened. Bruce peered inside. "It looks like a thin book of some kind."

Cyn snapped her head in their direction. "My journal?"

Scott raised his brows. "Could be." Using the tool, he peeled back the taped edge of the brown paper, lifted one end, and gently shook until the worn, faded journal slid out and landed on the table with a *thunk*.

Cyn stared at it with the same intensity she might have given a snake. "He took it." And then, with gritted teeth, "He stole my journal."

Bruce used the knife to turn back the front cover. Inside was a young girl's precise handwriting. It said *Private Property of Cynthia Potter.* New emotions gripped him. With Cyn, he stayed in a jumbled torment of indefinable feelings and urges. "You left it behind when you ran away?"

"Yeah." Her laugh was dry, chagrined. "I stupidly thought maybe someone would read it and know I hadn't meant to kill him."

Alyx Winston had been quiet too long. She crossed her arms beneath her breasts and shook back her long, dark hair. "Well, I say it's too damn bad the chump didn't die."

Cyn said nothing to that, and Bruce silently agreed.

Alyx elbowed Scott. "So? What are you going to do about this?"

Scowling, Scott rubbed his ribs where her pointy elbow had landed. "There's nothing I can do yet, other than get it tested for prints."

Rolling her eyes, Alyx said, "Swell. In the meantime, I have a plan."

Scott bodily removed her from the table. "No, you do not."

Cyn interrupted an argument by saying in an emotionless voice, "There's a marker in the middle of the journal. I didn't put it there, so he must have."

The men looked at each other first, then again, using great care, opened the book to the marked page. Next to Cyn's neat script was a message in bold red marker.

And then she died for her sins.

Alyx caught her breath. Cyn scraped back her chair and lunged to her feet.

Without a word, she paced away to the kitchen window.

Bruce wanted to find Palmer and kill him with his bare hands. He couldn't pull his gaze away from the horrid message, or what Cyn had written before it, when she'd been a girl of seventeen. He read aloud, "One way or another, I have to get away, and soon."

Scott put his arm around Alyx's shoulder, presumably to offer comfort. "You were certainly right about that, Cyn. He's not right in the head."

"He's evil," Alyx corrected.

Bruce watched Cyn. When she clammed up, she scared him. "Cyn is resourceful. She did get away, and now she's here, with me, where I can keep her safe."

"And I know how to get him."

Scott said, "No, you don't," and released her to put the journal and the wrapping in the plastic bag.

"I do, too," Alyx insisted. "Look at me and look at Cyn. We both have long, dark hair. Okay, so I'm taller, but I could slump."

"Forget it, Alyx." Scott glanced up at Bruce. "The postmark tells us that it was mailed from right outside Visitation, only two days ago."

Alyx didn't give up easily. "You could use me as a decoy."

Both men stared at her in shared horror.

"When he crawls out from under his rock to get me, you could be waiting —"

Scott smashed his hand over her mouth. He looked incredulous, outraged, and dumbfounded. "Don't. Even. Think. It."

Brows drawn, Alyx mumbled rapid arguments, but Scott wasn't lifting his hand.

Bruce drew a shaky breath. "Scott's right, Alyx. There's no way you could do such a thing."

Alyx jerked away. "I'd hurt him if he tried anything." She lifted a credible fist into the air. "I know the most lethal moves. Joe taught me."

"Oh, for the love of . . ." Scott turned his back on her and zipped the plastic bag shut.

Cyn laughed, and when everyone looked at her, she laughed again. "You really are as cocky as Joe, aren't you, Alyx?"

Given the look on her face, Alyx wasn't sure if she was being insulted or not. "No, of course not. Joe could take anybody. I know my limits. But I'm not afraid of this guy."

Cyn never missed a beat. "Joe is not invincible, regardless of what he thinks or tells you or what you believe out of sisterly duty, and I'm not afraid of Palmer, either. Not anymore."

Bruce had a bad feeling about her new attitude. "I'm sorry, but I like you better afraid. You're more reasonable."

"Reason has nothing to do with it. I'm tired of hiding. It's past time I stood up to him."

Bruce's temper almost snapped again. "You won't do a damn thing, Cyn. You'll leave it to me."

Scott yelled, "No one is going to do anything. I'm the damn law and I will not have vigilantes running loose through Visitation with harebrained plans to catch a madman."

Bruce subsided, even while knowing in his heart that he'd do whatever was necessary to keep Cyn out of Palmer's clutches.

Cyn glared at Bruce. "Dinner is ready."

Scott stared at the heavens, but Alyx smiled. "Let's eat!"

It was late that night before Bruce spoke with Cyn again. She'd been avoiding him, closing herself in the bathroom for a long shower, going online to research the colleges listed in the brochure she got, and to find out where she could take her GED.

If he spoke to her, she answered him, but she was still mad. No two ways about it.

It was time for bed, and Bruce wanted her. But more than that, he knew he owed her a sincere apology. He found her sitting on the side of the bed, braiding her long hair. She performed the chore without effort, proving that she'd been doing so for years.

"I like your hair loose."

She paused, glanced up at him, and then away. "Tough."

Bruce sat beside her. "We need to talk, Cyn."

"Yeah? About what?"

And she'd accused Alyx of being cocky? He shook his head and gave in to the grin tugging at his mouth. "I want to apologize."

Cyn fumed, then shoved him onto his back on the bed. She sat on his abdomen and grabbed his ears. "You can't mean it if you're laughing about it."

In one quick flip, Bruce put her to her back. "I was ashamed."

She quit fighting him and instead, grabbed his shirt and pulled his face closer to her own. "Because you were caught making out with me?"

He went right back to wanting to throttle

her. "No. You're my wife. I can . . . *make out with you,* all I want." He tried to figure out the best way to apologize, then he just spit it out. "I yelled at you."

Cyn blinked. "That's it? You yelled?"

"At you."

"Well, whoop-dee-do." Her lack of concern was palpable. "I'm not made of glass. I won't break just because you prove you're human enough to get pissed."

"It's more than that, and you know it. I shook you, and that's unforgivable. Never in my life have I manhandled a woman."

She made a face of disgust. "Drop the drama, will you? You didn't hurt me. If you had, I would've decked you."

Bruce closed his eyes. She was worse than Alyx. Worse than Joe, even. "Cyn, you scare me." He opened his eyes and tried to make her understand. "Palmer wants to provoke you, to get to you so that you let down your guard. I can't let that happen. I *won't* let it happen."

Her eyes narrowed. "Tell me why."

"Don't play games. You already know why. I'm your husband. I'm supposed to protect you, but I can't do that if you're determined to put yourself in harm's way."

For some reason, she looked both sad and resigned. Then she relaxed beneath him. "You mean in Palmer's way, right?"

Bruce nodded. He cupped her face and leaned down to kiss her. "Promise me you won't do anything dangerous."

Her fingers laced into his hair and gently stroked his scalp. "I promise." Then her fingers tightened. "But I want the same assurance from you. Scott said he'd handle it, and I want to give him a chance."

"If it's at all possible, I'll be happy to have Scott do the honors." He kissed Cyn then, and luckily, she kissed him back instead of pressing him. Because if Scott wasn't around, Bruce would do whatever was needed.

Scott knocked on their kitchen door two days later. Cyn had passed her driver's test, but wasn't able to go anywhere on her own yet. By the day, she felt more imprisoned and strained. Bruce did his best to take her mind off Palmer, but the threat of him loomed over them at every turn.

"Has Alyx left again?" Bruce asked as Scott came in alone. Cyn poured coffee.

Scott shook his head. "She's having dinner with Joe and Luna."

"Maybe she's planning to move here for good."

He grabbed his heart. "Don't even think

it. I get gray hairs every time that woman is around. If she visits much longer, I'll have to start dyeing my hair."

Cyn put sugar and creamer on the table, but didn't sit. She couldn't join in the idle chitchat. Not once had Scott stopped in just to visit. "You have news."

"That I do." Scott removed his hat and took his seat.

Bruce leaned across the table. "You got Palmer's prints off the journal?"

"Nothing on that yet. But Detective Orsen called. They have Palmer Oaks."

Cyn's mouth fell open. Thank God Bruce moved quickly, or she might have hit the floor. He caught her arm and slid a chair beneath her just as her legs gave out. "You're kidding?" Cyn asked, and her voice shook almost as badly as her hands.

"I'm serious as a heart attack. Palmer must have been close just long enough to mail the journal, because they caught him up north a good piece. He got drunk in a bar, made too much of a ruckus, and drew too much attention. A couple of uniformed cops got called and they arrested him." Scott paused with a worried frown in Cyn's direction.

"Hey," she said. "Don't hold back on my account."

"You look a little dazed," Scott admitted.

"Undiluted joy, that's all." And disbelief. She'd never quite imagined it ending so easily.

"Right." Scott grinned, sipped his coffee, and then continued. "Palmer not only broke parole, but a woman at the bar claims he tried to rape her in the parking lot, and she has witnesses."

Cyn's stomach turned over. "Was the woman hurt?" She had to know.

"She's all right. A little banged up. More emotionally shook than anything. It took two other guys to pull him off her. At the very least, Palmer will have an assault charge from it. And on top of that, they found plenty of drugs on him. And are you ready for this? He was also carrying a big knife."

At the mention of a weapon, Bruce reached across the table and took Cyn's hand. "Thank God they've got him."

Cyn shivered, her imagination going wild over the idea of what Palmer would have done with that knife if he'd gotten hold of her. "I hope he rots."

"He's being held without bail. With any luck, they'll be able to round up enough evidence to pin him with the murder charge, too."

Cyn couldn't quite take it in. "I guess this means . . . it's really over."

"Looks like." Scott gave her such a gentle look, that Cyn did a double take. "You might need to be questioned, and the trial will take forever, but he won't be able to bother you anymore."

Bruce gave Cyn a huge smile. "No more worrying. Now we're free."

But Cyn's mind had already jumped ahead. Bruce wasn't free. He'd married her to protect her, but now that reason didn't exist. She knew Bruce wouldn't leave her — but would he regret his hasty decision?

She decided that she needed to speak with someone unbiased. Someone who knew things she didn't. Someone she trusted.

She needed to see Jamie Creed.

Making plans was easier than executing them, though. The rest of that day, Bruce still stuck to her side. There were a lot of last-minute things to be done before services on Sunday. Cyn wanted everything perfect for Bruce, even though he told her time and again that it didn't matter — not to him, not to God, and not to the townspeople who were drawn together by faith.

It wasn't until the following morning that she decided she'd just use faith to find

Jamie. She wanted to see him, and so he'd be there, on the road where she'd first met him.

Bruce was cutting the grass when she strolled out to the yard and oh-so-casually mentioned that she planned to ride to the store. He used a forearm to wipe sweat from his face and nodded. "Give me twenty minutes to finish and I'll go with you."

"No."

Bruce lifted a brow. "No?"

"You're busy. I can handle it."

"I don't mind going. I need a break anyway."

Cyn hated lying to him, so she drummed up a small piece of truth. "Ever since I was fifteen and a half, I've been looking forward to getting my license and driving on my own. For a long time it seemed like that'd never happen. But now I have my license, and Palmer's out of the picture, so there's no reason I can't go to the store all by myself. We just need a few things."

He still looked undecided.

For good measure, she laid on guilt. "That is, unless you don't trust me with your car."

For an answer, Bruce fished the keys out

of his pocket and handed them to her. "It's *our* car, which isn't anything to brag about."

Cyn smiled. "I kind of like it. It's old enough to have character."

"Whatever else it might be, the car is dispensable. You're not. Be careful, okay?"

Cyn bit her bottom lip, and said a quick prayer. *Please, please, please let Jamie reassure her. She wanted him to swear that Bruce was happy with her, that he wanted to keep her as his wife*. She crossed her heart. "You got it, Lancelot. I'll just go get my purse and be on my way."

"Cyn?"

She paused.

"Stop and get some gas first thing. It's almost on empty and I don't want you to run out. I meant to fill it up yesterday, but I forgot."

"Sure thing."

With a flighty wave, Cyn darted back to the house. She had to get her purse and change clothes. She ran up the steps to their bedroom. The sooner she learned the truth, the sooner she could either relax, or make things right. How she'd make them right, she wasn't sure. No way would she leave Bruce. But she'd tackled bigger problems in her life.

For sure, she could handle one do-gooder preacher.

Bruce waited until Cyn was out of sight before strolling to the house and using the kitchen phone. He could hear her upstairs, changing clothes in a rush. He felt uneasy, more so after she'd called him Lancelot. She hadn't used that name since their marriage. That she'd reverted back to it now told him she felt defensive about something, and that made him wonder if a trip to the store wasn't her plan at all.

He'd bought himself a little time by asking that she stop to refuel. But it was still going to be a close thing.

He trusted her in that he knew she wouldn't run off with his car. But would she do something she thought was for his own good? Probably. In her own unique way, Cyn was more protective than he was.

He got his brother on the second ring.

"Bryan Kelly."

"It's Bruce. I need a ride."

"Okay. I'm on my way." Tires squealed, and Bryan said, "I was in town anyway. I can be there in five."

Leave it to Bryan to just agree, with no questions asked. "You don't want to know why?"

"I could tell by your tone that it's important. You can tell me all about it when I get there."

"If you see Cyn, don't tell her I called."

"Gotcha." Bryan disconnected the call.

A few minutes later, as Cyn pulled the aged station wagon away from the curb, she noticed that Bruce stood at the window, watching her, ripe with speculation. She wrote it off as unimportant. She hadn't called him names in a while and he probably hadn't appreciated her humor. That's all it could be, because if Bruce had known she wanted to see Jamie, he would've argued with her about it — or insisted on coming along.

Luckily, she'd been on enough trips with Bruce that she knew her way around the area. She found the road leading out of Visitation where she'd had her first introduction to Jamie.

She pulled the car off the road and put it in PARK beneath the shade of gigantic evergreens. She got out and turned a wide circle, looking everywhere, but Jamie was nowhere around. Undaunted, Cyn cupped her hands to her mouth and called out, "Jamie Creed!"

Her voice echoed again and again. Cyn

waited, but heard nothing. Not the rustle of weeds or leaves, not the crack of a branch. Nothing.

She put her hands to her mouth again. She was just about to shout when someone touched her shoulder.

Her shout became a shriek and she jerked around so fast she stumbled and fell on her backside.

Jamie stood there, his enigmatic ebony gaze boring into her.

"Good grief," she snapped. "You scared me half to death."

"With good reason. Why are you out alone?"

"I had to talk to you."

Jamie caught her hand and hauled her upright. "It isn't safe. Get in your car and go home."

She resisted his attempts to shove her back to the station wagon. "Just listen, will you? They caught Palmer. It's safe now."

Very slowly, Jamie let his eyelids sink down. "They never listen."

"They who?"

"Anyone." He opened his eyes to stare at her. "I told you not to trust anyone, to only believe it was safe when I told you it was."

"I know, and I trust you. That's why I'm here. I have to talk to you."

"You need to go. Right now, before it's too late."

Frustrated, Cyn shoved off his hands. "You aren't listening. Palmer is caught. He's in jail."

His gaze locked on hers, Jamie suddenly went on the alert. "I'm sorry. It's too late."

"What's too late?"

He moved so that she stood behind him, as if he meant to protect her. "It wasn't Palmer."

"Wasn't . . . then who?"

A voice she hadn't heard in a very long time said, "It's me, little Cyn. I've got you now."

Pinpoints of light exploded on her brain before darkness tried to close in. Reverend Thorne. But . . . that didn't make any sense. Why would he want her?

Jamie said, "Don't move. Bruce is on his way."

Oh God, that didn't help. She wanted Bruce as far away from danger as she could keep him.

After swallowing her fear, Cyn peered over Jamie's shoulder and there he stood, the man who'd made her mistrust men of strong religion, the man who'd made her doubt her own faith, her own worth.

Until Bruce.

Thorne was thinner than she remembered, and his hair was long and dirty and tangled. Beard stubble covered his face. In five years, his nose had grown and new wrinkles had worked their way into his face.

But his smile, a smile of malicious intent and vile joy, was the same.

Thorne had a gun.

Think, Cyn tried to tell herself, but she remembered that young girl, and she remembered how Thorne had verbally beat at her, calling her a slut and a whore and condemning her to hell for luring good men with her lusty body. She felt sick all over again.

"Thorne." Her voice was weak, and she corrected that, saying again, stronger this time, "Why, if it isn't the evil Reverend Thorne. What are you doing here?"

"Collecting you, of course." His words were slick with anticipation, smooth with absurd righteousness. "We never did get to finish our lessons, did we? And there's much you need to learn yet. Much that I, as your advisor, will teach you."

Jamie took a step back. "You're going to die," he said, and Cyn knew he wasn't talking to her. Jamie nodded. "It'll be the best form of justice."

The gun went off, and though Cyn jumped, Jamie never moved. The shot had been fired into the air.

"Get away from her," Thorne ordered.

"No, I don't think so." Jamie took another step back. "Cyn, keep moving."

"He'll hurt you."

"Keep moving."

Her heart nearly stopped. Jamie didn't deny that he'd be hurt. Had he already seen it? Did he even care?

Well, *she* cared, and she wouldn't allow him to be some damn martyr on her behalf. She started to step out around Jamie, but damn him, he knew her every move before she made it. He caught her and though he was a hermit, he was a man, and strong. He kept her held at his back.

Cyn thumped his rock-hard shoulder. "Get out of my head."

"I'm not in your head."

"Bull. You knew what I was going to do."

"Because you're a woman, and you care for others. I didn't need to read your mind to know you'd try to protect me."

"Oh."

Thorne stalked closer. "Come to me, Cynthia, or you'll force me to shoot him. Do you want to add a man's death to your other sins?"

"You're a man of God," she shouted, and it made her sick to utter the lie. There wasn't one iota of similarity between Thorne and Bruce. Her husband had the purest heart, while Thorne had the blackest of souls.

In a voice intoned with virtuous indignation, Thorne said, "You're a wanton, a prurient and deceitful whore. You used men, lured Palmer, and you tried to corrupt me. For years, you've played my weaknesses against me, tempting me, possessing my thoughts."

"I haven't even seen you in years."

"Not since you ran away from those who tried to better you." As he spoke, his rage increased, as did his voice. "God knows you need to be dealt with and no measly heathen will stand in my way."

He was completely insane. Stark, raving mad. "We . . . we thought it was Palmer."

That calmed him. He wanted to share his cunning, to gloat. "Yes. Unfortunately, Palmer grew weak. He didn't understand that we needed to find you. You ruined him with your defiance and the ugly scars you left on his face. I think he actually fears you to some degree. I was justified in using him as a pawn to see that good prevailed."

"Palmer is in jail."

He made a laughing, tsking sound. "I know. I'm the one who encouraged him to go to that bar, to drink too much. I knew he'd get into trouble, and once he was arrested, you'd feel safe. I've been watching the road ever since they grabbed him, going without sleep, just waiting for you to venture out on your own. And you did." He bit his lip, trying to contain his delight. "Lucky for me, there's only one main road. And it's secluded."

The only thing Cyn could think to do was to keep him talking. Thorne liked to hear himself, he liked to add drama and theatrics to his lectures. "Did you kill my mother?"

"I put the whore out of her misery." Thorne smiled with the memory. "I had hoped with Palmer on parole, they'd get back together and you'd return to your family so I could continue counseling you."

Counseling her? Is that what he called the verbal and emotional abuse he'd doled out with such verve?

"But Palmer didn't want her anymore, and you made no signs of embracing a family reunion." Thorne shrugged. "I rightly assumed that if your mother died —"

"Was murdered."

Thorne's smile was slow with satisfaction. "Yes. If she were murdered, then the cops would find you for me. I left the pathetic little note from you just to cement my success. The timing was difficult, and the waiting horrendous. But after the cops finished questioning everyone in that putrid little neighborhood, I was able to hide in an abandoned house and just watch."

"And then you followed us back here?"

"It wasn't difficult. God showed me the way."

Jamie said, "And people think *I'm* odd."

Thorne paid no attention to Jamie, but then, Jamie was so still, so . . . blank of expression or emotion, that he almost seemed nonexistent.

"I almost had you," Thorne remembered, "at that blasted smelly barn. I found the books and knew it was where you lived." His lip curled in disdain. "With animals."

"Now that's the pot calling the kettle black."

Again, he ignored Jamie's quips. "But when you started back, I saw that you weren't alone. Then you went and tricked a man into marrying you. Patience is a virtue, but my oh my, you did try my patience."

His face darkened, and he licked his lips. "Especially since I knew you were fucking him, using him up. You were, weren't you?" The gun wavered in the air in front of him, and Thorne's voice grew hoarse. "What did you do to him, Cynthia? Come clean. Confess your sins."

"I'm not telling you a thing. You're a miserable pervert. Why couldn't you have fallen down a flight of stairs or something?"

The aroused color leached from his face. "Whore. Get over here. Now."

Jamie shook his head. "Not happening."

"Please." Cyn pressed her hands to Jamie's back. "Let me go to him. You can find help and come back for me, but if he shoots you, then you can't help me at all."

Jamie never took his eyes off Thorne. "You're not going anywhere."

"She is, too," Thorne yelled. "She's coming with me. Only I know how to deal with her."

"Soon," Jamie told Cyn in a carrying voice that Thorne couldn't miss, "the reverend will be dead. He won't plague you or anyone else any longer. There's no reason to worry." Jamie's voice was devoid of alarm, as bland as oatmeal. He might have been discussing the weather.

Thorne stared in disbelief, then roared with hilarity. "Me, dead? I'm God's servant, you miserable reprobate. He protects me and watches over me. He —"

"He can have you," Bruce stated in a strong, deep voice, "when I'm through. That is, if there's anything left."

Chapter Fifteen

Cyn stared in amazement as Bruce strode out of the woods to stand in front of her. He was dressed as he'd been when she left him, shirtless and sweaty, his jeans covered in grass stains. He must have followed her the moment she left. But how? He didn't have a car.

Thorne went wide-eyed. "Where did you come from?"

"Your worst nightmare, of course." Bruce smiled, and before Cyn could stop him, he ended up in front of both her and Jamie.

"I told you it'd be okay," Jamie said.

Visitation was obviously ripe with nuts. "You *are* daft! Nothing is okay."

"Hush, honey."

Her incredulous gaze swung back to Bruce. How dare he show up now, when everything was a mess, and then have the nerve to give her such a ridiculous order. "I will not hush! What are you doing here?"

"You went off without me. You want to tell me why?"

Cyn stared at his back, at his loose-limbed posture that she knew meant he was prepared for battle. "No. It's not exactly a good time for a chat."

"Why not?" Bruce flexed his shoulders, curled and uncurled his fists in a most menacing way. "Thorne's not going anywhere, and if he tries to pull that trigger, Bryan or Joe or Scott — maybe all three — will fill him with bullet holes."

Thorne whipped around, looking in all directions. "You lie."

"I never lie."

Cyn had the hysterical urge to laugh. No, Bruce never lied.

Jamie, the fool, put a hand on Bruce's shoulder. "You haven't made things clear enough to her."

"How's that?"

Jamie turned to Cyn. "Tell him why you came to see me."

She shook her head.

"Fine." Bruce started toward Thorne. "I'd just as soon take care of him first anyway."

She did *not* want Bruce to do that. In a rush, Cyn explained, "I wanted to ask Jamie if you were satisfied with me." Bruce halted, but kept his back to her so he could watch Thorne. The man was still frantically trying to locate any other guns, but the trees surrounding them were so tall and thick that spotting anyone or anything was impossible.

"Go on."

Cyn swallowed. "I wanted to know if you regretted your deal."

"What deal is that?"

She could not believe they were discussing this now, with a madman threatening to shoot them, and Jamie listening in his blank, nothing-touches-me way that she didn't buy into for a moment. "Marrying me just to keep me safe."

Bruce nodded. "I see." He moved closer still toward Thorne. "You could have asked me, you know. You don't have to come to Jamie."

Visitation, apparently, led straight down the rabbit hole. "Okay, I'm asking now." She'd do anything to keep the reverend distracted, and to keep Bruce from rushing him.

"Of course I married you, and of course I want to keep you safe." Bruce shrugged. "I love you. No one is ever going to hurt you again."

Given that Thorne still had a gun, Cyn thought that vow might've been a little precipitous, but she didn't quibble.

Jamie leaned near her ear and whispered, "Told you it would all work out."

How could Jamie be so ridiculously urbane at a time like this? They had bigger problems. "He really loves me?"

Bruce let out a feral growl. "What in the world did you think? That I just like running in circles around you, trying to figure you out? You've made me nuts, Cyn." And then, more quietly, "But yes. I love you."

"Enough." Outraged, Thorne started toward them. Bruce matched him step for step, always staying in front of Cyn, until the distance between the two men was dangerously close.

Thorne's eyes were wild, his face flushed. Spittle formed at the corners of his mouth as he screamed, "You're heathens, sick and promiscuous and God will thank me for ridding the world of you."

He raised his gun, and it wasn't Bruce he aimed for.

It was Cyn.

Thorne focused only on her, as if no one else existed. His tone almost mournful, he said, "I hadn't wanted it this way, damn you. I wanted time alone with you, to make you repent. But —"

That awful threat went unfinished. Thorne had let Bruce get within striking distance, and strike he did. In one agile leap, Bruce landed hard against Thorne and they both went down to the gravel roadway.

The gun fell from Thorne's grip, not that Bruce noticed. He squeezed Thorne's throat with one hand, and with the other landed a heavy fist against his jaw. The man's head snapped to the side. Another blow and blood gushed from his nose.

Bruce's fists were fast and full of fury, landing on the reverend's face, his upper body, his gut. Thorne quit fighting by the third punch. By the fifth, he wasn't moving at all.

Sobbing, Cyn shook Jamie. "Stop him."

Jamie glanced down at her. "Why?"

"*Why?*" She shoved Jamie to the side and ran down the rough gravel road to where Bruce continued to rain blows on the fallen man. "Bruce! Stop it."

Either Bruce didn't hear her, or he ignored her. He pulled back his fist yet again, and Cyn grabbed his arm. His biceps were huge, knotted with anger. She held on with all her might. "Bruce, *no*."

He hesitated, breathing hard and fast.

"Please stop. He's done for. Please, for me, don't hit him anymore."

"He was going to shoot you."

Bruce's fury was a live thing. "I know." Cyn had no delusions about Thorne's intentions, but she knew Bruce, and he might regret his actions later. "He can't hurt me now. Please stop."

Bruce turned to her, saw the tears streaming down her face, and all his rage melted away. He released Thorne and came to his feet. His knuckles were bruised and bloody, but he paid no mind to that.

He cupped Cyn's face in tender, trembling hands. "You're okay, baby?"

Sniffing, she nodded. "Yes."

"Then why are you crying?"

She half laughed, half sobbed again. After all they'd been through, he had to ask that? "I swear, you are the craziest man I know."

Jamie cleared his throat. "Bad move, Thorne."

Bruce jerked around, saw Thorne had risen on one elbow and had the gun in his hand. One of his eyes was completely swelled shut, the other was open only a slit. Blood covered his face, trickling from his nose, his mouth, a cut on his temple.

In a barely audible slur, Thorne said, "Fucking whore," and then a bullet hit him in the arm. Another landed, and another.

Bruce pulled Cyn into his chest, turning

away from the gruesome scene, protecting her the best he could.

Howling, Thorne fell back in a dead faint.

Cyn blinked as Scott, Joe, and Bryan seemed to crawl right out of the forest around them. "You didn't lie."

"Never do." Bruce loosened his hold on her so she could catch her breath. His chest was sweaty, but Cyn didn't care. He smelled of freshly mown lawn, of man and security and she loved it.

She loved him.

She stared at Reverend Thorne, lying still as death. She felt Bruce's heart, beating strong and sure. Calm settled over her. "It really is over."

"Yes. The past is dead." Bruce tipped up her chin. "But your life, your future, is just beginning."

"With you."

He rubbed a thumb along her jaw. "You might as well understand now — I won't have it any other way. When I married you, it was forever. I love you and I'm never letting you go."

New tears dampened her cheeks, but they were tears of relief and happiness.

Joe strode over and removed Thorne's gun. Scott tapped him on the shoulder, and with a shrug of apology, Joe handed it to him. "Sorry," Joe said with a load of insincerity. "Habit."

Bryan checked the man's pulse. "He's alive, just barely."

"Figures."

"Knock it off, Joe." Scott pulled out his radio and called for an ambulance, while Joe and Bryan worked on Thorne to stop the sluggish blood flow from his wounds. With that accomplished, Scott graciously gave explanations to Cyn.

"There were prints on the wrapping from your journal, only they weren't Palmer's. I called to tell Bruce that the bastard after you was still loose, but Bruce wasn't home, so I called Bryan's cell phone."

"And of course," Cyn said, still a little dazed by it all, "everyone in Visitation just naturally carries a gun."

Bryan stood, looking so much like Bruce, but with such a different air. While Bruce had handled himself with competence, he wasn't nearly as at ease in the grisly, bloody situation as Bryan. "I gave all that up when I married Shay, but yeah, since trouble followed you to town, I've been armed."

"Not me," Joe said. "I had to borrow one from Scott."

Bryan pointed a finger at Cyn. "I told Scott that we were tailing you since you decided to skip off on your own."

"I did not skip," Cyn said, but she felt guilty because she had inadvertently endangered them all. "And I thought it was safe."

Jamie folded his arms over his chest. "You disregarded my warning. I told you that until I said otherwise, the threat would still be there. I told you not to be fooled."

Cyn winced. "Yeah, well, I remember that *now*."

"How'd *you* get involved?" Jamie asked Joe.

Joe rubbed his hands together. "I just lucked into this little dragnet. I was out shopping, minding my own business. Then Scott passed me in a hurry, so naturally I followed. We all met up down the road and came in through the woods."

Bryan shook his head at Cyn. "Once Bruce realized you might really be in trouble, I had to practically sit on him so we could make plans. He was all set to charge in like a damn hero."

"He is a hero," Cyn insisted.

And the men all nodded and laughed.

Bruce said, "I'm never going to live that down now, you realize."

Joe rubbed the back of his neck. "The thing is, I knew if you were here, and in danger, odds were Jamie was hanging around, too. And I figured he'd look out for you."

The ambulance sirens suddenly split the morning, halting all conversations. Cyn watched the paramedics work, trying to stabilize Thorne, but they were too late. Reverend Thorne faded away, just as Jamie had claimed he would.

It wasn't Bruce's beating, and it wasn't the bullet wounds. It was the rock Thorne's head landed on when he collapsed back. Not that anyone was suffering guilt or looking to escape blame. Reverend Thorne would not be missed.

It was just as the ambulance drove off that Cyn felt it. She moved away from Bruce and scanned the area. Jamie, the sneak, had separated himself and was ready to do his patented disappearing act.

Cyn stormed toward him. "Oh no, you don't. Not this time."

His back still to her, Jamie froze comically in mid-step. He even seemed to cringe.

"Not another single step, mister! I mean it."

Her determination grew as Cyn kept

walking, and then she was jogging, and finally sprinting. Jamie heard her rapid approach and turned in time to catch her when she threw herself against him.

She was bawling again, but she couldn't help it and she didn't even care. If even one of the big oafs staring at her said a single word, she'd sic Alyx Winston on him.

Jamie looked like a man sent to the gallows. Cyn didn't care about that, either.

She dried her eyes on his shirt and sniffed, then leaned back to see his face. Above his shaggy beard, his eyes were black with caution. Cyn smiled. "Thank you."

Jamie ill at ease was a sight to see. He all but stammered — then, in a voice too low to hear, he muttered something.

"What did you say?"

He scowled darkly. "I said it was nothing."

"Oh, it was something all right. Something wonderful — like you."

Jamie glared at Bruce. "Don't just stand there. Come and get her."

Joe nudged Bryan. "He's sort of lost his aplomb, hasn't he now?"

"Looks like it to me."

Scott sympathized. "A woman can do that to you."

Joe leaned around Bryan to stare at

Scott. "You're not talking about my baby sister, are you?"

Scott walked away, but not before saying, "You really do need to quit calling her that."

"Why?"

"Because her relationship to you ruins my good mood every time."

Laughing, Bruce strode over to his wife, but he didn't pull Cyn away. Instead, he embraced Jamie and Cyn both. "I agree with her, Jamie. You are one incredible man, and I can't thank you enough for being here with her."

Jamie cleared his throat. "I knew she was coming here and I knew Thorne would be here, too. He's been hiding in the mountains, creeping into town under disguise every now and then." He rolled one shoulder. "So of course I came."

Bruce stepped back and gently pried Cyn loose. She mopped at her eyes, and smiled a beautiful smile.

"If there's ever anything we can do for you, please let us know."

Instead of meeting her gaze, Jamie stared up at the late morning sun. "Sure." And without another word, he turned and walked, not so silently this time, into the woods.

Cyn watched him go, and for some reason, her heart was breaking. By choice, Jamie was so alone in the world. "He's a very special person."

"Much like my wife." Bruce put his arm around her shoulders and together they walked back to the car. "Know what I want to do?"

He'd whispered that question, so Cyn had an idea that it was something private. "Tell me."

"I want to go home and shower with my wife, then crawl into bed and just hold her, to reassure myself that she's fine, and that she's all mine."

Cyn nodded. "A great idea. Let's do it."

But a few hours later, when they were curled together beneath a sheet, Cyn grew contemplative again.

"What is it? Are you still upset?" Bruce pulled her closer. "It's not unusual to be shaken for days, even weeks, after such a terrible ordeal."

"No." Cyn put her cheek on his shoulder. "It's not that."

"Then what?"

"Jamie."

Bruce smiled and smoothed her hair away. "It's a good thing I'm not a jealous man."

"I love you, so you have no reason to be jealous." She pushed up on one elbow. "But we need to do something for him. He's hurting, Bruce. The kind of hurting that he lives with day in and day out."

"What do you suggest?"

She shook her head in frustration. "I don't know. Do you think he knows how much everyone cares for him? Do you think he knows that Joe and Bryan just like to bluster, and that Scott's only guarding his position? Does he know that he has respect and gratitude?"

Bruce stared out the window. "He knows just about everything, right? So surely, he knows that much. I think it's more that he doesn't want to be friends. He keeps a deliberate distance."

"He warned Julie that things would be happening in her life. Julie is so pragmatic that she dismissed it, but I believe Jamie. And I believe that he'll try to protect Julie as much as he can."

"Probably."

Cyn's conviction grew, especially since she knew she had her husband's support. "When Jamie shows up next time," Cyn said, "and he will, to help Julie with whatever's going on, I'm going to insist he stay and visit. I'm going to insist he accept our friendship."

Bruce pulled her back down and kissed the mulish expression right off her mouth. "Go carefully, honey. Jamie is a grown man with deep secrets that he might need to keep buried. Let him get used to you. And in the meantime, we'll let him know how we feel."

Cyn grinned suddenly. "You know, I've always tried to live in the present, without thinking too much about my future, much less anyone else's. Every day was a reprieve, filled with caution. Now . . . it's the oddest feeling, but I'm looking forward to growing old with you."

Bruce laughed. "Luckily I married a young woman who has a lot of years to go. I'm going to cherish each and every one."

Night settled onto the mountains with blackness so thick, so absolute, Jamie couldn't see his hand in front of his face. He sat there in his cabin, his back to the wall, his fireplace cold and empty, no lamps lit. And he tried to focus on the sounds of wildlife that surrounded him, the sounds that usually brought him peace.

He should have given up an hour ago.

But he was a man plagued by turmoil,

wanting what he couldn't have.

And he couldn't have friends. Friends would make him weak, would ruin his abilities, and that would put others at risk.

No, he told himself for the tenth time, I *can't* make friends. But, without even meaning to . . . he knew he already had.

And even the dark couldn't tell him what to do about it now.